Dawn of the Second Darkness

The Second Darkness - Book 1

Will Groberg

Rock Court Media

Book Cover by Sara Groberg

First edition 2025

ePub ISBN: 979-8-9931947-0-7
Paperback ISBN: 979-8-9931947-1-4
Hardback ISBN: 979-8-9931947-2-1

Rock Court Media, Sierra Vista AZ
https://www.rockcourtmedia.com/

https://www.willgroberg.com/

This story is dedicated to my daughters Ellie and Hannah. To Ellie for accidentally inspiring the title of the book and to Hannah for the many characters that originated with her suggestions.

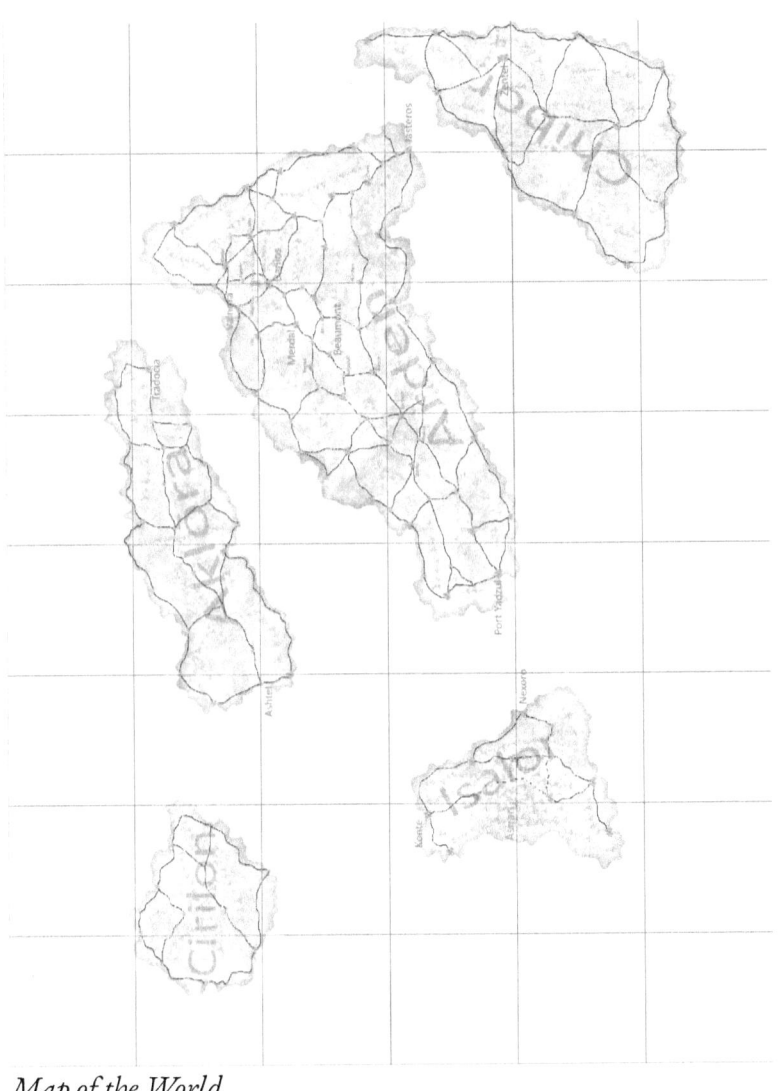

Map of the World

.

CONTENTS

Prologue - 800 years ago - End of the great darkness

Silence descended over the depths as the dust settled and the raging storm that had churned there for months calmed. No one had anticipated the costs. Of the nine grand archmages in the Halidar coalition, only three remained. The struggle had been difficult and brutal. At the start, they had to face thousands of minions and mind controlled thralls. Then they broke into the tower itself and confronted Vlastorn. It didn't go well. That failure led to them collapsing the pit and finally destroying the tower core. The endeavor cost them six of their number, leaving just the three of them.

The three remaining Halidar stood in a large central chamber deep in the bottom of the Tower of Sangar, a huge half mile wide tower rising up from the Pit. The Pit went all the way down to the core of the world, concentrating and carrying a massive quantity of magical energy that surged constantly upward to the surface. The Tower of Sangar anchored to the sides of the pit, tens of thousands of feet below the surface and extended upward, towering two miles above the plains of the Kingdom of Sangar.

The central chamber housed the tower crystal which gathered and concentrated the raw magical power from the Pit. Vlastorn had bound his soul to the giant crystal core so that if his body was destroyed, it would be reformed. Because of that, the only way he could be killed was through its destruction.

The three mages gazed at the wreckage surrounding them. During the preceding battle, the Halidar had collapsed the sides of the pit far below them, causing blockage that severely reduced the upward stream of raw magical energy from the planet core. Once the energy diminished, the crystal core and its protections weakened enough that the archmages were able to shatter it and defeat the overlord.

Evander, the youngest of the remaining Halidar, stooped and ran his fingers through the rubble. He had been very close to the other grand archmages. When the darkness first started, he and the others had been pursuing their own interests and projects, each a political leader in their own section of the world. They ignored the darkness at first, thinking it was just some fanatic project the arch-necromancer Vlastorn was working on. After all, he was one of their own, and as a general rule, archmages didn't interfere in each other's business. But when the darkness continued to spread and impact the other archmages' countries, the remaining nine banded together and formed a grand coalition to defeat Vlastorn.

Evander looked up at the other two remaining Halidar and then at the destruction around him. He had once thought that Vlastorn was his friend, but now because of him most of the coalition were dead. The anger of Vlastorn's betrayal clashed with the pain of having to destroy his friend, leaving him exhausted and confused.

"Is that it?" Dardanos's angry question interrupted his thoughts. "Is it completely stopped?" Evander stood up and looked at the dark haired earth and energy archmage. His face was crinkled in disgust and matched the confusion Evander felt. Dardanos paused, obviously searching for any energy signatures from the tower. "I don't sense anything."

From the side of the chamber, Rhondalyn spoke, her voice barely audible from exhaustion. "It's gone. No spell power signatures. No psychic vibrations. It's all gone. Just raw energy."

Evander looked over at her. Her tiny frame was curled up against the side of the chamber wall. She looked like she shouldn't even have the energy to speak. Her normal healthy and youthful appearance had been replaced with sunken eyes and taut stretched skin over a small bony frame. Their quest had taken an enormous toll on her. Sidoran, her husband of thousands of years and fellow grand archmage, had been killed when they first confronted Vlastorn a few weeks prior. Now that the overlord was defeated, the reality of her loss was starting to sink in. Evander wondered if she would ever recover. She sat there staring blankly like she wasn't even aware of the world around her.

After a moment, her eyes flitted to her companions. She spoke up in just more than a whisper. "How do we keep this from happening again?"

"Let me take care of it. This pit and the tower in it need to be destroyed." Dardanos growled.

Evander agreed but also knew that there might be valuable resources and people left in the tower., "We should empty out the tower's resources before we destroy it. Do you think there are any people still inside?"

Dardanos rolled his eyes but his voice softened, "Fine, we can check before we destroy everything. But let's be quick, I don't want to be here longer than necessary. Rhondalyn, do you have enough energy left to scry for anyone alive in the tower?"

Rhondalyn slowly stood. "Yes, barely." She shuffled a bit to center herself and performed a brief hand ritual to trigger the spell. A pulse of cool green light burst out from her hands and passed through the walls and floors. After a few minutes, small tracers of light flowed back to her and her eyes glowed the same green color. Once the tracers stopped returning, she took a deep breath and the light faded from her eyes.

She gingerly sat back down, "There are a couple hundred people in the top 10 floors. I think that's where he had most of the normal services and servants. I can't tell who is hostile or not, but they were all walking around without any direction, so I don't think they are a threat. There are also some small armed bands outside the tower on the plains that are working their way here, but I can't tell if they are his reinforcements, or if they are people who we freed." She leaned back against the wall, "I need to rest." Without saying any else, she curled up against the corner of the wall again, closed her eyes, and immediately fell asleep.

Evander looked over at Dardanos and raised an eyebrow. "Well?"

"Well what? You're the 'Great Leader'. Go do something about the people. I have to stay here and figure out what it is going to take to make this place nothing but a bad memory."

Evander frowned, but didn't respond as he turned toward the stairs. Dardanos was a naturally grumpy soul and the stress of the battle added to his aggravated mood. All of their nerves were on edge and they were more exhausted than they could have imagined.

Evander began to make his way up the tower, floor by floor. He had at least ten floors to climb before he started getting close to the first of the people Rhondalyn had seen. As he entered each floor, he sent out numerous pulses of light to help him detect the floor layouts. The tower was huge. Each floor could hold ten of the largest palaces he had ever seen, and was essentially a giant maze. As a precaution, he visited each stairway and set a monitoring light ward that would let him know if anyone other than him used the stairway.

Once he made it up to the tenth level from the top, he began to run into individuals and small groups of people. Most were simple servants, and seemed a little confused at what was going on. A few of them were catatonic. After stabilizing their minds and gathering their attention, he instructed them to follow him. When he had assembled all the people he could find on a floor, he led them to that floor's external exit, a high speed magical elevator that ended in a small building next to the base of the tower.

When he exited the elevator, he found himself in the middle of the bands of armed people Rhondalyn had seen earlier. These were people they had previously freed from the Thrall, and like most who had been freed, were angry, but he was able to quickly talk them down from their anger. Once they were calm, they took the servants and promised to help them settle into normal life as best they could.

After another few hours of searching, he was pretty sure he had found everyone. A few of his light wards had been triggered by servants who had wandered onto lower floors before he reached them. He soon tracked those individuals down and led them to the exits. Then, confident he had found everyone, he returned to the core chamber where Rhondalyn and Dardanos were still waiting. Rhondalyn was awake but still resting against the wall. She was still weak but looked much better than she had before. Dardanos was scowling and writing in a notebook in his hand. He apparently had been making notes the entire time Evander had been gone.

"Alright, I got everyone out that I could find. Will you check the tower one more time?" he asked Rhondalyn.

She nodded her head, stood, and again cast her spell. After a few minutes she reported "There are three more people on the ninth floor from the top, but they may be in some kind of a holding cell. We can probably get them when we leave."

"I suppose," he replied, then turned to Dardanos. "Are you ready to remove this blight from our world?"

Dardanos looked at his notes frowning and shifted uncomfortably. "I, ahem, may have been too optimistic in my estimate before."

"What do you mean?"

Dardanos pursed his lips, then frowned again. "There is still a lot of raw energy, both magical and non-magical, escaping from the core. I don't think I can actually shut it down completely enough to keep it from causing explosions and major problems. Instead, I think it would be wise to set up some kind of research and monitoring station near here to keep an eye on things and see if we can understand what is happening. My country was completely destroyed by this mess, so I guess this is as good a place to set up as any."

"So, you will be staying here in this region?"

"Yes, I think that would be for the best." he paused and looked around, "There is no reason to stay down in this hole anymore. We can go get those last people out, and then I can start making this place inaccessible." He started toward the stairs and the other two followed.

The three mages quickly found the last three people and Rhondalyn healed them, then they left the tower. As they walked, Dardanos picked up the conversation where they had left off. "So, what are you two going to do now?"

Evander pondered for a moment, then replied, "I'm going back to Chibor and will build a Tower of Light to prevent the darkness from being able to enslave the minds of people again. Rhondalyn, what about you?" They were walking slowly so that she could keep up in her weakened state.

She frowned wearily, "I'm going to get as far from here as I can. I never want to see or think of any of this again. I am the oldest of the three of us by quite a ways, and this took a lot out of me. It will take a lot of work and time to get my youth back. I think I will set up a little home in the mountains of Isalor and be a bit of a hermit for a few centuries. After that, I don't know. My sleep is filled with nightmares of this place and I would like that to stop. I think I will focus on that for a while. And beyond that, we'll just have to see."

Evander nodded and passed a look to Dardanos. He knew the toll the battle had taken on Rhondalyn and hoped she found the peace she was looking for.

They walked for miles to the crossroads. The group walked for a time in the silence of their own thoughts until they reached the main crossroads. Evander was to take the south road and Rhondalyn would continue west, while Dardanos was going to stay in the area and build a new city. They all embraced and said goodbyes, then Evander turned and started on his journey home. His chest swelled inside with the hope of a future without darkness. A future of light and peace.

CHAPTER ONE

RHONDALYN

SWEAT DRIPPED DOWN RHONDALYN'S face as she made adjustments to the complex equipment she was working on. Arlista handed her tools and equipment while Henry held the parts in position while she made adjustments and attached connections to the central flow controller of the grand array.

It was the final piece of a project she had spent the better part of a millennia working on. It had to be perfect. It would connect and coordinate all the other pieces on this side of the world, as well as the other parts that would need to be installed in the dark tower itself.

She received the final connector from Arlista, and then Henry helped her work it gently into position. With a smile, she looked at her two faithful assistants. She was grateful for them. They had been with her for nearly 500 years each. Their families had served faithfully before that. All over the vast underground chamber, massively complicated magical and mechanical devices were precisely arranged, each part of a powerful, yet delicate balance.

She finished up the last connection and thought back on the work that had been involved. It had taken nearly eight centuries of detailed planning, meticulous crafting, and the most difficult magical formulations she had ever heard of to get to this point. Building the chamber and drilling the shaft that descended deep into the crust of the world in preparation for the first half of the array had taken nearly a century.

Two more centuries had been spent building up secret technology and magical manufactories to enable production of the special equipment, starting with the spike. The spike itself had taken decades to design and build, and more decades to assemble in the shaft. Then came the other enchanted equipment that had to be aligned with absolute precision. All of it was now connected or aligned with all of the other special equipment to complete the array in the chamber.

The last few months had been frantic, but she and her people had raced to complete the chamber array. Now, they needed to make sure they had everything ready for the next step. All the remaining pieces for use in the dark tower were either finished or close to finished. If everything went as planned and foreseen, the huge planet spanning array would permanently override what the overlords did to create the darknesses.

She didn't know exactly how soon the second darkness would start, but it would be within days. Based on her magical readings and from what she had seen in her visions, she could tell that the new dark tower was nearing completion. She would have a very narrow window to find the people who she prophesied would be part of the mission to end the darkness. They wouldn't start moving until the darkness started, and they had to be found before the darkness overtook them.

She wished she knew just a few more details about them as it would simplify things for her. Understanding visions was generally a tedious and imprecise labor. These visions regarding the darknesses had been different from anything she had previously experienced in all of her more than 3000 years of life. She didn't know as much as she would like and there wasn't any time to try to get more. It was time to take the next steps. She still didn't know all the details. She hoped what she knew was enough.

She refocused and led her assistants in cleaning up the tools and they exited the great array chamber. It was specially warded to prevent anyone but a select few from entering. While others in her manufactories had done much of the work building all the components, the installation had to be done by the few who could enter the chamber.

They put everything away and she turned to Henry and Arlista, "It's time for the next phase. Get cleaned up and meet me in the conference room." They nodded their acknowledgement and headed off. Rhondalyn used magic cleaning spells to freshen up as she traversed the huge facility to get to the conference room. The chamber was a long way from the conference room and magical travel was completely blocked in the sections around the chamber as a security precaution.

Once she arrived in the conference room, she took a few minutes to contemplate what had led to this day. More than 800 years previously, she and her husband, Sidoran, knew what was happening because of her visions. He was another Grand Archmage specializing in shadow magic and teleportation. They had helped form the idea of a grand coalition of Grand Archmages to stop the first overlord and end the first darkness. The idea took a long time to catch on, but eventually, it did.

Before she joined the other Halidar, Rhondolyn was renowned as the world's greatest healer; she could heal almost anything. Even then, she could only be in one place at a time, which limited when and where her magic could be used. And some things or situations caused death quicker than she could heal. Still, getting her help was generally renowned as the best option anyone could hope for. She was also known as an unstoppable scrying mage who could look through just about any barrier or ward. Secrets thought to be undiscoverable were often disclosed when she was employed against them.

What only she and her husband knew was that her scrying wasn't only scrying. She secretly was the greatest magical seer the world had ever known. She didn't look at things only in the present, but both in the future and the past. She simply had to look before the current wards or barriers were set or after they went down. It would have surprised most of her colleagues to know the secret of her power.

Because of these gifts, only she and Sidoran knew that there would be a second darkness. They knew due to her visions. They were the strongest visions she ever had, and they came frequently and with incredible detail. They showed her how she could hijack the second darkness to end the possibility of darknesses forever. Unfortunately, they also showed that Sidoran was going to have to die in the confrontation to end the first darkness. He had to sacrifice himself to set things in proper motion.

His sacrifice was still hard to think about, but she had moved inexorably forward from the moment the previous darkness had ended. She already knew people she could trust, and she knew where she had to go. She had called select people to come and carve this place out of the heart of the largest mountains in the world. She called it Ashari. Some of her people just called it 'The Facility'.

Now the culmination of all her visions was about to start. She thought about the people who she would have to find and train and support in their mission to end the second darkness, but like most visions, there was still much uncertainty.

Her rumination was interrupted as Henry and Arlista arrived together. They entered and took their places across the table from her.

Rhondalyn looked at them both for a short time without saying anything. Henry asked, "You said it is time for the next phase."

Rhondalyn took a deep breath and nodded, "Yes, it is."

Arlista asked, "What do we know about them?"

Rhondalyn thought for a moment, then said, "We know there are six people in the main group. One comes from Isalor, four from Arden, and one from Chibor. There are two others that will join later, one who is already here in Ashari, and the other that will get here on their own. In addition, we will also send the security team that has been training. Henry, how are their preparations?"

"It is going well. Their training is nearly complete. They have already taken on a couple of small missions as part of their training, and they are fully equipped and have been for a while."

Rhondalyn smiled thoughtfully, "Very good." She then turned to Arlista, "How are the preparations for the others?"

Arlista frowned for a moment. Rhondalyn wasn't sure why. Then Arlista answered professionally, "The training rooms and evaluation equipment is just about all ready. We have about 98% of the armor, weapons, and accessories acquired and organized already, and are working on the last few items."

Rhondalyn worried that they wouldn't be ready, "You only have a short time before they get here."

Arlista nodded confidently, "Yes, I know. Our projections indicate we will be ready on time." She paused, open mouthed, like she was trying to find the right words, "Um, how will you find them?"

Rhondalyn raised an eyebrow at the question. Then she turned to Henry, "I need you to get Banosh."

Henry groaned and rolled his eyes, "Seriously? He is so childish!"

Rhondalyn ignored the hypocrisy in Henry's response, "Yes, but he is the most effective messenger that I have, especially when magic is required. Have him meet me in my personal lounge in one hour."

"Fine. I'll get him." Henry rose and headed to the door.

Rhondalyn then turned to Arlista, "Will you fetch the stones and bring them to me in my lounge."

"Yes ma'am." She rose and followed Henry.

Rhondalyn followed them out the door shortly after and went to her private lounge. While she waited for Banosh, another of her people, a woman named Betty, entered with tea and served her without speaking. She left the room and Rhondalyn's eyes followed her out. She shook her head as she thought about the strange and challenging path the woman would soon experience.

Arlista soon entered carrying six rough clear stones, about the size of a small apple. She brought them over to Rhondalyn and held them out. For a moment, Rhondalyn looked deeply at them, then selected one, "Please return the others to storage." Arlista nodded and left.

Eventually, Henry escorted Banosh into the room.

He entered and bowed with a flourish of his hat, then stood formally and asked, "What need have you of me, my lady?"

She made herself not roll her eyes at his dramatics, but he had always been dramatic even as a child. "I need you to find someone for me, and have them come to the hunter's shack."

She ignored the joke that she knew was coming before he even opened his mouth, "Is there someone specific or would just anyone do?" he asked with a grin.

Without bothering to acknowledge his question, she said, "The person you must find is a ranger. They are especially skilled with bow and stealth, but most rangers are. This ranger was orphaned as a young child, and has raised himself into what he is today. He is young for an elite ranger, and has a habit of delaying before answering questions. To know for certain, you must have him hold this stone."

She held out the small stone to Banosh. "It will light up when it is touched by the right person and no one else. You will find this individual in one of the rangers' lodges near Ishron here on Isalor. Give him these two platinum coins and tell him there will be more when he meets me at the hunter's shack."

Banosh looked at her, then mischievously asked, "How much in the way of dramatics is warranted?"

She thoughtfully responded, "Not too much, but some would probably be good. Once you have found him, return and let me know how it went." She looked at him, playing to his mischievousness, "I have a special bonus for you if you can beat him back here after he has accepted the invitation. Do you have any questions?"

"No, my lady. I will go at once." Banosh replied. With that, he turned and was gone.

Rhondalyn sat there for a while, deep in thought. Eventually, both Henry and Arlista entered and waited. She turned to them. "Henry, make sure the production of tower modules is on track. Where is it at presently?"

"It's on track and we are still targeting 160%."

"Very good. Henry, keep on that and don't let it fall behind. Arlista, double check everything with the training facilities. Both of you, keep me apprised daily on where things are at." Both assistants nodded and left to comply with her instructions while Rhondalyn returned to her rumination.

The visions didn't detail the losses and struggles the world would have. The first darkness had destroyed a great many cities and people. If only there was a way to stop them before it started, but there wasn't. The visions had been clear on that point. She contemplated how it all might turn out and hoped it would be worth it. After a while a deep yet quiet voice that seemed to come from nowhere and everywhere at once asked "How confident are you that this plan will work?" The sudden voice didn't seem to disturb Rhondalyn in the least.

"I wish I could be certain, but even seership has its limitations." she responded. "I just hope we can get everyone on the team that needs to be here."

"I have never known you to be wrong, not when the visions are so detailed."

She took a deep breath, "No other visions in my life have been like this. I can't even begin to compare them." She shook her head, feeling completely overwhelmed. Then she decided to change the subject, "How are your preparations coming?"

"Oh, they are coming along fine. 800 years is a long time to dedicate to even the largest projects. Of course, I don't have to tell you that. Your projects are of a greater magnitude than mine. If mine fail, they simply make life more inconvenient and complicated. If *you* fail, life as we know it is over."

A single tear formed in her eye and trickled down her face, "I know. That is all I can think about." She looked out at the empty room and forced herself to regain her composure, then got up and went to help her assistants.

Chapter Two

Micaela

Micaela wiped the sweat from her neck with a towel as she walked out the artists' entrance at the back of the big top tent, reviewing in her mind the routine she had just spent the last three hours practicing. She was a trapeze artist, and she and her team had been preparing for the final trapeze act of the grand opening of the new circus season which would happen in just a couple of weeks. Things were going really well. Out of 25 tries, they averaged 23 of the difficult catches and returns successfully. She was confident that by opening night, they would be reliably at 25 out of 25.

She wound her way through the small artists tents to reach her own. She collected her change of clothes and hurried to the showers. She had an exciting afternoon planned. It would take her three hours to reach the top of Survey Hill overlooking the city of Danlos and the Wizards tower. It was the only nearby location that was taller than the tower. She loved the view from there, and tried to do the hike several times a year when they were not traveling. After cleaning up in the shower tent and changing her clothes, she deposited her soiled practice outfit at the laundry and headed out.

After walking around the side of the city, she started up the trail that repeatedly circled around the prominent hill before reaching the top. She stopped each time she reached the face of the hill that looked out over the city. To the left, she could see the large circus encampment. On the far side, separated from the city by a good sized clearing, stood the wizards tower. It was beautiful, tall, and constructed of mixed types of rock with windows and balconies periodically placed on the sides. The top had crenelations placed in the parapet, each topped with blindingly white stone.

Micaela loved looking at the tower. She looked out at it with a smile from the second highest trail overlook on the hill. What an amazing sight. Knowing the view from the top was even better, she continued around the hill on the last loop before she reached the top. Just as she reached the back side of the hill, a blinding flash filled the air. Shocked, she braced herself against the unknown, but was still knocked down when the ground shook violently.

Her mind reeled in panic and confusion, but before she got up, the ear splitting roar of a massive explosion pummeled her, followed by an overpowering shockwave that assaulted her from both sides. The ground continued to shake for what seemed like a long time, but was probably only a handful of seconds. She looked out over the top of the hill to see a huge shaped plume of smoke, dust, and debris begin to mushroom up into the sky.

Having hit the ground hard, she felt lightheaded and tried to regain her focus. Despite being shaken with a few scrapes, she wasn't seriously injured. *What was that?* She thought. The ground finally finished shaking.

Relieved, she stood up and began to dust herself off. She started up the trail toward the top of the hill, but after about twenty seconds, a deeper rumbling began to shake the ground again, though not quite as intense as before.

She quickly stopped, not wanting to get knocked down again. The shaking came with a deep sound that seemed to grate and grind at the very air around her. It was loud enough to hurt her ears. She tried to make sense of it, but couldn't gather even the faintest idea of what was going on. It continued for what seemed like forever. At first it was surprising, but soon her surprise was replaced with fear and irritation.

She was able to stay on her feet despite the shaking ground and carefully hurried to the top of the hill, which was not far from where she had been first knocked to the ground. As soon as she crested the hill, her vision was met with massive devastation. The Wizard's Tower was gone, and smoke was coming from hundreds of places across the city. Most of the buildings nearer the tower were broken or crushed and many were only rubble. She stared in horror at all the destruction. *Am I dreaming? How can this be real?*

As she stared, trying to comprehend what she was seeing, she noticed that in the far distance, another tower, far larger and all dark stone was slowly rising from the ground. It continued to grow, reaching far above where she stood at the top of the highest hill near the city. The tower had begun belching huge plumes of dark smoke that was spreading out to make an ominous black cloud that was spreading outward in every direction. The smoke from the city was also rising up and drifting toward the black cloud.

Micaela didn't know how long she watched the scene, but she gaped in disbelief until suddenly, the dark tower stopped rising with a heavy thud, then the shaking stopped. She looked out over the city at the new tower. She realized that people she loved and cared about were down there in that mess. She could see that the big tent of the circus had partially fallen and was damaged.

In panic, she turned and ran back down the trail, far faster than was safe. The trail lower on the hill had been damaged by debris in a few places, but she quickly made her way around them. It took her less than an hour to reach the circus encampment.

Many of the smaller tents had been knocked down and a few people were trying to beat out fires. She decided to delay checking on her own tent and proceeded to the big top. It was partly on fire, and there were massive tears in it. Some of the main poles were down or broken so that the tent drooped extensively in many places. Some parts were all the way on the ground. Out to the edge of the encampment, there were many animal cries, and it sounded like the animal trainers were trying to capture an escaped lion or other large animal. The two other big side tents were down and also on fire. There didn't seem to be anyone even trying to fight those fires.

Micaela didn't know what to do, and she looked around in dismay. She felt compelled to try to help, but didn't know what to do. She realized it might be best to ask someone who would know. She ran around the large tents to the group of wagons where the management of the circus organized everything. The Circus Boss's wagon had been smashed completely somehow. The Circus Matron, Freya, was sitting on the ground outside the Ringmaster's wagon, which had been pretty badly damaged. As she ran up, she could see that the Ringmaster was lying on the ground and mostly covered in blood, and Freya had a bandaged and splinted leg.

Still trying to catch her breath, she gasped, "Matron, what happened?"

Freya turned to her as she approached. The small thin middle aged woman winced as she moved. "Micaela! You seem uninjured. Where were you for the last hour?"

"I had climbed Survey Hill and was behind the hill when the ground started shaking. How is this possible?"

"The tower exploded, don't know how. Not sure I ever will. Just wanna take care of our own. What could you see from up there?"

"The wizard's tower is gone! All the way to the ground! There's smoke and fires all over the city, but the worst is close to where the wizard's tower was." Freya nodded like she somehow expected all that. Micaela continued, "Then there is the new dark tower growing out of the Pit! It is huge!"

Freya suddenly looked panicked, "What did you say? What dark tower?"

Micaela didn't know why Freya would be worried, but confirmed what she said before, "Yeah, a huge new tower rose up out of the pit. It is dark and smoke is pouring out the top and making a dark cloud."

Panicked worry flooded the matron's face and she reached up to Micaela, "Help me up!" Micaela reached down and gently helped her to her feet. The matron pointed, "Over there!"

Micaela helped her move over where she had pointed and then turned her around to where they could see the top of the new dark tower.

Freya's panic and worry seemed to get worse. "Oh no! We have to get everyone away. All those that can travel." She moved, but realizing she was not very mobile, she stopped struggling and looked intently at Micaela. "Listen carefully. We don't have much time! Get those who are able to travel, gather as many wagons as you can and get them rigged up, and get the people on and head toward Jasteros. We need to get everyone to the Tower of Light. It may be the only thing that can protect us now."

Freya's words and reaction caused a feeling of doom to fall upon Micaela. Freya was obviously terrified about something. Micaela hadn't thought Freya was ever afraid of anything, but now she was preparing for everyone to flee. She helped her sit on a trunk and then was about to run off to obey, but stopped. "What about you? And him?" she pointed at the unconscious Ringmaster on the ground.

"I don't think he's gonna make it. Get everything together, then come get me. My leg is broken, but I think I can survive a ride on a wagon for a while." She smiled weakly, then said, "Now git, and get those wagons ready."

Micaela obeyed and took off. She ran to the horse pens and found that less than half of the horses were uninjured. The horse-master was nowhere to be seen. The hauling wagons were behind the horse pens and she could see that some had been damaged. She found some good wagons and quickly grabbed the harnesses and prepared to hook up the horses. She had helped hook up the wagons once the previous year and she struggled to remember where everything went. As she struggled, one of the drivers named Korel ran up. "Hey, what do you think you're doing?"

She held up the equipment she was struggling with, "Freya said to rig up some wagons and get as many of the people who can travel on them. Will you help me please?"

He looked at her in frustration, "You're doing it wrong." He grabbed the gear from her, "Here, let me!" With his help and direction, they were able to get things hooked up much more quickly.

She was grateful he came along, cause it would have taken her forever. She turned to him, "We need to get as many people who can travel as possible and get them on the wagons as quickly as we can. After you hook up the horses, can you help me look for people?"

He looked at her like he thought she was a little crazy, but after glancing at the mess around them, nodded, "Yeah, I can do that." Then he turned toward the horse pens.

Micaela headed toward the personal tents. She ran between them, checking for people. She directed anyone she found to grab what supplies they could and meet at the horse pens. After about twenty minutes of searching, she had found one full family, who had miraculously avoided any injuries, and six more people who were in good enough shape to travel. There were others who were still alive, but who would not be able to travel.

She continued through the tents. When she got to her own tent, she just kept going, since there shouldn't be anyone in there. It was partially knocked down like many others. Once she completed the small tents, she went to where she had seen people who had been fighting fires at the Big Top. She told them what Freya had said and then went to report in.

When she appeared, Freya asked "What were you able to do?"

"I found two workable wagons, and maybe fifteen or so people who could travel. Korel helped me set the wagons up. They will be meeting at the horse pens."

Freya retorted, "Well, come on girl, pick me up. We need to get out of here before that storm arrives. See that weird colored lightning. I don't think we want to know what happens when it strikes near us." Miceala spun around, looking at the storm clouds. She hadn't noticed it before, but there was a lot of lightning coming from the edge of the storm. The lighting was a vibrant mix of red, purple, and green. It didn't seem like it should be possible for lightning to be that color.

Turning from the storm, Micaela stooped down and picked up the Circus Matron. She was heavier than she looked. Micaela carried her carefully while Freya harped about things to avoid. "Watch out for that post!" "Care not to trip on that!" When they arrived at the wagons, she put Freya up where she could ride and see everything at the same time.

People were just starting to get loaded. Freya immediately took charge from her perch on the wagon. "What supplies do you have? Do you have tents? What about food? How about water skins?" People answered the best they could and just went about trying to comply. Before too long, Freya ordered, "Ok, we need to head out now! Right now! Everyone get on! If you aren't on, you get left behind!"

Micaela got on the second wagon along with the family she had found and a couple others. The father's name was Pentar and he had plenty of experience driving wagons. As they drove around the city, Micaela sat there thinking about what had happened. In the adrenalin-fueled rush, she hadn't had time to think about everything, but now that she was sitting still, the feelings of panic and worry rushed in. She hadn't found any of her team. She didn't know if they were alive or dead. Her whole life and everything she had worked for was effectively gone and she had no idea what would happen next. Emotion began to overwhelm her and she started to cry.

The youngest child of the family soon joined her, while the child's mother, a woman named Segrid, tried to comfort the young girl. Micaela was scared and confused and didn't know what to make of everything. She never would have believed that the Wizard's tower could have been destroyed. It was a symbolic anchor for much of her life.

Then there was the new dark tower and the dark cloud that was forming and spreading. Why had Freya been so afraid of it? Seeing Freya's reaction made her even more worried. Now they were fleeing, but to where? Freya said something about the Tower of Light, but Micaela only barely remembered anything about it. *Wasn't it on another continent?*

She vaguely remembered stories about the Great Darkness, but it never seemed real to her, even though she had grown up right next to where it had started. Now it seemed those stories had come back to life. She didn't know what to think.

She also realized that she might never see anyone she knew who was not on the wagon again. A huge sense of loss swept over her, and she began to cry and shake again. Segrid scooted over to her and rubbed her back to comfort her. She didn't say anything, but it helped a lot. Before long, she fell asleep, not realizing how tired she was from everything.

She woke up just after sundown, but before it started getting really dark. They had circled around the city and were headed south east toward the port of Jasteros. The storm raged with green, red, and purple lightning behind them. She couldn't tell how fast it was moving, but she was confident they didn't want to get caught in it.

It would soon be getting too dark to see. Almost everyone was sore and most of them had minor injuries. Freya whistled and both wagons slowed and pulled off the road. Once the wagons were stopped, Freya had someone boost her up where almost everyone could see her. "We need rest." She said loudly enough for them all to hear. "We will forage and make a light dinner. We start moving in the morning as soon as it is light enough to see the road."

Several men jumped off the wagons and quickly set up two large tents. One was dedicated to help treat those who needed more first aid. Pentar and his son Thanosh set up a large fire. Sigrid and her daughters Frieda and Vipora were assigned with Micaela to forage what they could from the forest next to the camp and the road.

They searched through the forest in the dim twilight and found a few patches of edible tubers and close by was a small berry patch. Micaela took the berry patch, but had it picked clean in only a few minutes. She turned to Sigrid, "I'm going to look for more berries further down the road." Sigrid nodded but didn't say anything.

She found another small berry patch a few hundred yards further, and quickly picked that clean. There weren't enough berries for everyone yet, so she continued a little deeper in the forest. After a few more minutes of searching by lantern light, she found a large patch of berries. She figured it would provide more than she needed and started picking.

Micaela was focused on berries and the bag she was gathering them in wasn't full yet. She had heard the other three call out that they were going back to camp. Micaela decided she didn't have enough yet and kept picking. While doing so, she kind of zoned out. She was pulled out of her trance by a scream from camp. Alarmed, she grabbed the lantern and started running back, trying to see what the matter was.

As she ran back to the camp, she looked up and could see the edge of the storm had caught them. It had been much quicker than she expected. Lightning flashed occasionally in the area around them, but almost seemed to be targeting their camp. As she got closer, she heard what sounded like fighting and indistinct yelling and screaming. As she ran up to the edge of the camp, she was bewildered at what she saw.

One of the tents was on fire at the back, while the burning wood from the campfire was scattered around the clearing. One of the men, possibly Gaiten, was swinging a large burning branch at something that she had trouble making out. There were others running around and fighting, with lots of yelling. Suddenly, something large moved into the light. It looked like a skeleton of a very large person, perhaps seven feet tall.

Gaiten swung the large branch and hit the skeleton in the head which slightly knocked it back, but didn't seem to damage it at all. The skeleton blocked his next swing with an arm and hit him in the chest with the other arm. Gaiten went flying out of the light, and the skeleton followed after.

Skeletons? Where did skeletons come from? Like so much else that had happened that day, it didn't seem like it could be real. The impossibility of it all made her think she was dreaming or crazy. The skeletons didn't have weapons, but would just bludgeon with their fists. She moved toward where she could see Korel fighting.

Korel wielded an axe and seemed to be doing well against a couple of skeletons when another appeared out of the darkness and stuck him across the back of his head. Micaela froze in shock and horror. The skeletons were swarming everywhere except where she was. The members of the company seemed to be going down fast.

Suddenly, a large purple lightning strike hit the ground only a few feet from her and she jumped back. As her vision began to recover, she saw a couple more skeletons forming from the ground where the lightning had struck. Even before they were fully formed, they started clawing their way across the ground toward her. She screamed and turned and ran back down the road.

Fortunately, she had kept the lantern. As she ran, she noticed a large animal off the side of the road. She was about to run past when she realized it was a horse. When they had stopped to camp, they let the horses out to graze in a field near where they had been foraging. In the dim lantern light, she had found one. The horse was skittish from the lightning and the noise, but she called out to it and it seemed to recognize her voice. She ran to it and quickly climbed onto its back and it took off.

Using the lantern, she was able to follow the road. It didn't take too long to outpace the storm and the skeleton, and she paused the horse and looked back. It mostly didn't seem real, but just enough that she started to weep again. She still didn't think there was anything that could be done for anyone. They were probably all dead.

Her weeping turned into greater sobs as she sat there looking at the storm. The lightning was getting closer again. She wiped her eyes and headed in the direction of the Tower of Light. Maybe she couldn't have helped those she knew, but she could warn as many people as possible on her way.

CHAPTER THREE

NERIAN

NERIAN HURRIED DOWN THE road toward the Royal Palace of Zentel on his way to his post at the Tower of Light. He double checked his armor to make sure he fully looked the part of a Royal Knight Lieutenant of Zentel. He had worked hard to become the youngest officer the royal knights had ever had. His diligence and dedication had been amplified by his numerous other advantages, establishing him as the standout knight of his generation.

He looked around at the early morning sky and noticed that it was later than he expected. He sighed in relief after quickly checking his watch and concluding that he would make it on time... as long as he didn't stop for anything. He had spent the night at his family's estate after visiting his mother the night before. The change in his normal environment interfered in his normal rhythm, causing him to sleep in. So he had to hurry.

As he descended the hill on the main road from the southern flats district, he looked at the Tower of Light sticking up behind the palace and the nobles district. It was majestic and blindingly white in the early morning light. The tower was legendary. It had been built to prevent another darkness and to spread enlightenment through the world.

Nerian glanced back at the road, navigating around a butcher's cart that was making early morning deliveries. There weren't too many people out and about yet, but the city was already starting to wake up. He could smell fresh bread baking somewhere close by and a few people were arriving to open their shops and stores.

He crossed the bridge over the river and approached South Palace Road. As he approached the outer palace wall, its height began to block his view of the mountains behind it, eventually even blocking his view of the Tower of Light, which rose nearly half a mile in the air. He turned to follow the road toward the main gate at the intersection of South Palace Road and Tower of Light Avenue.

Fewer people walked on that road because the offices of government bureaucracy that occupied most of the buildings wouldn't open for a couple of hours still. Suddenly, blinding light filled the air. He flinched back and shielded his eyes. His arm still covered his face when the massive roar of an explosion and a heavy concussive wave of compressed air surged past him, causing him to stumble and almost knocked him down.

His eyes began to recover when a second even larger blast wave surged back the other direction, throwing him into the outer palace wall at the side of the road. His helmet and armor dampened the blow, so he avoided being badly injured. Even then, his head swam and black dots scattered across his vision. He could hear a few loud crashes and realized that some large chunks of the palace wall were crashing to the ground around him. He quickly moved away from the wall and back onto the road while blinking to try to clear his vision.

As soon as he was away from the wall, another explosion rang out. It was smaller, but felt much closer. Large chunks of masonry tumbled from the top of the palace wall, and a smaller one bounced into his leg. It hurt, but he could tell that his greaves had prevented any broken bones. He had barely noticed the stone that hit him, as his eyes were still trying to recover from the blast.

Somewhere inside, he knew he should be doing something, but the blow from being thrown into the wall was still interfering with his thoughts. He rubbed his face, trying to clear his mind. Slowly, like light gradually increasing when coming up from deep water, his mind began to comprehend what he had just experienced.

Explosions! The last one had to be from the palace! He drew his sword and started running, but his bruised leg slowed him down. His mind now raced faster than he could run, and he began to look around, half expecting to see invading armies appear everywhere.

As he approached the main palace gate, he slowed. He had run past several people on the road who had been injured, but his main responsibility was protecting the kingdom. Still scanning for possible enemies, he rounded the corner to see the gate. Koz, another knight and one of his best friends, was lying on the ground, partially propped up against the damaged gate.

Nerian quickly sheathed his sword as he knelt and Koz's side. He could see that his lower thigh was severely injured and a lot of blood covered his leg and the ground underneath him. Someone had tied a cloth around it to contain the bleeding. Koz was conscious, but in extensive pain. Nerian started speaking to Koz, but realized he couldn't hear himself, or anything else for that matter.

Koz held up an empty vial, presumably from a standard issue healing potion and then pointed to Nerian, and then to his ear. Nerian got the message and pulled out one of his own potions and quickly drank it. He could feel the fast action potion start affecting his head, his ears, and his leg. A loud pop was the first thing he heard, followed by ringing and then the noises around him began. They were faint at first, but quickly became louder.

"There, can you hear now?" Koz asked with a pained grin.

Nerian struggled to deal with the overload of thoughts, feelings, and emotions that assaulted him. "I hadn't even realized my hearing was gone." He looked around at the debris on the ground around them and asked, "Any idea what that was?"

Koz looked at him like he was crazy, then pointed, "The tower blew up!"

Nerian followed his finger, trying to comprehend what he said, "What?" His eyes scanned the distance, trying to realize what was off about what he saw. Then it all snapped together in his mind. The Tower of Light was gone. "Bu.. bu.. but.. That's not possible!" he stared at the empty space where the tower should be. "How?"

Nerian continued staring, unable to accept what his eyes were telling him. Thoughts circled in his mind, unable to reach a conclusion. Somewhere in what sounded like the far distance he thought somewhat was talking to him. The tiny distant voice said, "Hey! Are you okay man?" Nerian was unable to respond. "Nerian?" the voice continued. Nerian had based his entire life plan around the tower, and it was gone! The voice became forceful, "Lieutenant!"

Nerian came to with a start, and looked down at Koz, who was still sitting on the ground. Koz looked at him with a puzzled expression, "Dude, snap out of it. We have trouble and you're the only one who is mobile at this point."

Nerian felt like the entire world rushed upon him in that moment as he realized the importance of Koz's words. He shook his head to clear his thoughts, "Ok, what do we do?"

Koz looked more concerned, "You're the senior officer, and you're asking me?" Koz looked at him in annoyance, "Well, to start, check on some of the injured people around us. Then, go check out the palace and see who you can find alive. Maybe look for the King or the Royal family. Find some more knights. Everything needs attention, so just pick something and do it. Oh, and if you find a healer, can you send them my way?"

Nerian stared at Koz. How could he be so casual about everything? And yet, he was right. There was a lot that needed Nerian's attention right then. He realized he hadn't handled the shock of the situation well, but he was determined that would change that instant.

Thinking about what Koz had listed, he looked around. Most important was to find the king, but almost as important and more pressing was to help those he encountered who needed help. There had only been a half dozen people close to the palace gate when the explosions had happened. At least one was obviously dead, but several others looked to be in pretty poor shape.

He checked his belt and realized he only had two more health potions, then looked back at Koz. "Do you have any more health potions?"

Koz nodded and pulled two more from his belt. "Yeah, here." Nerian took the potions and turned toward the injured people he could see. One was unconscious with a large head injury, but was still breathing. Nerian knelt and forced the man to swallow a potion.

Next he approached a middle aged couple. The slightly injured man was yelling "Stay with me!" at the woman, who was bleeding from her abdomen and appeared on the verge of passing out.

Nerian quickly offered a potion. "Here, give her this health potion. It may be enough to stabilize her." The man grabbed the potion, ripped the cork out, and got the woman to drink it.

Looking at the others that were close by, and knowing he should probably save at least one potion for when he got into the palace, Nerian decided that he could only help one of them. One appeared to be more injured than the others. He thought the others would probably heal eventually, but the one man needed urgent care. He used Koz's last potion on him, then turned toward the palace and started to run.

The pain in his leg from earlier was mostly gone and only slowed him a little bit. As he approached the main entry hall to the palace he slowed and again stared. The entire entry hall was just rubble. The entry hall had been large enough that grand balls were held there. It appeared that it had exploded outward and he vaguely recalled the second explosion.

He approached the main doors and found the bodies of two more knights there. They had been on duty guarding the doors, but had been killed when it exploded. A sense of guilt washed over him and he had to remind himself that there wasn't anything he could have done. Their armor hadn't saved them from the shrapnel and the impact.

In spite of the destruction, three of their health potions had survived in their belts. Nerian took those, then started around the north side of the palace toward the royal residence. He stopped cold with a grim frown when he saw the north side of the palace. It was completely smashed. He wouldn't be getting in that way.

He circled back to the south side until he reached the main section of the palace where the throne room was. It still stood, but there were very few intact windows. He briefly reflected on the irony that breaking into the palace like he was currently doing was one of the things royal knights were supposed to prevent. He refused to feel guilty about it and was sure the King would understand.

After going through the broken window of a clerical room, Nerian made his way into the maze of hallways that made up the center of the palace. He turned toward the shattered entry hall and found the doors for the throne room still intact. There should have been two knights guarding them, but considering the circumstances, they could be anywhere. He tried to open the main doors to the throne room, but they didn't budge.

He decided to kick them in, but again, it was like kicking solid stone. The doors were not magically enhanced and should have easily opened. They never should have withstood his kick. Nerian was puzzled about the door, but it was not as important as finding the king and helping people. He would find another way in.

The next closest entrance into the throne room was through the balcony. He went back to the hall outside the main doors and went up one of the grand staircases to the next level. As he started down the hallway there, he could see that it was blocked by debris and what could potentially be a large boulder.

Retreating back to the stairs, he decided to try the south side balcony and see if he could get in there. He halfway expected the door there to be blocked or damaged, but it opened silently. From the back of the balcony he could see that the opposite balcony was completely destroyed and the boulder he had seen blocking the entrance was actually a giant chunk of stone from the Tower of Light. It had smashed much of the north side of the throne room and completely blocked the main doors.

Nerian vocalized his amazement, "No wonder I couldn't get the doors to open." He looked down onto the floor of the throneroom. The throne was intact, but empty. He hoped that was a good sign, but he really couldn't be sure yet. There were less than a dozen people in the room, with perhaps half of them either dead or unconscious.

Nerian worried that too many important leaders of the kingdom might have died. He needed to help. He caught the distraction and pushed away thoughts about long term recovery, making himself focus on the current crisis. He quickly made his way to the front of the balcony and used a decorative tapestry as a rope to get down to the main floor.

One of the bodies on the floor was another knight, and Nerian quickly made his way to his side. He found that the knight was alive, but unconscious with head injuries and a broken arm. Nerian vaguely recognized the knight as one of the new rookies, but couldn't remember the young man's name. He searched the knight's belt and found two unbroken health potions. He moved the rookie so he could administer the health potion, then gently leaned him back on the floor.

He checked the others who weren't moving and found three of them dead. There were two others who were not. One was a young noble and the other was the King's steward, Theibold. After administering health potions to both of them, he checked on the others who were conscious. He felt pressure to keep searching for the king, but knew he had to help those he encountered who were injured.

One noble woman was in complete hysterics and the man with her was trying to calm her down. Once the woman was calmed, he turned to the man, a minor noble, based on his clothing. "Do you know where the king is?"

The man glanced up at him, stress and worry etched into his face, "He hadn't arrived for the morning court audience yet when everything happened."

Nerian nodded, "Thank you for your help." Nerian then went in search of the king. The door into the administrative offices that exited behind the throne was still in good working order, so he went through into the narrow private hall that connected the offices to the throne room.

As soon as he entered the small hallway, he noticed a sickly green gas filling the hall and offices. Nerian reflexively slipped on a magical breathing mask that all Royal Knights carried. He really didn't like the look of that gas. Miraculously, he hadn't breathed any of it. He cautiously moved down the hall towards the king's office. There were several offices along the way, most with their doors open. He noticed bodies of some of the royal pages in one of the offices, and one of the accounting assistants in another.

The gas was obviously lethal. It seemed to want to rise slightly toward the ceiling, and it gave him an idea. The hallway had three exits. He opened both the exits that went into larger hallways that ran along the sides of the palace. Those larger hallways had windows in them that were probably broken. If he propped the doors open, it might create a cross breeze that would blow the poison out and allow it to dissipate. He quickly propped the doors open before entering the king's office.

He didn't want to open the door and let the gas into the king's office if there wasn't already gas in there, but he had to check, just in case. He stood next to the door with his hand on the handle. It seemed his idea was working and the gas was thinning. Once the gas had dissipated enough, he opened the door to the king's office. He realized he had been worried for nothing, since the gas was much thicker in the king's office. He left the door open and looked around the desk. The king was lying on the floor.

Nerian gasped and rushed to the king's side, "Your Majesty!" He feared the king was dead, and that seemed even more impossible than the Tower of Light exploding. The king was one of the Halidar. He was immortal, wasn't he? He reached to check the king's pulse and the king stirred. Nerian released a breath he hadn't realized he was holding. The king was alive. Everything would be okay.

King Evander rolled over enough to see who was at his side and squinted. "Nerian?" He coughed with pain.

Nerian was shocked at the sick and weakened state of the king. He looked around at the thick green gas. "I have to get you out of here!"

He picked up the king as respectfully as he could while still hurrying and took him out into the nearest large exterior hall, called the Garden Hall. He checked to make sure the gas wasn't pooling around them and then set the king down gently where he could lean against the wall, hoping it would help. He removed his mask, "Is that any better, your majesty?"

King Evander leaned his head back against the wall and looked at Nerian through slitted eyes, "It's no use. There is no cure for this poison."

The very concept of the king dying was painful for Nerian, "But.. You're a Halidar. You can fix this, right. You're immortal! You can't die."

Evander squinted at Nerian, "Where did you get that idea? Some things even Rhondalyn can't cure. This is one of them! Nerian! I am still dying! Nothing can stop it. My power only delays it some, but it doesn't stop it."

Nerian didn't want to believe the king's words, but he also knew the king didn't lie and was never wrong. His chest felt tight and he found breathing difficult. He managed to squeak out, "What do we do?"

The king looked at him with concern, "Tell me, how bad is the damage?"

Nerian felt a brief moment of panic. He didn't want to be the bearer of bad news, but knew he had to speak the truth. He struggled for a moment to organize his thoughts into something like a coherent summary, "The Tower of Light is gone. The entry to the palace is destroyed. There is destruction and death and injuries everywhere. Anyone who was in the offices is dead, except you. I tried to help a few people including some like Theibold who was injured in the throne room."

The king coughed again, then looked at Nerian, deep in thought. After a minute he said, "The only purpose in destroying the Tower of Light would be if someone is trying to create another darkness. Stopping that is more important than anything else."

He stopped and struggled to reach his breast pocket. He retrieved something with his hand closed over it. He closed his eyes and focused. A light briefly surrounded him. He then opened his eyes and held out his hand to Nerian. "I have a high commission for you to fulfill."

Nerian looked at the engraved glowing eight sided token in the king's hand and listened to his words. What the king held out to him was an eight sided engraved coin like token with a glowing gem in the center. The gem glowed with enough power to light a small room. He recognized the token. The king's tokens and the high commissions that went with them were legendary. All guards and military in Zentel, and even in all of Chibor knew what that token meant. It was impossible to forge, and it only glowed when activated by the king. He had only seen one activated once, and it was the Royal Knight commander who held it then. Now he was being handed one.

The king looked deep into Nerian's eyes, "Gather up to a full squad of healthy royal knights and journey to Danlos on the continent of Arden. Seek Dardanos, my fellow Halidar at his tower. Help him in any way possible to make sure the tower of Sangar is not being rebuilt. If you find that there is a new overlord, do everything you can to stop them."

Nerian couldn't look away from the king while he spoke. He felt chills and a strange energy running all across his skin. He felt energized and focused like never before. He held up the token, not even remembering having reached for it. Almost without thinking, he said, "I will do so."

He started to stand, but then stopped himself. He couldn't just leave the king. What if he really was dying. He had to try to find help. "Your majesty, I know I have to go, but can't leave you here alone."

The king answered sadly, "Nothing can save me. This mission is more important than me. It may be more important than anything. As you try to gather your squad, you may find those who are too injured to accompany you. You can send one of them to accompany me."

Nerian nodded and turned. It bothered him to leave the king alone when he might be dying, but he had a high commission. He had to pursue its objectives over everything else. First step, find other healthy royal knights.

Chapter Four

Nerian

Still struggling with the decision to leave the king, Nerian began his search for other royal knights. He realized there was another royal knight in the throne room who might have awakened at this point. He went back through the royal offices, noting that the sickly green gas was mostly dissipated, and what little was left was only along the ceiling.

When he got to the throne room, he found the knight was starting to stir, but not really conscious yet. He checked on him, and noticed that Theibold was sitting up, blinking. He figured he should report the King's condition to the steward and approached him. "Steward Theibold?"

The older man looked up at him and recognition flashed in his eyes after a moment, "Lieutenant Nerian. Can you help an old man up?" Nerian reached down and helped Theibold stand.

"I need to report the condition of the king." he said, trying to keep emotion out of his voice.

Theibold looked him in the eye with worry on his face, "What happened to the king?"

Nerian took a deep breath before he began, "I found him lying on the floor of his office which was filled with a sickly green gas. He said he has been poisoned and that there is no cure. I took him to the garden hall and opened the doors to the private hall to air out the gas, and it seems to be working. Be careful though, the other offices and the private hall also had some of that gas and anyone who breathed it other than the king died." He gestured to the knight who was starting to sit up, "I'm getting that knight and assigning him to accompany the king." Theibold looked deep in thought as he listened.

Theibold glanced darkly up at Nerian, "The king said there is no cure?"

Nerian nodded, "Yes sir."

Theibold blew out a large breath, "Well that's not good. What else happened?" He gestured to the massive stone occupying the one side of the throne room, "I see we have redecorated."

Nerian frowned. He really didn't want to go through all that again, but reluctantly answered, "Yes sir. It appears to be a large chunk of the Tower of Light, which exploded and is now gone. Additionally, the entry hall blew up too. There are a lot of dead and injured and damage is nearly everywhere."

Theibold's eyes grew so wide, Nerian thought they would pop out, "The tower EXPLODED?!?"

Nerian nodded grimly, "Yes sir."

Theibold held his head with both hands, "Why would someone blow up the Tower of Light?!"

Nerian started fishing in his breast pocket for the king's token, "The king said the only reason to do that would be if they are trying to create another darkness." He fished the token from his pocket and held it up for Theibold to see. "He gave me a high commission to gather a squad of healthy knights and go to Danlos and help Dardanos stop or end the new darkness and fight the new overlord."

Theibold's mouth hung open as he stared at the token. After a few seconds he closed his mouth and stared at Nerian again. "Well, get going boy! High commissions are serious business!"

Nerian wanted to get someone to help the king first. He was very worried, "What about the king?"

Theibold pointed at the knight who now was awake and trying to sit up and failing due to his broken arm, "Assign that knight to assist the king. I will take care of everything else here. You need to get started on your commission. Do you know where you will search for healthy knights?"

Nerian shook his head, "I hadn't got that far. I guess I'll start here in the palace and then check the main barracks. I doubt there will be anyone healthy closer to the tower."

Theibold frowned regretfully, "Very well. That's probably the best approach. Get going."

Nerian had to stop himself from saluting, since the Steward was not in the chain of command, "Yes sir." He turned and approached the knight who had finally managed to sit up. "What is your name, Corporal?"

The corporal looked up at him, "Karl, sir."

Nerian reached down and lifted Karl by his good arm, "Karl, the king has been poisoned and says he thinks he will die. I left him in the Garden Hall. Go find him and do whatever you can to help him. Probably get him out into the fresh air of the Gardens"

"Yes, Sir! What about these people here?" Karl waved at the people remaining in the throne room.

"The Steward will take care of things here. You help the king. If you encounter any healers, see if they can help the king first before attending to anyone else."

"Ok! Where can I find you, sir?"

"The king has given me an assignment that I must take care of." Nerian held up the token from the king and Karl's eyes grew wide. "He charged me with putting together a special squad for a critical mission, but I need knights who are not badly injured. If you run into any other knights that are not badly injured, have them help you or search for others. Regroup in the gardens."

"And the people, sir?"

"We'll get to them. For now, I will have Senior Corporal Koz, who should still be at the main palace gates, send any additional Royal knights to the gardens as well. So far, all the Knights I have encountered are too severely injured to go with me. I will send any other knights I encounter to the gardens to join you."

"Yes, sir" the corporal saluted as Nerian turned away. He exited the throne room and headed back through the halls. He heard Karl following him. Once in the main halls, Nerian pictured in his mind all the different sections of the palace where he might find royal knights. Unfortunately, the first places that came to mind were either places he had already checked, but there was a small knights barracks alongside the royal residence.

The one brief look at the royal residence that he had showed that it had been mostly destroyed by the giant rock that now sat in the throne room. Still, there were probably sections that were only partially destroyed, and therefore might have knights that survived. He jogged through the palace halls, checking different sections.

He found two knights near the treasury, but they both had significant injuries from a damaged section of roof that had fallen on them. They still held their posts, but did so from the ground. If someone had thought to rob the treasury at that time, they probably could have gotten around the two.

A little later he found that the residence barracks was only partly destroyed. Out of sixteen knights that had been stationed there, eight were present and alive. Several were completely immobilized by fallen walls and ceilings, and the others had spent the time since the explosions digging them out. One of the knights was another lieutenant named Jeffrey who had just been freed from the debris when Nerian arrived.

Jeffrey had a broken shoulder and large injuries on one leg, but he still had taken command even before he was completely free from the rubble. When Jeffrey saw Nerian, he sighed a great relief. "I'm glad someone is uninjured. How did you escape?"

Nerian looked at him flatly, "Luck." Then he explained the situation, "I don't know how much of this you already know, but the tower has been destroyed, as well as the entry hall. There is a giant chunk of the tower filling up a large portion of the throne room."

Jeffrey was shocked, "What?!"

Nerian ignored his outburst and continued, "The king has been poisoned, and I have had another knight take him to the gardens. Theibold is managing the search and rescue operations near the throne room. I have told all the knights except the two guarding the treasury to help with the search and then assemble in the gardens. If any healers can be found, they are to go immediately to the gardens to help the king."

Jeffrey was still shocked, "Wait, where are these orders coming from?"

Nerian pulled out the token he had received, "The king. I am going to check the main barracks now. I hope it fared better than those of us here, but I'm somewhat doubtful about what I will find. Get everyone here to help with the search and then we will meet in the gardens in half an hour."

His next step was to go check the main barracks next. More than half of the Royal Knights lived in the main barracks, so he might find some there, but felt concerned because the barracks sat between the palace and the tower on the edge of the nobles district. It probably had been badly damaged.

When he got to the main gates, Koz was still there. Nerian gave him an update. "I found the king. He has been poisoned and doesn't think he will survive. He gave me a mission. I also found some more injured Knights in the palace and currently have them checking for others and taking care of the King. If any knights arrive here, send them to regroup in the gardens." He looked Koz over, "How's the leg?"

Nerian could tell Koz didn't want to think about it, but he answered anyway, "I'm not sure I'll be able to keep it. I hope so. It hurts but isn't bleeding anymore. I need better treatment than just a healing potion."

Nerian considered that. He hadn't seen any healers. Most of the healers would have been in the nobles quarter, the knights barracks, or the palace. He hoped some had survived. "If I see any healers, I will send them this way. I'll check back later. If I can, I'll have someone come and relieve you." Koz was obviously in pain, but he looked better than he had earlier.

Koz nodded, "Thank you. I will wait here and keep tabs on things the best I can until you send a replacement."

Nerian jogged toward the main barracks. There were a few injured people on the road, and he gave health potions to a couple of them. When he arrived at the main barracks, he was dismayed. There were some sections standing, but most had collapsed and were broken. He quickly started going through the ruined buildings.

When he had first seen the destroyed barracks, he was fearful that no one had survived. He was relieved to discover that royal knights were known to be tough for a very good reason. More than half of the knights who had been there had survived.

He found that while all were injured, many had survived and been able to get to their health potions. There was evidence that a few had survived the initial destruction but then succumbed. That saddened him, but it wasn't nearly as bad as he had expected.

The most tragic part was that the command building had been pulverized by another large stone from the tower. He found not another single officer among the knights that lived beside himself and Jeffrey.

He organized the remaining knights and then directed them to assemble in the palace gardens while he went to check the tower barracks. His trip there took longer than he expected because the scale of destruction increased greatly as he approached where the tower once stood.

The tower barracks was the only building besides the tower itself that had occupied the grounds proper. It was also where he normally lived, and the only reason he wasn't there was that he had spent the night at his family's estate. As he got closer, his fears materialized. The only way he could identify where the barracks stood was by analyzing debris patterns and piles of crushed rock. Nothing larger than his fist had survived at all.

There were no other survivors.

He stood there numbly for several minutes. There was nothing left. Not even any of his normal belongings besides what he had on his person survived. All the rest of his platoon was completely wiped out. He wiped his face and found that tears ran down his face leaving trails in the dust there.

Nerian knew there was nothing he could do. He had a high commission, and to fulfill it, he had to travel further than he ever had. He wasn't even sure if he would ever see his home city again once he left. He pulled out a handkerchief and wiped his face as best he could, then turned back towards the palace.

When he arrived at the gardens, he quickly identified the gathering of knights. He had arrived just after those from the barracks due to their being injured and slow. He could see Lieutenant Jeffrey and he approached with some concern. "Where's the king? I don't see him."

Jeffrey looked up at him, surprised at his sudden presence, "A small group of knights and a healer are trying to treat him in his private garden." Jeffrey pointed the direction they had gone, and Nerian quickly moved to follow.

As he navigated around the concealing hedge, he could hear voices but couldn't make out what was said. Urgency was held in the tone, even if he couldn't discern the words. He sped up and arrived around the last corner, just in time to see a healer place a blanket over the king's head. Nerian froze and stared.

All sound had ceased and the world hardly moved. He couldn't so much as shift his eyes from the blanket draped over the body of his king. *NO! This can't be real! The king can't die! He's an immortal Halidar!*

Slowly the world began to move again and sound reappeared. One of the knights looked up at him with a tear streaked face. It was Karl. Karl made himself stand taller and started walking toward Nerian. As he got closer, he managed to squeak out, "I'm sorry Lieutenant. We tried everything we could. We couldn't save him." The last was barely more than a whisper.

Nerian felt tears on his own face as he closed the distance between them and put his hand on his good shoulder. "Thank you for trying." He said softly. Then he spoke louder so the others could hear, "Thank you all for trying. The king himself had said he would die. I appreciate your efforts. Let's gather with the others." Nerian led them all back to the gathering of knights.

As they arrived, he could see Lieutenant Jeffrey was getting reports from and giving instructions to different search groups about the search. Nerian looked around. Every single knight was injured with broken arms, splinted legs, bandaged heads, or other significant injuries. A quick estimation let him know that more than forty percent of the knights were not there, either dead, or too injured to make it there.

A thought occurred to him and he turned to Karl and the knight next to him, "Both of you go to the main gate. Karl, if you can take Koz's place and if you.." indicating the other knight, "if you can help him back here." They both saluted and left. Nerian watched after them and thought for a moment, then turned and walked over to Lieutenant Jeffrey.

Jeffrey looked up at his approach, "How can I help you?"

Nerian frowned for a moment, "You may have heard by now that the king is dead. Did they find any of his family?"

Jeffrey shook his head grimly, "Two bodies, the rest are missing."

Nerian sighed, "I guess that means for now, we have to assume the Steward is in charge. I am heading to his office, then I will be leaving, meaning you are the ranking knight officer. I wish you luck."

As Nerian turned to leave, Jeffrey called, "You too! For what it's worth, I think you have the harder task." Nerian shrugged and headed back into the palace. He decided to start looking for Theibold in the royal offices and he made his way there.

Theibold was in his office next to the king's office when Nerian arrived. There was no sickly green gas anywhere to be seen. A few of the palace staff were just leaving as Nerian entered. "Lieutenant," Theibold greeted him.

"Steward Theibold," Nerian responded. He stood as straight as he could, "I bear ill tidings.... The king has died."

Theibold stared at Nerian without any other response for over a minute. Nerian could tell that he was trying to process the ramifications of the news. Finally he spoke. "What of the royal family?"

Nerian shook his head, "We have found two of them dead, and the others are missing."

Theibold pursed his lips as he processed the information. "The nobles council?"

Nerian shrugged, "We haven't even looked yet, but if they were in the Nobles district, then they are likely dead as well. I went through there when I checked on the tower barracks. Very little is still intact or even standing."

Theibold's expression had been grim when Nerian arrived, and with each piece of news, it fell even further. At that point, he looked like he was carrying the whole world on his shoulders. His voice was just above a whisper, "What about you? Have you been able to gather a squad of knights?"

Nerian's body wanted to shake, but he forcibly held it still. He responded quietly, "There are none who are well enough to make the trip."

Theibold, who had been standing and trying to keep a strong posture the whole time, slowly lowered himself into his chair. He leaned forward and buried his face in his hands for a minute. Then he looked up as Nerian sat in a chair across from him. "What do we do?"

Nerian shook his head sadly, "I don't know. I haven't even left the city and already I am failing my commission. I was hoping to get advice from you."

Theibold sat with his mouth closed, his eyes furtively darting around the room. At long last he looked back at Nerian, "It seems we both have challenges ahead of us. I have a few thoughts if you can wait here while I get something. It might take about ten minutes."

Nerian gestured with one hand and a shrug, "Sure, I guess." Theibold stood and left the office, limping as he went. Nerian sat and waited, trying to anticipate what the Steward would say. About ten minutes later, he returned and handed Nerian a good sized leather bag. It was very heavy. Nerian looked at it cautiously, then looked at Theibold as he sat back in his chair.

Theibold looked across the desk at him, "You can use the power of wealth to help you in your mission. I think I understand the implications of what your commission is about, and while you can't flat out buy a solution, there is enough there to greatly speed your progress. Consider hiring mercenaries, bribe other kingdoms, hire assassins, mages, buy what you need, and so forth, but be cautious. While it may seem like a lot, it won't last all that long once things get expensive."

Nerian looked into the bag, and there were bundles of rolled coins. Many of them were platinum coins. There were many rolls of gold coins as well as enough silver and bronze that he couldn't imagine what he couldn't purchase with them. He wasn't sure what to say. It was an enormous sum. Greater than most treasures of legend. He coughed as he stared and tried to understand what he was being entrusted with. "Um, are you sure?"

Theibold waved off his concern, "We have far more than enough here. If what the king feared happens, stopping it will be the only way to save us, regardless of what we spend locally." Nerian stared wide eyed, hardly believing what was happening. Theibold gestured to the door, "Now get going. Be careful. Stay focused, and remember that it won't last as long as you think it should. Wars and epic quests are unbelievably expensive."

Nerian stood, feeling alone and overwhelmed. He appreciated the support, but from here on, he expected he would be alone. He needed to get supplied before he left, but the barracks had all been destroyed. There wasn't much he could get in the palace, other than a horse. He went to the stables and got a royal charger, since it would be able to support him better than other horses. Then he rode to his family's estate.

The main gates were closed and securely barred. He continued to the servant gate and noticed one of the family servants rush out just ahead of another that was rushing in. He tied off his horse and went in, almost running into one of his mother's guards. The guard jumped back in surprise, "Master Nerian!" he exclaimed.

"At ease. The main gate is barred, so I came here."

The guard stammered for a second, "Ah.. ah.. Of course sir."

Nerian looked up at the servant's entrance to the manor and could see one of the servants look at him with wide eyes and duck away. *I wonder what that was about?* He approached and entered, but didn't see the servant again. When he reached his mother's drawing room, she was already walking toward him with concern written all over her face.

Her voice showed even more worry than her face, "Nerian. I'm grateful to see you, but shouldn't you be out protecting the king and the city?"

He wasn't sure where to start. There was too much, so he just dove in, "You probably already know the Tower of Light has been destroyed." She nodded as he continued, "I am the only survivor from my platoon. The king was poisoned and gave me a high commission before he died."

Horror flashed across her face and she looked like she was going to faint. He quickly stepped forward and wrapped his arm around her to support her. "Here mother, sit down until you feel better."

They sat and she leaned against him. She spoke softly, her confusion evident, "That is beyond terrible, but.. why are you here instead of out there working?"

He sighed heavily as he thought about how to explain it to his mother, "All the barracks were destroyed and there are no ready supplies for my mission. I stopped here to get supplies and to let you know I will be going on a mission very far away."

She turned and looked at him, "How far away?"

He shrugged, "Arden. At least."

She eyed him suspiciously, "How long do you expect this mission to last?"

He realized that he didn't know, and paused to figure out how to explain it. Finally he said, "I don't know. Maybe forever. It's a desperate gamble against overwhelming odds. I don't even know how to properly go about it, but regardless, it is my high commission and I must do it." He pulled the king's token from his pocket and she stared at it wide eyed. He added, "I worry about you."

She waved him off, "I'll be fine. Your brother and sisters have everything well in hand here. You just focus on your mission." She stood, seemingly recovered, "Now, what supplies do you need before you go off to save the world?"

CHAPTER FIVE

ROBERT

ROBERT SIGNED THE DOCUMENT and placed it in the only empty bin on his desk. The entire rest of the space was covered with bins and piles of papers. Requisitions, requests, orders for the guards, reports of lost or misplaced supplies, and requests for clarification on just about everything. Three days ago, the doors to the new tower were sealed and general orders went out to all the staff. He had been one of the few who knew about it all beforehand, but still, there had not been enough time to get everything straight.

The staff had been instructed to pack everything they used and move it all into the tunnels far below ground. What most of them didn't know is that those tunnels continued for a couple miles and came out in a new tower that was entirely below ground for the first day. Everything that could be moved ahead of time had already been moved, but anything that was part of their normal operations had to be moved in that one day window.

Robert had been one of three directing the logistics of the move, and had ordered the guards to help move all the kitchen and facilities staff with all their own supplies and equipment. They had made it before the deadline, barely. Robert hadn't been the one to plan the relocation, but he was the one who had to make sure it all worked out.

They had to complete the move before they collapsed the tunnels and destroyed the old tower. Robert hadn't liked the plan the first time he heard it, and hadn't grown any fonder of it with time. The explosion of the old tower had mostly been muffled inside the new tower, but no one had missed the new tower rising thousands of feet upward. No one had been allowed to unpack anything until the new tower reached its final position. For a time, it felt like the vibrations were going to shake the entire world to pieces, but eventually it stopped and power surged through the tower core.

Robert knew the explosion and the raising of the new tower had caused a lot of death, destruction, and panic in the city outside, and would negatively affect the world as the storm and news of it spread. Dardanos had assured him and others who had concerns that it was necessary and that it would all be made better in the end. Once the tower had finished rising, he hadn't had much time to think about everything outside, since inside was such a mess.

It seemed everyone was panicked because they could not find something that was misplaced in the rushed relocation. People were constantly getting lost in new parts of the unfamiliar tower, and search parties for lost workers were a nearly constant thing. Fortunately, the workers couldn't leave the tower and were magically restricted to the top 20 floors.

The downside was that each of those floors was a mile and a half long if one went all the way around the tower and a couple hundred feet from one side to the other. There were no main hallways that followed more than a small part of each circumference, so getting lost was more than easy, even for those who had some idea where they were.

Robert reviewed the next several reports, which were actually about search parties finding lost workers and where they had gotten to. One of the kitchen helpers had gotten almost halfway around the whole tower circumference because she got turned around and was sure she was going in the right direction. By time she figured out she wasn't where she thought she was, she panicked and just kept running, in the wrong direction of course.

Perhaps it would be better to just set up checkpoint barriers around the main working sites like the kitchen and the laundry. Robert thought about that as he moved to the next report. Another lost person, no, people. A whole search party was lost. "For crying out loud!" He complained out loud to himself, "Can't these people get anything right?"

Next was an issue where half of the supplies for the top floor kitchen had ended up in the laboratory freezers 20 floors below and a third of the way around the circle. They only had 2 people available and the kitchen staff was too busy preparing food even though they were missing several key ingredients. Robert quickly wrote out his orders.

"Delay dinner for the floor by half an hour. Order all kitchen staff who are missing ingredients to take serving carts and follow the guards who know the way. They are to load up everything they need first, and then anything else that they can fit on their carts that belong in the kitchen." He finished writing out the order, put it in his outbox, and rang a little silver bell. One of his clerks ran into the room to gather the outbox items.

"Handle this one on top first. Take it directly to Sargent Cooper on the top floor." he ordered the clerk.

"Yes sir. Right away!" The clerk responded and practically ran from the room. Robert realized the clerk was one of the new people and that he didn't even know his name. He shook his head in frustration at the chaos. He continued working through the reports, requests, and other documents.

It seemed that all rational thinking had ceased amongst the staff once the tower had started shaking and rising out of the ground. Fortunately, most of the staff had no idea how high exactly the tower now stood over the plain. It was high enough that the ground was partially obscured by clouds and haze, made worse by the fires that had resulted in the destruction of the old tower and the storm that raged and expanded out from the new tower. It was regrettable that there was so much destruction, but Dardanos had assured him it was necessary that they were rumored to be dead.

Robert didn't want to think much about the implications of this new tower and everything that came with it. Dardanos had even had people start calling him "Overlord" and would berate anyone who called him by his name. Robert had worked for Dardanos for a couple of hundred years, the wizard's magic keeping him young, but he feared that the old Wizard was beginning to lose his sanity. Robert couldn't ignore all the similarities between the current new tower and the legends of the Great Darkness. Dardanos, or the new Overlord as he wanted to be called, had assured him it was all for the best cause, but still the worries nagged at him.

Several hours later, he was almost finished with the bulk of the urgent issues and his aide Kaltha came in with his dinner. "You have been working too long sir, if I didn't bring you something to eat, you would starve." She lightly scolded him as she put the tray on his desk.

"Thank you Kaltha, I just have too much to do. I am used to running a very orderly operation and this whole thing has just been a disaster." He frowned and then took a bite. He paused after clearing his mouth and said "Here, can you take care of these issues?" He handed her a big stack of papers from the corner of his desk. "Just sign my name on them and handle them however you think is best. If you are really unsure about something, come and ask me."

"I can do that, but I don't know if you will be available for me to ask. I was also told to pass the message that The Overlord wants to see you." She emphasized the title dramatically. It was good to see that he wasn't the only one who felt it was a bit ridiculous.

Robert did his best to hide his frustration, "Ok, do you know where I am supposed to find him?" he asked and then took another bite.

"I would assume in Central Command. He really hasn't been out and about much today. I think he has been pretty busy in there. Every time I am on that floor, I see his research staff running in and out like ants in a line."

Robert nodded, "Ok, as soon as I finish eating, I will go." She left with the large stack of papers. He was glad she was so capable. That was about a third of the remaining mess he still had on his desk that she just walked out with. He soon finished eating and left his office.

His office was four floors above Dardanos's, no, he corrected himself, the Overlord's Central Command. The way the floors were numbered was counterintuitive. The top floor was numbered 1, while the floor with Robert's office was numbered 12 and the floor with Central Command was floor 16. The four floors below Central Command were reserved for researchers, while anything below that was strictly off limits for everyone except the Overlord and two of his key research assistants.

When he reached the 16th floor, he was able to make it quickly into the block of offices and meeting rooms that surrounded Central Command. There were still a lot of people rushing here and there despite the late hour and he didn't want to get in their way so he sat in a chair waiting for a pause in the rush. He looked around, and could see the hallway that led to the control room. It wasn't as busy as it had been two days earlier. Soon, he heard Dardanos's voice call out brightly, "Robert, don't wait out there all night, come in."

Robert walked into the huge suite of offices, big enough to hold a small battle in. "I didn't want to interrupt everything going on. Am I really not interrupting anything, sir?"

"Oh, you know me better than that. You might have to wait until I get a break from the hustle and bustle, but I will always have time for you." Dardanos was in quite a cheerful mood.

Robert had to check himself and remind himself to think of his boss as 'The Overlord'. "I was told you wanted to see me."

"Yes, you run my intelligence operations as part of the guard corps, correct?"

"Yes, that hasn't really changed in decades. Is there something you want confirmation on?" Robert was puzzled by the avenue of questioning.

"I have a mission of the utmost importance that needs to be run. It must be undertaken by someone I trust implicitly. That person is you." The Overlord's strangely happy demeanor took on a more serious tone.

"What of the chaos of getting everything organized in the new tower? It is still quite the mess and I have a lot of work left to get it running as we are used to."

"Have Kaltha handle things. You already have her managing a lot of things. Have captain Griesh report to me directly in your stead for anything that is not directly related to standard operations. As for intelligence, I expect you to give me regular reports using communicators. Your people can keep you up to date the same way." The instructions indicated that he would be on a long journey and gone for a good amount of time.

"Where am I going?" he asked to confirm his suspicions.

"I have detected some strange magical emanations that appear to be coming from the High Reach Mountains on Isalor. I don't know what Rhondalyn is doing, but whether she means to or not, what she is doing is strong enough to possibly cause complications with our plans. I want you to make your way to Isalor and find where she is holed up. She is supposed to be a hermit these days, but hermits don't do things that cause such strong emanations."

"Ok, anything else you want me to do there?"

"Find out what she is up to. If she has some kind of organization, infiltrate it, recruit someone from the inside of her operations if possible. I want to know everything about what she's doing."

Robert stood up a little taller, "Yes, Overlord. I will begin preparations at once."

"Have Geron help you coordinate with my research staff to make sure you have all the best equipment we can provide you. We want you to have the best probable outcome for this mission. Keep in mind, Rhondalyn is one of the Halidar. She is not to be underestimated. Even if she is not involving herself in what we are doing, she can be dangerous and disruptive."

"Yes sir!" Robert left the office, collecting Geron, one of the Overlord's personal guards on his way. They went to meet Terlan, one of the chiefs of the innovation group from the Overlord's research staff. They spent the next two hours going through a multitude of equipment upgrades and devices to help him on his mission.

By time they were done, he had bundles of communication devices, scrying tools, trackers, ward stones, ward breakers, and even a newly developed storage ring that could store everything he was given as long as it wasn't too high energy. Terlan then replaced his clothes with several new outfits enhanced with unobtrusiveness, camouflage, powered stealth, environmental resistance, and a hardening armor effect in case he was struck. Lastly, he was equipped with a whole armory worth of weapons.

He wondered, *Do they think I am going to fight a whole army?* He had a fire sword in his preferred style and length, two special daggers, one which canceled magic, and the other which paralyzed his target with only the slightest nick. On top of that was an automatically reloading crossbow with multiple cartridges of shadow bolts, fire bolts, ice bolts, lightning bolts, poisoned bolts, regular sharpened bolts, and a special anchor bolt with an attached rope and retracting belt clamp.

As if that wasn't enough, he had several cases of specialty hand thrown bombs. Some of them caused blinding caustic smoke when they hit. Others released knockout gas, and the worst were poison gas. Fortunately, each one came with an antidote vial, but it all made him feel rather nervous. He wouldn't have been able to carry a third of it if not for the storage ring. He hadn't known about it ahead of time and was quite surprised when they showed it to him.

After getting his equipment fully upgraded, Robert returned to his own office. He spent the next hour keying communicators and attuning the devices he was given. Then he gave instructions and communicators to his subordinates, had the kitchens provide him with several containers of provisions, and requisitioned adequate funds to provide for any eventualities he thought he might run into on the journey.

He paused in his office foyer and looked around, trying to think of anything he personally needed to handle before he left, but he had good people taking care of everything. As he thought about leaving, he realized that since the floors where he was no longer connected to the tunnels, but were instead more than a mile and a half in the air. He wondered, So, now that we are so high in the air, how are we supposed to get out of here?

He eventually ended up back at The Overlord's office since no one else knew. When he entered, The Overlord looked up and asked "Yes, weren't you supposed to be leaving on a mission?"

Robert responded with a bit of redness in his cheeks. "Yeah, I am all ready, but, um, I don't know how to leave the tower now that it is raised. How do I get out of here?"

The Overlord laughed and smiled, "Here, I need a break from my desk. Let me show you. You're going to like this. Coming back in will be very similar, but in reverse." They made their way to the back of the overlord's central command and entered a heavily fortified receiving area where two of The Overlord's personal guards were manning things.

"Ok gentlemen, we are going to make the first regular use of the new entrance to the tower. Robert, come this way." The Overlord gestured to an alcove further into the room. As he passed the two guards, Robert could see they had a view of what seemed to be a window looking out at ground level. We have three of these transporter rooms. One is larger for dealing with supplies and large deployments.

Once Robert stepped into the alcove, a strong magical pulse triggered and one of the guards did something that Robert couldn't see. A bright blue magical shell flashed all around the interior of the alcove and he felt like the world paused. Then, the shell cleared and he found himself in what appeared to be the same alcove, but with the entrance now behind him. Out of the entrance was the ground. As he walked forward, he heard the Overlord's voice from the alcove. "Good luck Robert. Check in tomorrow around sunup. We will schedule our further touchpoints then." There was a click, and then nothing more. Just an empty alcove that went nowhere.

"What a way to enter and leave the tower." thought Robert. Then, he walked out and started on his mission.

CHAPTER SIX

FINN

THE HAMMER RANG OUT as a young man pulled the door to the smithy open. He entered and stood back, waiting for the blacksmith to finish what he was doing. The old grizzled Blacksmith looked up from where he was working all alone, his apprentice nowhere to be seen. "Ho there Finn, can you pump the bellows for a bit? Carlisle had to run an errand, but I have some urgent orders to get out."

Carlisle was Master Ganslow's apprentice. Finn quickly went to the bellows and began to pump. His hand was smooth, his arm strong, and he felt comfortable with the experience he had with it. The coals soon began to glow brighter and Master Ganslow moved the object he was working on back to the hearth and plunged it into the coals. "That's good for now." Finn stopped pumping. "When I lift it out to the anvil, take these tongs from me and hold it steady. I have another part to add to it."

The blacksmith added another piece of metal to the coals in the hearth, and then pulled the original object out and moved it to the anvil. Without asking any questions, Finn seamlessly transitioned to holding the tongs the blacksmith had been using. Ganslow picked up a smaller set of tongs and fished the other piece of metal out of the coals. It was much smaller and already glowing red. He moved it to the other piece and began hammering the two pieces together. Soon, the blacksmith moved the whole object back to the coals and Finn returned to pumping the bellows.

The process continued and another small piece and then another was added to the device. Finn still didn't know what it was for, but he figured it was following some design the blacksmith had in his head. About that time, Carlisle returned and he and Finn swapped out. "Thank you for your help, Finn." Master Ganslow said. "If I didn't already have an apprentice, I would offer you the job, but, it will be a while before Carlisle here has moved on to his own shop, and I figure you will be long gone by then."

"That's alright Master Ganslow. I don't know that blacksmithing is really my calling in life. I think it would wear on me before too long. I just don't have the right passion for it." Finn smiled slightly as the blacksmith looked up at him. "I do like to help out, but I don't think I will ever sling a hammer the way you two do. Is there anything else I can help you with? Deliveries to be made?"

"Oh, yes, over on the finished shelf, there is a bundle of tools wrapped in canvas that need to go to the carpenter. Can you take them over? I will settle the accounts later myself."

"Sure thing Master Ganslow." Finn went over to the finished shelf, identified the right package and hefted it. He then swung it up onto his shoulder and headed out the door.

The carpenter's shop was a couple streets over in their small town of Mijople. The bulk of the merchant district filled in the distance between. Several people greeted Finn as he carried his load, and he greeted them back by name.

He soon arrived at the Carpenter's shop, opened the door and entered. "Good morning, Isan. Where do you want me to put these tools from Master Ganslow?"

The carpenter looked up from the furniture he was working on. "Good morning, Finn. Put those over on that table there. I will sort them out in a bit."

Finn placed the heavy bundle on the table and then turned to Isan. "Is there anything I can help you with today," he asked.

The carpenter stopped what he was doing and reached into his pocket. "Um, yes, here, take this ticket and the pushcart down to the sawmill and pick up this order of lumber, please." Isan went back to his work and Finn went out the back door to get the pushcart. The trip down to the sawmill and back took about 45 minutes. Part of that was loading up the lumber, but the longest part was pushing the cart back. It was a heavy load, but Finn never complained.

He was grateful that he was allowed to help so many of the different crafters in town. He had been helping people out now for about 5 years. When he started, few wanted to trust him with the work, and those that did probably allowed him to help more out of sympathy than anything else. It was pretty well known that his father had recently died in those days and he and his mother were in need. The sympathy had increased when his mother had become sick.

Prior to that, they lived very comfortable lives and his mother always had money for anything they wanted. The money came from his father and was to ensure he had a proper upbringing for the son of a Duke, even if he was an illegitimate son in this case. His mother paid for tutors and trainers and made sure he had opportunities of just about every kind to make sure he had his choice of careers and could decide his own future.

They still lived a fairly simple lifestyle despite the financial backing they had. Mijople was where she grew up, so when things didn't work out with his father, she returned there. His mother often used some of the money she received to support various crafters and tradespeople in the town when they were having a hard time, even though they often didn't need what she ordered and she would often give the items away. That had all changed when Finn was about twelve years old. They received word that his father had fallen ill, and then that he had died. After that, there was no more money. There was a rumor that his father had been poisoned at the orders of his wife, the Duchess, because she hated that he provided for his illegitimate son and his former mistress, but Finn had never believed it.

He and his mother then had to find ways to earn a living. She took up working in the tavern, and helped the tailor at times. He had started doing odd jobs for the various crafters in town. That worked for a while, but then his mother became ill. They used everything they had to get medical help, but nothing worked. She soon died. Finn did have the small cottage where they lived, and since he didn't know anything else, he continued doing odd jobs for people.

Doing the odd jobs eventually turned into a regular routine where he frequently checked in with different people. They even taught him some of their trades. The blacksmith had wanted him for an apprentice, but Finn really didn't want that life, and fortunately, the blacksmith was already obligated with his current apprentice. The young carpenter had discussed him becoming an apprentice there, but didn't push the issue when Finn indicated that he didn't want to pursue that field either.

The tavern keeper, the city guards, and a hunter had all expressed interest in having him apprentice with them as well, but in each case, he turned them down. He still kept his route doing odd jobs, and sometimes larger opportunities would come along, which he loved, but he always returned to his routine.

After fetching the load of lumber, the carpenter had him help hold various pieces of wood in place while the carpenter attached them on the cabinet he was making. After that, Finn said goodbye and he moved on with his route. Next, he checked in with Bojerus at the tavern, where he was asked to help the cook prepare vegetables and other ingredients. Then the tavern keeper had him go pick up various orders from some merchants and the brewer. Part of the deal with the tavern keeper was that he always got a free lunch when he was helping.

Next, he stopped by the hunter's lodge and checked in with Gesh, who was the most successful hunter in town, and also a cousin of some sort. Gesh didn't need help that day, but was planning a multi day trip the next week that he wanted Finn to come on. After that, he went by the city guard's barracks, where he cleaned equipment and sharpened blades and polished boots.

Lastly, not too long before dinnertime, he checked in with Staynor who was supposed to be back in town. Staynor was a trader who would run longer trips to and between larger cities and would often pick up things people and merchants in town couldn't produce locally. Staynor let him know that he would be leaving the next day on an emergency run to Beaumont, a large city on the far side of the duchy, and he wanted Finn along.

Finn found himself retracing his steps letting everyone know he would not be available for the next couple of days since he was going on a trip with Staynor. Finn had been to Beaumont a couple of times, and it always seemed like an adventure. He loved seeing the larger buildings and shops and the special goods that were almost never seen in his town. He headed home early to try and get extra sleep so he would be well rested to start the journey.

The next morning, he met Staynor at his warehouse while it was just starting to get light. Staynor had his big wagon out and already hooked up and pulled by four draft horses. It looked like whatever they were picking up would be heavy. Because it was an emergency trip, Staynor had only arranged for a small amount of cargo for the trip out. Finn loaded it up quickly, and then they hopped on and started driving.

The big wagon was not as smooth as his normal wagon, but it could carry a lot more. At first, Finn just enjoyed the ride, watching nature, and feeling fairly content that this trip would provide a nice bonus in his earnings. After a time, Staynor spoke up. "So, Finn, you are... what, 17 years old now?"

"Yep, 17."

The old man glanced at him out of the corner of his eye. Finn could tell that Staynor wanted something more than just a hired hand, but the old man was quiet for a bit before he spoke again. "You've been doing odd jobs for five years now, I figure. That about right?"

Finn tried to not feel nervous about where this was going. "Yeah, about five years. You were one of the first to hire me."

"Yeah, I remember that. You might not know this, but your mother was a distant cousin of mine."

Finn glanced at him, feeling a little uncomfortable. "No, I didn't know that."

"Yep, she was. We weren't all that close most of the time, but when things got rough, we knew we would always be there for each other. She helped me finance my first wagon, back before you were born. Twisted the arm of that fancy father of yours or something like that."

"I didn't know that. She never talked about him."

"Well, I think he loved her, but she wasn't a noble, so he had to marry someone else, or some such nonsense. That monster he married never did like it much, and hated that he still took care of you two. Once their child, I guess he would be your half brother, was about 5, your Father got sick and she took over running everything as regent and he died shortly thereafter."

"I don't think I have ever met either of them." Finn was curious, but still wary of where this conversation was going.

"Rumor says that the witch has always had agents in Mijople, and that after your mother died, some of those agents left."

"What are you saying?"

"Oh, maybe nothing, just that your father got sick and died and nothing could cure him, and then your mother got sick and died and nothing could save her, and the witch had people around in both cases. Don't know if it really is as it seemed, but just interesting to think about."

"You think she had my mother and my father killed? With what, poison?" Finn was getting a little upset. He hadn't really ever thought about it, and his mother had never talked bad about his father's wife.

"Well, I don't know, I just hear things, but pretty much every time she has a problem with someone, that person or someone close to them gets sick and dies. One or two could be coincidence, but I hear patterns of more than a dozen with the same symptoms and then death and the only thing connecting them all is that she was involved."

"Why are you telling me this?"

"Well, it is hard to know for sure, but there have been some folk move back into town recently that might have some connection to your father's duchy. I am not saying they are involved, or that they are here to get you or something, but it might be worth thinking about." The old trader looked like he was casually talking about something as mundane as the weather. Finn was wide eyed and still trying to process everything.

"So, what should I do?" he asked, hoping for some advice.

"What do you want to do?" The old man answered.

Finn was feeling very alarmed by where the conversation had gone, "I don't know. I don't want to die, how about that?" Finn was exasperated.

"Well, with you being 17 and all, it might be time you figure out what you want out of life, and then go out into the world and seek it. Doing odd jobs for folk won't always take care of you well."

He tried not to sound too defensive, "I know that. That is why I save just about everything I have earned the last several years."

"Oh, that is very good. You looking to buy some kind of shop or something?" Again, Finn felt like Staynor was still skirting around the real issue.

"I.. I don't really know what I want. I just know I need to have money to live and so I save everything I can."

"Well, you have lots of learnin', and you have tried your hand at lots of stuff, so perhaps the challenge is that you have too many options. Most younguns only get one, maybe two options. They learn the trade of their folks or perhaps show high aptitude at some other trade and get picked up as an apprentice. You show lots of aptitude in lots of things, and you have turned down quite a few apprenticeships, so I ask again. What do you want to do?"

"I still don't know." Finn thought he now understood what Staynor was trying to get at.

"Well, perhaps you can take this trip and spend some time thinking about what you would like to do, and where. I figure staying in Mijople may not be good for your health. I recommend going a long way away from the Duchy of Horshon and your stepmother."

"Stepmother?" Finn had never really thought of her that way before.

"Yeah, that is what she is, and an evil one at that. You need to go far enough that you are completely out of her influence. Those of us who care about you in town will miss you, but not so bad as if you up and got sick and died."

"I guess that makes sense. I just don't know what I want to do. I can't really picture myself doing any one thing for the rest of my life. I don't have any idea where to go either. I don't even know what my options are."

"Well, think about what you do know. Do you feel passionate about any of those things? If not, are there things that seem like they might be interesting that you don't really know. If so, try those out, and maybe you'll find something you have a passion for. If that don't work, maybe try combining some things and doing something new."

"I... " Finn didn't know what to say about that. He tried to come up with ideas, but nothing really felt right. Maybe he was approaching it wrong. An idea struck him, "How did you decide what you chose to do?"

"I always liked to travel, and I always liked talking to people. I also got a thrill when I made an especially good trade, so those things kind of fit together. I spend a little less than half my time on the road, visiting and talking to people, always looking for good deals. I usually deal with the same people in each place, but every trip I meet someone new. It fits me and I like it. What are the things you like? If you can find a way to put those together into a trade or craft, that will be your answer, or at least closer to one."

That gave Finn a whole lot more to think about. "I will have to think about that. Thank you."

"Don't mention it," the old man finally smiled. They rode in silence for a long time after that, and Finn's mind circled and circled. He had a limited time to figure out his path and get away from his step-mother. If he didn't move on, eventually she would get him. Possibly with sickness or poison, or maybe something else. He didn't even know who her people were, so it wasn't like he could effectively avoid them.

That led back to the other main point. What did he enjoy? Well, everything, sort of. He loved doing new things, but he also loved doing things well. He loved being able to step into almost any situation and be able to function competently. He did like talking to people, and he liked his time thinking while working on things. Finn also loved adventure and seeing new things. He liked to take care of people and he liked seeing things run properly.

Finn thought about all of that for a long time until they finally arrived in Beaumont in the early evening. Staynor rented a room for them at the Inn where he usually stayed, then left to check on the orders for the trip. Soon he came back and they left together to unload the wagon at the merchant that had purchased the goods he had brought with them. Afterward, he spoke to Finn, "The order we are supposed to pick up won't be ready until at least tomorrow night. They are late with it, but with all the refugees, supplies have been disrupted a bit." Looks like we will be staying two nights, lad."

"Ok." Finn replied, then crinkled his nose while asking, "Refugees? What refugees."

"Well, seems like there is some kind of great storm like the one from the legends that is destroying a lot of things off toward Merdal and Sangar. Some people have been fleeing and telling all sorts of unbelievable stories, but few of them really match up, so it is hard to know what is real. What is real is that they are clogging the roads and delaying supplies, which means we will be here an extra day. Is there anything special you want to do tomorrow morning?"

"Um, not really, I want to window shop, maybe, but I really don't want to spend anything I don't have to."

"Smart of you, boy. Ok, feel free to wander around tomorrow morning, and meet back here at the Inn around lunch time, and I will buy your lunch at the tavern next door, since the Inn serves its food there."

Finn was surprised. "Ok, thanks. That is very kind of you."

"Nonsense. You are stuck here working for me, so I will pay for your expenses. That is how a proper businessman does things. Make sure you cover the responsibilities that are yours." Staynor really was as good a man as you could find.

"Ok, thank you." With that, they both went up and went to sleep.

CHAPTER SEVEN

FINN

THE NEXT MORNING, AFTER an early breakfast, Finn set out to look at the goods in all the shops. While doing so, he kept thinking about what it was he wanted to do for his life. Each different type of shop offered different possibilities, but running a shop didn't seem very enticing. He also thought about what kind of crafter would make each of the different amazing things he saw, but while it all seemed amazing and wonderful, he couldn't picture himself focusing his life in that way.

He returned to the Inn and caught up with Staynor as he went into the tavern. Staynor seemed to be in a bit of a grumpy mood. "They got their supplies, but don't think they can finish everything until tomorrow morning. We won't be getting home until very late tomorrow night."

"Well, it could be worse. What if we came all this way and they told us they couldn't deliver. Has that ever happened?"

"Yeah, of course it has, but not very often. That breaks trust, and business runs on trust. If you can't trust someone, then you can't adequately make plans. Things like this do happen, but good crafters and merchants work very hard to deliver on their promises, cause if they don't, they stop getting orders." Staynor's mood had slightly improved, just talking about things.

"I can see why it works that way." Finn said. "Is there something you want me to do this afternoon?"

"No, go ahead and go sightsee. Maybe you can go past the Duke's castle and think about how your life might have been different if you had grown up in a place like that, cause if things had worked out differently, you would've."

"You know, I hadn't ever really thought about that before. I will do that." Finn spent the rest of the afternoon visiting shops and walking past the Duke's castle. He assumed that his father would have had a similar castle, and he tried to picture living in a place like that. Mostly, his mind just boggled at the size of it and he wondered how often he would have gotten lost.

The afternoon wore on, and he returned to the Tavern a little early. Staynor had reserved a table already, so he sat and waited for his employer to join him. While he waited, he watched a bard come in and talk to the tavern keeper, whose name was Orvindo. Then the bard began to set up for a performance that evening. The bard noticed him watching with curiosity and asked, "Have you never seen a bard before?"

"No, I mean, maybe, but they don't come to our small town. I have never seen one set up to perform and it all looks really cool."

"You play an instrument?" the bard asked.

Finn felt a little intrigued and embarrassed at the same time. "No, that is one thing I have never learned anything about. I can whistle, but I don't think people want to hear that."

"Do you sing?" The bard raised an eyebrow.

Finn's face fell just a bit. "I don't know how good I sing, but I have sung a few songs a time or two, but never for anyone else, just to keep myself company while working at times."

"Well, maybe I can listen to you and let you know if you have potential. Do you think you would want to be a bard?"

"I am supposed to be figuring out what I want, but I have a lot of options and not really any clear direction, so, sure, I'm game, but I don't know about being a bard. It seems like a rough way to live."

"It certainly can be, but there are a lot of good times too. It has to be a passion though."

"That seems to be my biggest problem. I don't know what my passion is." Right then, Staynor arrived and glanced at the bard as he joined Finn at the table.

"You thinking you might want to be a bard?" Staynor asked.

"I still don't know what I want, but I figure it can't hurt too much to find out what all my options are." Finn stood and then went over to the Bard, who had gone back to setting up his mandolin. "So, how do we do this? Do I just sing some little song I learned as a kid and you tell me if I stink at it or not?"

"That would work, but first, remember to try to sing clearly and strongly and don't worry about who else might hear. That will determine a lot of how this goes."

Finn fixed in his mind what he was going to do, and then made himself relax. The whole situation was making him feel tense. Then he sang one of the children's songs he learned when he was younger. The bard had stopped everything else and was focused solely on him as he sang. It was short, and there were only two people besides him, the bard, Staynor, and Isolde the barmaid. She apparently had been listening, because when he finished she clapped and cheered. Finn felt his face turn bright red and he wanted to run away, but he also wanted to know what the bard thought.

The bard turned to him, "Not bad, if you feel like that is the life you want, you could do halfway decently. Probably not be entertaining lords and kings in their palaces, but you could probably handle a tavern like this with enough practicing, but you would need to learn to play an instrument to make a living at it. My name is Finnias, by the way."

"I am Finn. Kinda similar. I don't know if I want to learn an instrument, but singing seemed ok. It made me really embarrassed when Isolde started clapping and cheering, so I don't know if I would like that."

"I understand. It probably doesn't mean anything. Most of us feel embarrassed the first time we get cheered for, but it grows on you. Are you planning on staying for the whole performance?"

"I think I would like to, unless Staynor needs us to go somewhere."

Staynor had been listening in and spoke up. "No, kid, we can stay the whole performance if you like."

"I'd like to." Finn grinned from ear to ear.

Finnias turned to include Staynor in the conversation, "Would you mind if I joined you at your table after my performance?"

Staynor deflected the question back to Finn, "What do you think, Finn?"

Finn answered enthusiastically, "Yeah, that would be good."

Finnias smiled, "Great, hope you enjoy the show."

Finn returned to his seat and Staynor just looked at him like he was trying to read a book. Finn wasn't sure how to feel about it, but then felt Isolde arrive at his side. "What can I get for you this evening?"

Staynor ordered for them, "Oh, just the special for each of us. And juice for the boy here. I'll take an ale."

"Sure thing" she responded, then turned to Finn. "You really do have a nice voice. I enjoyed your singing." Finn felt himself turn red again as she left to return to the bar.

"Hmm, you seem to have an admirer." Staynor teased, then became just a bit more serious. "She seems like a nice girl, but I doubt you would want to settle down in this city, and always be careful to not just fall for a pretty face. You need to really get to know a girl before you get that kind of serious."

"Yeah, I don't think I have any intentions like that here. I once was interested in a girl that stayed in the Inn back in Mijople, but I don't think she ever even noticed me."

"Don't take it personally. It takes special conditions for mutual interest to form, and even then, that doesn't mean it can or should go anywhere. Take your time and be sure from both an emotional and mental place before you commit to something like marriage."

"Yeah, that whole subject still makes me squirm inside, so, I am not worried about that sort of thing any time soon."

Right about then, a loud strumming came from Finnias's mandolin, and he began to sing an intro song. Several more people had taken seats at tables as it was getting time for the dinner crowd. Finnias sang some common folk songs, and soon the tavern had filled up quite a bit more. He stopped at that point and introduced himself to the crowd. He announced that in light of the recent talk and rumors, he was going to sing some songs about the Legend of the Great Darkness. That got a mild response from the crowd and he began.

The songs mesmerized Finn. They told of the power of the great wizards in the past, and that one named Vlastorn became power mad. They told of the great tower he built, and then the Storm that came from it. The song told of the destruction and darkness from the storm and how it enslaved the people.

Then, he sang a song of the Halidar, with verses about each of them. Aspheron, the elemental archmage, who had fought the darkness directly, but then was lost. Thelanor, the great arch paladin, who helped free the people from the darkness. Ferozel, the arch Spellsword, whose magical blades defeated the hordes of monsters. Nitara, the arch void-mage, who banished the evil to the void. Sidoran, the rogue shadow wizard, who sacrificed himself to defeat the overlord.

Evander, the arch light-mage who survived and built the tower of light so they would never have another darkness. Rhondalyn, the arch healer who kept people alive so they could end the darkness. Dardanos, who destroyed the dark tower after the overlord was gone, and who then began his endless vigil to protect the people.

The music was over, but Finn still sat entranced, with all the parts of the stories running through his brain. He just kept going over it again and again. It just spoke to him in ways that nothing else had. He wasn't sure what to make of it. Suddenly he was pulled out of his reverie by laughter right next to him. He hadn't even noticed that Finnias had joined them at the table. Then he realized that must have been a while ago because Finnias already had a plate of food in front of him.

"You ok there lad?" Staynor asked. "I haven't ever seen you get that distant before."

"Uh, I'm ok. That was just... amazing! I haven't ever heard anything like that before, and those stories. Just, Wow!"

"Have you not heard the stories before?" Finnias asked with complete seriousness.

"Well, when I studied history, I read a little about that, but it was more like, 'This happened, that happened, these people were involved, and it all ended and everything is good now.' It didn't really make it seem real, but your songs sure did!" Finn was still somewhat dazed from the experience.

"How much of that is accurate?" asked Staynor, "Do you know?"

Finnias waved his hands like he was trying to demonstrate, "Well, I try to be as accurate as I can, and I dug those up doing research in Danlos itself, which is where Dardanos has his wizard tower, or, I guess I should say, had his wizard tower if the rumors are true."

"Wait, he is still alive?" Finn was incredulous.

"Yes, or, he was. I don't know what the latest rumors mean. They say his tower was destroyed by a great explosion, and a new dark tower came up out of the ground, and a new Storm has come out and is causing destruction and so forth. I don't know how much is real. It could all be people imagining things based on the legends, but yes, he is real, and was alive not that long ago when I last visited the city."

"What about the others? How many of them lived?" Finn's enthusiasm was running away with him.

"Well, from what I heard, Evander went to Chibor and built the tower of light, which is supposed to prevent another darkness, and Rhondalyn went to Isalor to the high mountains and became a hermit, since her love Sidoran was killed defeating the Overlord Vlastorn. I haven't heard of anyone seeing her for a long time, but since those old archmages basically don't age, I assume both of them are still around."

"Is that for real?" Finn's mouth hung open after his question.

"As much as I can tell. I have never traveled to the other continents to verify, but I have spoken to those that have. The Tower of Light certainly is real. I haven't ever talked with anyone who claimed to speak with Rhondalyn, but some of those I have talked with claimed to have spoken with those that have."

Finn felt completely overwhelmed. Somehow this story resonated with him in ways that nothing else ever had. He didn't have a passion to sing about it or tell the story, but somehow, he wanted to go there. If Dardanos's Tower had been destroyed, and it was under some kind of Storm, perhaps that wouldn't be the best place to go, but maybe he could go to one of the other continents and try to meet one of the other living Halidar.

It wasn't quite a life purpose, but it called to him the way nothing else ever had. He would think about this a lot more on the trip back and during the hunting trip with Gesh after he got home. Traveling like that was not a trade or career path, but it was something that maybe he could use to figure out his future path.

Finn didn't ask any more questions that night, and Finnias and Staynor talked for some time until they all got up and returned to their rooms. Finn's head still buzzed with excitement and he didn't have much to say. Staynor kept looking at him strangely, but he didn't say anything. They soon went to bed to prepare for their busy next day.

Staynor woke Finn up even before it began to get light. Finn quickly got ready and made sure he had all his things. They got the wagon ready and the horses hitched before the sun came up. Staynor had ordered breakfast to go, which seemed like some kind of egg and sausage sandwich, and they ate as they drove to the manufactory that was making the goods that had been ordered.

At this point, Finn realized that he didn't even know what it was they were picking up. "Um, Staynor?"

"Yes?" the old man answered

"What are these things we are picking up?"

"They are special support beams for the new bridge being built up the road from Mijople. The locals wanted to take a stab at it, but the locally made items were complete failures. These had originally been ordered, but they thought they could do it cheaper the other way and put these on pause. That didn't work out. The bridge has to be done on a tight schedule, or a lot of people could lose their jobs. That is why this is an emergency run."

"Oh." was all Finn could say.

They got to the manufactory not long after that. There were 32 support beams that they had to load. They were long and heavy and made of wood and metal. The first thing they had to do was install braces on the side of the wagon so they didn't lose their load mid journey. That was the hardest part for Finn, and they were both completely drenched in sweat by the time they were done.

Then, they started loading the completed support beams. Each one took between five and ten minutes to load. Thirty of the thirty two support beams were finished when they finally caught up. The thirty-first was done only a couple of minutes later, and then they ended up waiting over an hour for that last one to be complete. The support beams had lots of parts and the process of putting them together was a combination of blacksmithing, woodcrafting, and a few other things that Finn had never done. It looked like at least a little of it was magic.

He had never learned magic. That had been one thing they had not had the resources for him to learn when he was young. If they had been able to provide it, he would have only had a year or two of learning before his father died, so he wouldn't have been able to get very far. He wondered how he would feel about doing magic if he ever got a chance to learn. It might be something to look into.

When the last support beam was finally complete, they quickly got it loaded. Then they had to secure their load. There were a lot of ropes and braces involved, but Staynor knew his business and Finn knew to follow instructions as precisely as he could. Soon, they pulled out and were on their way home. It was almost lunch time by then.

Fortunately, the ride home was uneventful. Finn was deep in thought most of the trip. He kept pondering on what had happened to him when listening to the stories and music Finnian had played and sung. He pondered on how to combine different skills to find or create his passion. He wondered how working with magic might be, and if he would want to learn or even include it in whatever it was he was trying to come up with.

At one point, he realized that Staynor had been watching him even more closely than he had been watching their load. Finally, only an hour or two from home and when it was starting to get dark, he couldn't take it any more. "What?"

"What do you mean, 'What?'" the old man asked.

"You have been looking at me strange the whole ride home. Care to share?" Finn realized he was being perhaps a bit too bold, but he bit back the desire to correct himself.

"I was just wondering what you have come up with? What are you thinking of doing about your stepmom's possible assassins and then how that little concert last night factors into it. Would you tell me?" Staynor's manner at this point was more gentle than Finn recalled ever seeing before.

"Well, I still don't know what I want, but that whole thing last night hit me harder than anything else I have ever felt. The weird thing is, I don't want to be a bard, or to sing, or make music. It wasn't the music that hit me, but the message it contained. It felt like I was being called to do something, but I can't go back 800 years to do anything then, and I certainly am not the equivalent of the Halidar in our day."

"I have no idea how that factors into what I want to do with my life, but I get a sense that I may be doing a lot of very distant traveling. That would probably take care of the stepmom problem, if it's real. How I factor everything else in, I still have no idea. I did get the idea or feeling or something like that about perhaps I should consider looking into learning magic or .. I don't know. I am not really clear on that or how it all fits together." Finn shrugged and held his hands out indicating that he was at a loss.

"Well, it certainly seems you have your work cut out for you. I hope you figure it out pretty soon." Staynor sighed.

Finn looked down the road ahead of them without focusing on anything. "I have a hunting trip with Gesh in two days, and I'll be thinking about it during that trip. I'll let you know when I come up with something and what it is."

"I'd appreciate that." Staynor smiled.

Chapter Eight

Cecilia

Cecilia entered the Merdal thieves guild hideout number two with a wide smile on her face. Her return from the headquarters and primary hideout had been somewhat chaotic, but even the mess in the streets hadn't dampened her mood. She had delivered a proposal for a heist on the Royal Treasury of Merdal that she had spent weeks preparing and it had gone well. Most heists didn't require approval of the guild chief, but big things affecting noble's treasuries and main branches of other guilds did.

It was odd in a way. She loved the kingdom of Merdal, and overall, her time there had blessed her life, but she felt that she was running out of room for improvement. She had ideas and dreams and would need ridiculous amounts of coin to fund them. It was time to establish her local legend and move on. That had led to the idea for the big heist.

She knew she needed to get to work. The chief of the thieves guild had signed off on her proposal, and it would take a lot of meticulous planning, special equipment, and the best team she could put together to pull it off. Then she would retire, at least from being a thief. She had risen as high in the guild as she could without replacing the chief, and she certainly wasn't interested in doing that. She wanted to do something else with her life. She wasn't sure what, but it wouldn't be in Merdal and it wasn't being a thief.

She gathered her planning materials and her kit, then sat down in her office to plan in more detail. She left the door open so she could call out instructions to any guild members that came through. After focusing on the objective, she stepped through what would be required. As she pictured the task and how it would bring change, she took a moment to think back to how she had come to Merdal in the first place.

She had grown up as the daughter of one of the dukes in the kingdom of Blahn. It was a neighbor with Merdal, but the two kingdoms did not have good relations. Her father, Brone, ruled over a duchy called Beaumont, which boasted one of the most beautiful castles on the continent. Despite its beauty, it held mostly nightmares for her.

She had endured an extremely strict and often brutal upbringing and doubted she had ever been loved by her parents. They certainly had as little to do with her as possible. She had only been permitted into her mother's presence once a month and her father's once a quarter. She could count all the conversations she had ever had with her father on two hands.

Instead, she suffered through an endless line of strict governesses, tutors, and school masters who seemed to only delight in making her miserable. Her one benefit was being privileged to have beautiful clothes and being able to shop frequently. Six years previously, when she was fifteen, she had been 'forgotten' by the governess while being fitted for new clothes.

While everyone else in the elite dress shop was busy about other things and were ignoring her, she decided to wander off in the high class shopping district and see how long it took them to respond. She actually had no idea how long it took before they noticed her absence, but she had wandered openly in the area for a long time before meeting some other girls.

The girls she met had some kind of adventure planned and invited her along. She joined them and had the best day of her life to that point. They hiked and had a picnic and ruined their dresses playing in a mountain stream. When she finally returned to the elite shopping district late that evening, she was set upon quickly by her father's guards who quickly rushed her before her father. That was one of the conversations she had with him.

He was furious, and went on and on about how she could become damaged goods by being out among the riff raff, and that her sole value as the daughter of a duke was to be a bargaining chip for political gain. After being restricted to her rooms for a month, she was finally let out, but she had to keep a full time bodyguard named Rasdal with her at all times.

Rasdal took it upon himself to be her constant overseer. Her tutoring time was doubled, and she wasn't allowed to do anything that she found enjoyable. If Rasdal noticed her smiling or looking even peaceful for a few minutes, he would eliminate whatever she was doing from the list of allowed activities. The one time she tried to stand up to him, he knocked her down the stairs and she ended up severely injured.

Once she had been bandaged, she ran through the castle and forced her way in to talk with her mother, Janice, who was not happy about the disruption. Still, she blurted out, "Rasdal pushed me down the stairs and broke my ribs!" She expected her mother to take her side.

Her hopes were buoyed when her mother said, ""I will speak with your father about it." Right then, Rasdal burst into the room behind her, his face full of murder. Her mother turned to the man and said with irritation, "Rasdal, you are to keep her from causing problems. If you can't handle her, then you will be replaced!" Cecilia felt her blood run cold. She thought her mother would care. "Also, she loses much value to us if she is injured or maimed. However you deal with her, there should be no blemishes or lasting injuries."

Rasdal nodded, "Yes, duchess." Then he turned to Cecilia with a cruel grin. "Back to your rooms!" Cecilia quickly turned and followed his orders. She feared what he would do. Apparently there was a limit to what was allowed, but it really didn't protect her much. Regardless, her mother had kept her word, as only hours later she was summoned along with Rasdal to her father's study for one of the other conversations she had with him.

She hoped her father would at least protect 'his investment', as he had once called her. When they got there, it did not go well. Her father was very unhappy, apparently with her. "You are such a troublesome child! Never fear, we have started negotiations which will see you out of our hair in a year or two." A sense of doom descended around her. Were they going to force her to marry? And apparently to someone she had never met. Not that she had met many young nobles.

Just when she thought it couldn't get worse, her father turned to Rasdal. "I want you to keep a closer eye on her. No broken bones. No visible bruises, but feel free to teach her some lessons, but make sure she doesn't lose any value for these negotiations. If we do this right, we will gain great influence when she weds the widowed king of Kornech."

The nightmare she was living became much worse after that. The king of Kornech was old, but had no living heirs. It also had strict laws preventing women from ruling or even inheriting anything. Rumor had it that the previous three queens of Kornech had been imprisoned and then executed when they did not provide male heirs. Picturing herself being forced into such a predicament terrified her.

A marriage to such a beast was not something she could agree to, not that she would have much of a choice. Somewhere deep inside, she found a new resolve. She would not sit there and have other people dictate her life. She immediately started trying to figure out a way to escape. She came up with a few ideas, but despite multiple attempts to get away from Rasdal over the next few months, she remained his prisoner.

She always tried to escape from the castle, but after the failed attempts, she realized her best chance was to escape while out in the city. After learning the treaty requiring her marriage was in the final stages of negotiation, she was forced to start preparations, which meant shopping trips. Of course, Rasdal always was with her, and it was nearly impossible to get away from him. One of the few times she could get a small break from him for just a few minutes was when she was being fitted for dresses and other clothing.

One of the assistants named Kolana, who often helped her at the dress shop, had been friendly with her for a long time. Additionally, Cecilia could tell Kolana didn't like Rasdal at all. Since an assistant always had to be her when they did fittings and measurements, she had a chance to plead for help. Kolana was willing to help, but what Cecilia needed would not be cheap and Kolana didn't have the means to cover it.

Ironically and fortunately, Cecilia had access to a large amount of gold from previous years before Rasdal had taken over her life, and no one had ever thought to check what happened to it. When she returned to her rooms, she immediately began putting together a plan. She wrote several sets of instructions for different people and figured out a way to hide the letters and gold under her clothes so that Rasdal would not suspect what she was up to.

When she went in to be measured again, this time for the wedding dress, at first Rasdal insisted on coming into the fitting. She did her best to throw a complete fit, which wasn't too hard considering how much she hated him. Fortunately for her, the shop owner, a refined lady of higher class named Jonora, threw a fit right alongside her, and Rasdal grumpily gave in and waited outside the fitting room.

In the fitting room, Janora spent the next five minutes ranting about Rasdal, and Cecilia made a point of letting her get it out of her system. When Janora calmed down, she had Kolana go to the fitting room to help Cecilia prepare while Janora fetched a catalog of dresses to let Cecilia browse through and pick a style. Cecilia quickly gave Kolana the letters and gold before Janora got back.

There would only be one shot at the escape, and it would be the last time they were out for the final fitting. Kolana would set up some little flags in a park that Cecilia could see from her window. The flags indicated which parts of the plan were ready. Out of six flags, the first four went up later the same day she had given Kolana the letters. The fifth went up the next. It took three days for the last, and most critical flag to go up.

The dress shop was down a side street from the elite shopping district. When she got to the shopping district, she and Rasdal exited their carriage. She noticed a wagon of goods that was stopped at the top of the street that they had to walk down. She also made eye contact with one of the people working on it and was a little surprised to see that it was Kolana, wearing a wig and dressed as a common laborer. Cecilia discreetly nodded as they entered the street.

They were about fifty yards down the street when there was the sound of something breaking behind them and people yelling. She turned and could see the wagon barreling down the street, out of control. Rasdal had also turned, and calmly used his arm to push her out of danger, while he eyed the runaway wagon. She used the moment to push him from behind right into the path of the wagon at the last moment.

Despite his large size, the heavy wagon swept him away in front of it. Eventually it crashed into the side of a building, but Cecilia had already run the other direction to a waiting carriage which had a change of clothes, a wig, makeup, and a pack with food and provisions. Kolana was already in the carriage and directed the driver to take off. Cecilia looked out the window and down the street where the wagon had hit Rasdal and could see him trying to run with a bad limp and glaring at her from far behind.

She had been sure that the plan would work if she could just get away from Rasdal for long enough. She wondered if she should feel bad about pushing him in front of the racing wagon that had come down a narrow street they were on, but for some reason she didn't. He had been injured, but not so much that he didn't try to chase her. Still, she got away and her plan worked out.

They had only stopped briefly once she had changed clothes, put on the wig and made herself up in a way that would disguise her appearance. She had brought all the remainder of her money. Half of which she paid Kolana before the girl exited the carriage. As the carriage pulled away, Cecilia called out her thanks again and then tried to calm herself down before they got to the city gates.

One of her worries was that word of her escape would get to the city gate before she was through, but it turned out to be unfounded. The carriage was waved through after the guards briefly checked the occupant, who didn't look like anyone they would recognize due to her disguise. There were two drivers on the carriage, and they drove through the night, only stopping to rest the horses twice.

She knew she still had a chance that she could get caught, but eventually they made it to the border with Merdal. Since Blahn and Merdal were not on friendly terms, but also not actively in a conflict, she did have to wait for a few minutes at the border, but the forged documents from the pack and her disguise helped her through without complication.

Finally, she was able to relax. She planned on going to the capital of Merdal which was also called Merdal. The carriage entered the city and stopped at the central square to let her out. She had to pay them the rest of her payment, and then she was free. The carriage pulled off and left her standing in the central square, trying to decide what she should do next.

Somehow, in all her planning, she hadn't thought too much about what to do after that point. First, she decided she needed to swap her remaining money for local currency. She proceeded to a bank that she knew did business in both kingdoms and for a small fee, swapped all her gold for various denominations of the local coin. She decided she needed a change of attire and then to find a place to stay temporarily.

She had enough coin to keep her for quite a while if she was frugal. Still, she needed a new look that would look less 'noble girl victim' and more 'don't mess with me adventurer'. She circuited the main square, and found a store providing clothes and provisions for adventurers and soldiers. She went in to see what she could afford.

The prices were steep, but still she left with bags holding a leather form fitting rogue outfit in grey and black, as well as a couple of throwing knives and two daggers. None of it was magically enhanced and it was all pretty basic, but she thought it looked good. There had been a couple of questionable characters in the store, so she opted to change once she found a room to stay in.

She headed across the square to what looked like a passable but not too expensive inn, dodging multiple people who were rushing through the square in the late afternoon rush. She even had two of them bump into her before she could get across the square. She had seen both of their faces clearly, and thought it was odd, but continued onward. Once she reached the inn, and requested a room, she realized that she had been robbed, and knew exactly who had done it. All her remaining coin was gone.

The innkeeper nodded understandingly, but couldn't give her a room if she couldn't pay. He did let her use a bathroom to change her clothes in and offered to hold the bag she put her old clothes into for a day

Once back out on the street, she went to where she had been bumped into the second time. She was quickly grateful for the magic lessons she had endured all those years. While she doubted her natural power would ever make her a full mage, she had enough ability to cast some spells. She hated the boring lessons, but had learned a few useful spells, including one simple tracking spell.

In seconds, she was following the magical prompts and followed them to an alleyway. The tracking led her to the back of the alley and up the pipes in one of the corners. It took her quite a bit of effort, but she managed to get to the top. She had to cast the spell a second time because the first one had timed out.

She followed the trail along the roofs for a ways and then back down to the streets. She continued until the trail led her into what looked like an abandoned building. She did her best to move quietly and she continued following the trail. It went down into the basement and then through a hole in a wall that had been hidden. She made it through and continued until she heard some voices.

Both of the people who had bumped into her were there. A boy and an older girl, not too much younger than herself. They were congratulating themselves, along with several other people about the successful grab. She decided to not make herself a target and stay hidden for a minute, but to get their attention by speaking in a loud voice.. "Congratulations on stealing my money! You can keep it, but it has a price."

Several of the people there started jumping up and looking around cautiously, but the girl simply asked, "What's the price?" The others all stopped and looked back at the girl in confusion.

"You are going to teach me your trade, and provide food for a few weeks until I have learned enough to handle that myself." The girl smiled thoughtfully but agreed, and the lessons began.

At first, Cecilia thought the girl and her fellows were trying to kill her or make her give up, but she didn't. She learned a lot and became strong and skilled. Within a week, she was successfully earning enough to provide for her food. After a month, she was formally inducted into the thieves guild. The types of training available expanded, and she was tested and found to have natural abilities with ward and barrier cracking spells. She advanced steadily, but more importantly, she found a place where she quickly began to fit in and feel at home.

The only problem was thieves. They really couldn't be trusted. Yes, there was comradery, and even a strange kind of family bond of sorts, but she knew that any of them could turn on her at any time. She never told any of them her backstory, other than she had chosen to come to a new kingdom and city and start a new life. After several years of being on edge, she was looking forward to finding a more stable and less risky way of living.

That was why she wanted to do this heist of a lifetime. The royal treasury. It would be hard. In the time she had been considering it, she had found several independent sources of information about what to expect and compared their information. She had even gone so far as to have a corrupt mage scry into the building as far as they were able to verify details that she had been told.

With everything she had learned, she had a route and the timing figured out to pull it off, but would need at least five other people to help. Any one of them could ruin the whole thing, so recruitment would require extreme discretion. She dug into the details and barely noticed when a large group of guild members came in, talking excitedly.

After a bit, one of them stepped into her office. It was Hank. One of the team leaders, "Hey, have you seen the weird storm thing?"

She looked up, feeling a little annoyed at the disruption, "Storm thing? What are you talking about?"

The young thief suddenly looked a little apprehensive, "There is this big black storm with all sorts of multicolored lightning. It's heading this way. There were some people who came running through the city screaming about monsters and skeletons and that everyone should run. Should we do something?"

She made herself wait to respond until she could keep a passive face, despite her irritation, "Have everyone stay down here. We are underground, but not vulnerable to flooding. We can head up and see what bonus goods we can pick up once it blows past. Have everyone practice skills in the meantime. Don't disturb me unless it is a real emergency."

He nodded and turned back to the others in the main room. Soon, they were all practicing either in the main room or in some side rooms. Cecilia returned to her planning, trying to figure out any contingencies that might be needed. She continued until she started to get tired. Her head felt fuzzy and she was having trouble concentrating. She looked out and realized it was too quiet in the hideout for everyone to be training.

She entered the main room, and saw there were only a few people there. Where had everyone else gone? She looked at Hank, who was stumbling toward the stairs. He had a vacant look on his face, and somewhere inside, she knew something was wrong, but couldn't identify what.

She called out to him, "Hank, where are you going?" He didn't act like he even heard her. She found herself stumbling after him, trying to figure out what was wrong. He went up and through the exit, but didn't secure any of the doors as he went. She made herself follow procedure and secure everything. By the time she reached the last exit and made it to the street, everyone around her had the same blank vacant look on their faces.

She knew it was wrong, but she couldn't bring herself to care. Only a single coherent thought came through. *Someone is trying to control me.* It gave her just enough edge to resist the impulses to pick up some debris and start cleaning the street. She vaguely concluded that she needed to get out from the cloud. It was taking everyone over.

She wandered down the street, doing her best to stay focused. When she saw a horse that wasn't pulling a cart or wagon, she moved toward it. It barely seemed to react to her presence at all. She again fought the impulse to find a wagon to fasten to the horse, and instead climbed on and spurred it forward.

The horse wasn't super responsive. It seemed to be affected by the same mind fog as everyone else around her. Still, it did exactly as she commanded. She headed toward the lightning in the far distance. She had to get out from under this storm. She didn't know why, exactly, but it was the one thought that stayed with her. She rode all that day, and kept going that night. The horse wasn't fast, but it kept going as long as she could.

It was getting light by the time she reached the storm front. The storm wasn't moving fast and hardly any rain fell, but just ahead of her, she could see major bursts of colored lightning burst out from the edge of the storm. She spurred the horse into a gallop. Lightning fell close to her, and some kind of beast reached for her from the side, but the horse outpaced whatever it was. The horse kept galloping for several minutes until they both burst out into the clear morning light. As soon as the light struck her face, the fog over her mind lifted completely. At the same time, the horse seemed to awaken as well.

It looked back at her, and when it didn't seem to recognize her, it started trying to buck. She managed to get it to calm and then carefully climbed off. She could tell that the storm would soon catch up to her again. She needed the horse to cooperate a while longer. She talked to it and pointed at the storm. It looked and again started acting a little skittish, but eventually let her climb back on.

She hadn't even directed the horse where to go when it took off at a solid run away from the storm. Later in the day, they stopped so the horse could eat. She realized that she hadn't brought anything with her. She had her kit, simply because she had picked it up out of habit, but she hadn't brought anything more than pocket change and had no food. She didn't have a change of clothes either.

There were some villages up ahead, and she made sure to acquire a change of clothing that looked more normal. She also found someone who would share a little food with her. In the second village, she found a pack that someone had left unattended. It didn't have much in it, but worked well to hold what she acquired.

At one stop, she started considering what she should do. She was headed directly down the road toward Blahn, where she was still wanted as a runaway noble. She definitely didn't want to go to Beaumont, where she would likely be recognized. She decided to take another route and travel through a different duchy of Blahn where the major city was called Parnul. She would have to figure out how to restock there.

In just under a week, she made it to the border of the kingdom of Blahn. She joined with other refugees fleeing the storm when crossing the border and then rode ahead of them all. Three more days of travel brought her close to Parnul. When she could see the city in the distance, she stopped to evaluate her plan. She could tell the horse was in poor shape. She had ridden it too hard, and needed to find other transportation. It saddened her slightly, but she let the horse go in some fields.

She wanted to get away from the storm for good, so she planned to head as far as she could on the continent of Arden. First, she had to get into Parnul without attracting attention, and figure out a way to resupply. She wanted to blend in with the other refugees, but there weren't many who had made it that far yet, since she had ridden ahead of most of them.

Still, there was a slow moving line to get through the gate. She waited in line, and when she got to the guards, she gave them generic answers that she figured would work. One of them looked at her a little longer than she expected, but she acted like she didn't notice. He finally looked away as though he had decided she wasn't of concern, and she had to force herself to not sigh in relief.

As she walked away from the gate, Cecilia subtly glanced behind her, just to make sure the gate guards weren't paying any more attention to her. She was just a traveler passing through, and they needed to believe that. She had never intended to be back in the Kingdom of Blahn. She was grateful that she didn't have to pass through Beaumont, though. She was already uncomfortable with the lower possibility that someone in Parnul might recognize her. She didn't intend to stay in Blahn any longer than was required.

She started thinking about what she should do. She needed new tools and a lot of money. While in Parnul, she had to find a way to get some quick coin, and then take a carriage as far from the Storm as she could get, which on the continent of Arden, meant Port Yadzul.

First she needed to scout out the city without arousing suspicions, which shouldn't be too hard, then she would need to determine her targets and find a place to operate out of. She would need equipment, so she needed to identify potential contacts amongst the local thieves and get things squared away there. She would also need to convert what she picked up into enough immediate coin to pay for the carriage, which wouldn't be cheap.

CHAPTER NINE

CHARLOTTE

A DARK HAIRED GIRL named Charlotte walked across one of the many fields surrounding Ethalor Manor. She worked at the Ethalor Manor in one of the border baronies of the Kingdom of Merdal. She served the Baron, who owned the Manor, as a milkmaid and took care of a small herd of milking cows. She had been there for a long time, having become a ward of the Baron when her parents couldn't pay their debts. When she was first taken, she was taken to the manor and assigned a place among the lowest level of servants.

She couldn't do much at first, and they had her scrub silverware. If she got distracted, she got beaten. If she was too slow, she got beaten, and if she did a good job, they let her have leftovers from the meals the Nobles had not finished. She quickly learned to do a good job.

As she got older, they shifted her role several times until she was assigned as a milkmaid. She had to feed and milk the cows and help make things like cheese. It was hard work, but it had made her strong and she had learned some important skills that she could use later in life if she ever got out of her indentured servitude. The earliest she would be able to do that was when she turned 18, which wasn't for a few years, since she was just approaching her 15th birthday.

While working in the field herding the cows back to their pen after letting them graze in the pasture, a group of seven people came running to the edge of the field and didn't even slow down as they climbed through the fence. "Hey! This is Ethalor Manor, you can't just climb through the fence! I will have to report you."

A young man diverted from his path to speak with her. "I am sorry miss, but I don't care. We are going through and not stopping or the Storm will catch us. It destroys everything that it touches, so, go ahead and report us, but we will be gone before anyone comes to look for us, and you should run too. Get what supplies you can and flee, or you will die to the storm like so many others."

"What are you talking about?" She remembered asking.

He turned and pointed. "See there on the edge of the horizon, a dark storm. It doesn't look like much from here, but when it comes, and it will come, it will bring monsters and destroy everything in its path. We have been running from it since it destroyed the Kingdom of Sangar. Now I have delayed too long. It doesn't stop, just always keeps coming. The only thing to do is outrun it." With that, he turned and ran faster to catch up with the others who were already leaving the other side of the pasture.

Charlotte was not sure what to do, but she figured she would do her duty once she got the cows in their pen. She had lost a few of them who had run off while the young man was talking. She managed to get five of them in the pen right away, but the three troublemaking cows, Daisy, Maggie, and MooMoo, were doing their best to keep away from her. They were usually obnoxious, but they seemed especially spooked for some reason.

Eventually she got them cornered, and threw ropes around their necks and then tied them to each other with a single lead on Daisy's nose ring, since Daisy seemed to be the ring leader more often than not. Early on, she had learned the trick to tie them to each other, and she learned very quickly that a 1000 pound cow can pull around a 110 pound girl like she weighs nothing. Once the cows were in the pen, she ran back to the manor house to report what she saw and heard.

She stood outside the office door, building the courage to knock. She had been fearful of Verlina, the stewardess of the manor, for as long as she could remember. She never knew what new punishment Verlina would impose. Beatings, starvation, various forms of torture, she had been through it all.

Still, she would rather be reprimanded for being overzealous in reporting something than being punished for not reporting it. She finally took a deep breath and knocked. She heard angry footsteps move across the floor toward the door, and then it opened. "What?!"

The anger in Verlina's voice made Charlotte jump, even though it was always there. She quickly blurted out "There were some young men who climbed through the fences on the northwest pastures. I tried to stop them and told them they couldn't cross the Manor lands, but they mostly ignored me. One of them told about a great Storm that is coming this way that brings destruction and monsters or something like that, and then pointed it out. He said it has killed a lot of people and destroyed a lot of towns. I didn't know what to do about it, so I am reporting it to you."

The woman scowled and swore, then turned back to Charlotte. "How long ago was this?"

Charlotte tried to control her trembling hands. "Um, about 25 minutes, ma'am."

"Why in the world are you so abysmally slow! Next time move faster!" She wasn't even looking at Charlotte as she berated her.

"What should we do about the Storm? I could see it, and it seems to be coming this way!" Charlotte's concern over the threat from the storm temporarily overrode her fear of Verlina. She immediately regretted it.

Verlina's yelling increased several levels, "You stupid girl! Your concern is not some overblown storm! Your concern is getting those cows fed and milked and the milk taken to the larder! It had better be there on time, or it will be lashes for you! Now get out of my sight you worthless slug!!"

Charlotte ran to get back to the barn, trying not to cry. She wasn't worried about finishing on time, but every time she had to talk to that woman was a new adventure in trauma and abuse. Why did I open my mouth? She thought. She tried to calm her nerves as she ran. Soon, she arrived and moved the first cow to the milking stall. She put feed into the trough and started milking. When she had first been assigned, it took her forever and her arms were eternally tired, but now she knew what she was doing and had a grip that most soldiers would be jealous of.

She consolidated the milk from each cow into the large tank on the milk wagon that she would take to the larder. Once she had finished the last cow, she fed the bull, a ferocious and aggressive beast named Blaze. Blaze had killed people before, but he was a prize bull whose offspring were highly valuable. He always tried to intimidate her when she fed him, even if it was just ramming or kicking the gate of the bull pen.

She finished up everything she had to do, and then started pulling the milk wagon up to the larder. The larder was a large room at the back of the manor where a lot of the food was stored and processed. The larder keeper was an old man named Leofric, who despite his coarse appearance, was actually kind and soft hearted. He seemed to have a sweet spot in his heart for Charlotte, since he always gave her some kind of treat when he could.

On her way up to the larder, Charlotte could see the storm was getting much closer on the far side of the Manor. She wasn't sure, but she was convinced she could feel the power of it, even if it was still a little distant. She wasn't sure when it would get there, but she was feeling more worried about it. She told Leofric about the storm and what the young man had said, and a little bit about what Verlina said.

Leofric looked at her with concern for a short while. "Hold on." He walked back into the shelves of the larder with a burlap bag. He started throwing various things into it. She noticed him adding some hard cheese, some jerky, some dried fruit, and some nuts. "Take this." He handed it to her, and then seeing her shocked expression added, "Just hide it in the barn somewhere, and if nothing comes of this storm, then bring it back when it is over, but if it turns out bad and you have to run, take it with."

She was alarmed at that. "But what about you?"

He gestured to the larder around him. "I will be fine. An old grump like me will often survive when others don't, so don't you worry. You just take care of yourself."

"Ok." she responded, fighting back tears.

Just then, there was a huge crash of thunder. It sounded like it must have hit the Manor above them. They both looked at the ceiling and then each other. Leofric ordered, "Quick, get to the barn. Hide and keep safe. And remember, if you have to run, take the bag."

Charlotte burst from the doors and she could hear him bolt them behind her. The storm was over the far edge of the manor and there was a lot of lightning. She ran to the barn and barred the doors, then ran through the cow pen to a little hidden alcove at the back of it. It was too small for the cows to use, but she had found it was a good place to stash things she wanted to save for later.

In the distance, she could hear the thunder, and a lot of crashing and banging. Occasionally, she could hear a shout or a scream. She worried that those young men were right, and this storm would destroy everything. She could hear the thunder, then screaming, then lots of things getting smashed. She wanted to know what was happening, but she was too scared to climb out and go look. Soon, it sounded like the lightning had moved on and passed the barn. There were still a lot of sounds of destruction and screaming.

Then, as the sounds of screaming and fighting died down. She began to wonder if it was a good time for her to come out. Suddenly, something slammed into the barn doors. It slammed again and again. Charlotte watched in fear through a small crack from her hidden alcove. The doors were not designed to withstand a lot of beating, so soon they started to crack and finally burst open in pieces. Standing in the entryway were three skeletons.

Her mind struggled to make sense of what she was seeing. Bones couldn't stand up like that on their own, could they? Then, they started moving. She barely held in a scream, and backed away from the crack she had been watching through. She heard them start hammering on the gates to the pens. *Why don't they just open the pens, they aren't locked.* She worked up the courage to peek through again. They were just hammering on things with their fists, but it looked far more effective than even hammers.

The wooden gates splintered and chunks chipped away from them. There was only one skeleton attacking the gate to the cows pen while the other two were attacking the gate to Blaze's pen. Charlotte wasn't sure what was going to happen, but a strange morbid curiosity arose in her mind as she wondered who would win between them and Blaze.

Somehow, Blaze could tell when the gate was weak enough for him to crash through it. He bellowed a deafening challenge and blasted through the gate, throwing the two skeletons all the way out the barn door. It didn't slow him down at all and charged the other skeleton that was pounding on the gate to the cow pen. It didn't go flying like the others had, but she could both see and hear that some of the bones in its leg were cracked.

Blaze went berserk about then, and kept switching which skeleton he was trying to crush. The skeletons for their part started pounding on Blaze. Charlotte could tell that it was hurting Blaze, but it was also breaking the skeletons. After several minutes, Blaze was able to catch one of the skeleton's skulls between his full charge and a heavy-duty post. The skull exploded, and then the skeleton stopped moving. The other two skeletons had continued to pound on him. At this point, he had many bloody gashes in his side and she could tell his strength was flagging. He managed to destroy one more skeleton completely before he finally collapsed. The last skeleton continued pounding on him until Charlotte was fairly certain he was dead.

Then it turned back to the cow pen and continued smashing the gate to pieces. Once it did, Daisy and Maggie rushed through the gate and past the skeleton. The skeleton turned to chase them when MooMoo charged it from behind. It was knocked down, and MooMoo tried to trample it. Despite the cow's size and strength, the skeleton was able to get back up and started pounding on MooMoo. The cow panicked and fled.

The skeleton paused for a minute, then turned back to the cows that were still in the pen. It cornered several over to the side, and had just killed Candy with a single blow to her head when Charlotte decided she needed to make a break for it. She quickly gathered what she had in the alcove and waited for the skeleton to be as far away as she thought it would get and turned so it couldn't see her. Then she ran. The skeleton seemed to sense her anyway, and turned, leaving the cow it had been attacking injured, but not dead. It started moving directly at her, and she ran.

She reached the end of the pasture, and decided the young men had the right idea. She climbed through the fence, tearing her clothes on the wire, and headed for the closest edge of the storm, trying to get out from under it. It would be dark before too long, and she thought that perhaps if the skeleton was hit by sunlight that it might die or break up in pieces or burn or something, so she did her best to keep running. She wondered how it might deal with the fence, but apparently something about its fists was sharp enough to just snap right through it when it hit it.

The skeleton did not move nearly as fast as it originally had. It appeared that the damage it took fighting Blaze slowed it down so she could keep ahead of it without too much trouble. She jogged and ran for about thirty minutes until she got close to the edge of the storm. She was now out in the forest quite far from buildings and people and there wasn't any lightning. She broke into a sprint and burst through into the sunlight as a huge sense of relief flowed through her. She was sure that it would somehow stop the skeleton.

She continued to run, however, so when the skeleton followed her out into the sunlight and wasn't stopped, destroyed, disabled, or anything like she expected, she was dismayed but not caught. Instead it just kept pursuing her. She shrieked a little when she saw it continue and decided she would just keep running. She had no idea how long it would take before it stopped, or if it never would. She continued running and jogging, slowing down to a brisk walk at times to catch her breath for three and a half hours more.

The sun had set, but fortunately the largest moon had come up and was keeping it bright enough that she could see. At about the four hour mark from when the skeleton had broken into the barn, she had looked behind her to see the skeleton fall forward and its bones disintegrated into dust. She stopped and stared. Had she made it? She had. Her mind struggled to make sense of everything, but it was too unreal to believe.

Her body hurt, and she hadn't even begun to figure out what was going on. The one thought she held onto was that she needed to follow what those young men were doing. Just get ahead of the storm and keep ahead of the storm. She tried to think of moving forward, but she was exhausted and needed somewhere to get some rest. She wasn't sure how far she was ahead of the storm and was sure she didn't want to get caught up in it again, but she didn't know how much longer she could keep going.

She decided she would try to find someplace that would make a decent shelter for the night so she could sleep a bit. It took her another hour, but she finally found a place she felt good about. A large tree in the forest had a burned out hole high enough that she had to climb to get to it.

There didn't appear to be anything living in it, and it was clean enough and away from anything that couldn't climb well. She knew she had to sleep soon. Giving in to her exhaustion, she climbed in and promptly fell asleep.

She woke up suddenly with a sense of doom falling over her. The air was charged and she could somehow feel the storm about to reach her. She leaned up and peered out of the hole she was sleeping in. The storm was almost upon her. She grabbed her bag and quickly climbed down. When she reached the ground, she almost fell over because of how much everything hurt. Holding on to the tree's rough bark, she looked backward at the storm, and made herself continue onward. She realized she didn't have to go too fast to stay ahead of the storm. Somewhere between a fast walk and a slow jog would work, but she wanted to get much further ahead to give her a chance to rest when needed.

She jogged ahead of the storm, and when she felt far enough ahead, she slowed to a walk and dug into the bag that Leofric had given her. As she chewed on the hard dried fruits and jerky, she wondered if Leofric was okay. He seemed confident that he would be fine, but how could someone prepare for the disaster that was the storm? She hoped he would be ok, but the thing for her was to keep going. After her breakfast she started running again at a slower pace so she didn't tire herself out.

Chapter Ten

Ewan

Ewan looked around the lodge at the smiling rangers. They were celebrating his birthday, even though he had no idea when his actual birthday was. When he was just reaching his teenage years, one of the rangers had made a big deal about him not knowing it and the group had selected a birthdate for him, seemingly at random. Somehow, the date had stuck and they celebrated it every year. It hadn't been a big deal to him at the time, but he appreciated the comradery and closeness he felt.

He and the other rangers were responsible for preserving the forests, searching for lost people, and preventing poaching, destruction, and even wildfires. They also had to hunt fugitives who thought the forests and mountains of Isalor were places to hide out.

Ewan was young for a ranger, and the youngest elite ranger ever. He had an early start, since he had done much of his growing up in the ranger's lodge. As an orphan, he didn't have many prospects in life, and he had too much integrity to join the gangs in the cities. He loved the outdoors, but with a passion to be strictly obedient to laws, he didn't want to become some kind of hermit that hid and poached his way through life.

When he was eight years old, he decided the orphanage was not going to help him much, so he ran away and left the city. He was fascinated by the rangers he had seen only a couple of times. Even the city guards showed respect to the rangers. The rangers didn't work for the king, but for all the kings. He didn't quite know how that worked, but he wanted to be part of them. He found out where a ranger's lodge was supposed to be, and headed out into the woods. It couldn't be too hard to find, right?

He had gotten lost, and no one knew he was even out there. He couldn't find the lodge, and being rangers, they left little in the way of tracks that he could follow. He had survived by eating berries and roots, but was getting desperate. He didn't even know the way back to the city. Finally overcome with despair, he figured he was going to die, and he sat down on a rock overlooking a nice valley and had a good cry. He cried long enough to attract the attention of someone passing by.

He really hadn't been too far from the Ranger's lodge, but without knowing how to enter or being guided, it was intentionally impossible to find. The person who had heard him crying was one of the rangers, and decided to check it out. When he found a little boy crying his eyes out, he assumed the child had been lost from some traveling group. To his surprise, the boy was an orphan, and no one would have ever come looking for him out in the wilds. Even more to his surprise was that the boy was intentionally trying to find the ranger's lodge because he wanted to be a ranger.

Not really sure what else to do, the ranger had brought him to the lodge to ask the lodge master for guidance. The lodge master had been inclined to send the boy back to the city to an orphanage, but the boy had pleaded and begged to be given a chance to show he could be a help to the rangers and someday even become one. The lodge master had a soft spot for the young, and relented by giving him a two week trial. If he didn't prove his worth, he would have to go back to the orphanage.

The boy didn't even need two weeks before he had made himself a necessary fixture of the lodge. He cleaned, chopped wood, served food, helped take care of kills that hunters brought in, and anything else that might need doing. The lodge master had expected the boy would soon tire and give up, but the boy never did. Within three months, the boy was being sought to help different rangers with various tasks. Within six months, some rangers were taking it upon themselves to start training the boy. One of them made sure he knew how to read. The lodge master eventually taught him how to help keep the books for the lodge.

By the time the boy was twelve, he was joining on hunts. When the boy was fourteen, he had rescued some lost nobles. At fifteen, he had helped capture a notorious fugitive that had camped out in their part of the wilderness. At sixteen, he had passed all the tests except for age to become a ranger, and after months of negotiation with the lodge master's council, an exception was finally made. The next year was an active forest fire season, and the young ranger had been instrumental in stopping a fire from reaching their lodge. At 21 years of age, he had reached the elite status as a ranger. Most rangers didn't become elites until they were in their thirties or later.

Suddenly, a strange man just appeared inside the lodge. No one had seen him approach or enter. He was just there. Addressing the rangers present, the man asked a few questions about a special ranger he was looking for. 'Did they know of a ranger who had been an orphan as a child? They were young. This orphan had raised themselves into a ranger of high excellence. They had a habit of delaying before answering questions.'

The man had not even finished his description before everyone else in the lodge was looking at the young ranger. The man simply walked up to Ewan and held out a stone. "Just hold this for a few seconds, just to be sure."

The young ranger didn't know what else to do, so after a pause, reached out his hand and took the stone. No sooner did it hit his palm than it began to glow. More than glow, it shined with a brilliance that rivaled the sun. He was startled, but didn't let himself drop it, as it seemed much more than just special.

The strange man reached out and picked it out of his hand and it became an ordinary white crystal stone once more. "I need to speak to you in private. Will you agree to that?"

The young ranger looked around at the shocked and curious faces of all the other rangers, and thought of the brilliance of the stone in his hand, and then agreed. "Yes."

The lodge had a meeting room that usually was reserved for the lodge master, but the lodge master motioned for them to go on in. Once the door was shut, the strange man turned to him and without sitting said, "You have been identified by a great seer as one who will be instrumental in defeating one of the greatest evils this world has faced in thousands of years."

The ranger looked at him, wondering if he had heard him right.

The man continued. "I cannot tell you all the details, but you must go to the high mountains, in the Rockfield Valley. You will find a small canyon on the northeast side where the mouth of the canyon is marked by three split pines growing in a row on the left side. Go two and a half miles into the canyon, and where the canyon starts to narrow, behind a large boulder, you will find a small hunter's shack. Enter the shack and wait, and someone will be with you within a day. You must come alone."

The strange man reached out to hand him something. "This should cover all your expenses for the trip and far beyond. She said to tell you there is much more where that came from, not that it should be your main motivation." Ewan looked in his hand and then had to look again. There were two platinum coins. He had only seen one once, and had never touched one. Now, two were sitting in his hand. He looked up to protest that it wasn't necessary, but was startled by a bright flash around that strange man, and then the man was gone.

Ewan rushed from the meeting room, looking for where the man went. The other rangers all had stopped what they were doing and looked at him in silence. Ewan looked back in confusion, "Where did he go? Did you see where he went?"

One of the other rangers who had been looking at him answered, "What're you talking about? Nobody's been through here."

Ewan froze for a minute until the lodge master called, "Ewan, come over here, sit down, and tell us about it. You look like you've seen a ghost."

Ewan returned to the seat he had been sitting in before the strange man had appeared. He looked at his closed hand that was holding the platinum coins. Then, making a decision, he lightly slapped the coins under his hand onto the table and slowly removed his hand.

The response from the others around the table was sudden.

"What the ..?"

"Are those ..?"

"What have you got yourself involved in, boy?"

Ewan shook his head slowly, trying to make sense of everything. "I have to face some great evil, or something like that. I have to go to rockfield valley to meet someone to be told more, or something like that. It's all so confusing."

One of the older rangers spoke up, "That's platinum coins there, son. They don't just grow on trees. And did that fancy man just up and vanish on you?"

Ewan looked up, "Yeah. He said a few words, handed me the coins, there was a bright flash, and he was gone. I feel like I should follow through on this, but would that be stupid?"

There were several murmurs but the lodge master held up his hand. "Ewan, you have been like a son to me, and several others here. Any time strange things like this or when platinum coins are involved, there is always trouble involved, but we didn't become rangers to avoid trouble. If you feel like you need to follow through, you may want to listen to that feeling, just keep your guard up."

Ewan could see the wisdom in his advice. He picked up the coins from the table and nodded, "Ok, I'll go get ready."

CHAPTER ELEVEN

CECILIA

STANDING AT THE EDGE of one of the commercial districts in Parnul and feeling uncertain, Cecilia went back over the plan in her mind. She had just enough funds to pay for a room for a couple of nights, but that was it. She didn't have many of the tools that she liked to use, but she could make do. She started walking around, looking at the goods in the various shops, trying to decide what her best options were. While doing so, she made sure to keep an eye out for anyone who might be a local thief that she could get information from.

She started in a general merchandise shop, but it was not a great shop and didn't do enough volume to make it worth hitting. Next she visited Istron's Fine Goods, which looked a little more promising, but the goods they had were too large, heavy, and fragile, which would make it impractical for a quick hit for money making purposes. Renzer's Armory had higher end goods, but were too heavy and anything that was especially valuable would be distinct enough that it would make it hard to offload.

She also checked a potter, a clothier, and a furniture store, then decided to try a more upscale commercial district.

It only took a few minutes to find out where the better stores were located. In the higher end merchant district, there was an alchemist's shop, a custom jewelry store, a high end clothier, another furniture store, an overpriced general goods store, a gem merchant, and a shop called The Magical Goods Emporium. She visited the jewelry store first, but like it said, it was all custom work.

The clothier had expensive goods, but they wouldn't be all that valuable for reselling. She did grab a nice outfit and an expensive bag as she went out the door that she could change into later. There was a small ward that was supposed to stop that kind of theft, but it was easily bypassed by the skills and spells she had gained through training in the thieves' guild of Merdal. The furniture store was nice, but the goods were far too heavy and bulky, and very distinct with the carpenters' marks making them easy to trace.

The general goods store did enough volume that it might be worth hitting if they keep their funds on site, but while observing, she saw bank guards picking up a large deposit, so that wouldn't work. The alchemist was a possibility, but after looking at the gem merchant and especially the magical goods place, she was sure she wanted to target those two.

The gems were all high grade, but standardized. While they were very valuable, they were also very portable. The magical goods store had probably the most high end goods. She was concerned that the proprietor might be some kind of full mage, and she didn't want to mess with one of those, but it was probably better to check both to get to know what she was dealing with better.

After changing into the nice Lady's outfit she swiped earlier and while working her way through the crowd from the gem crafter to the emporium, she noticed a small disturbance and watched as two young men took off running with a mostly concealed red coin purse and quickly disappeared in an alley while people yelled from where they had been. Soon some city guards came to investigate but they didn't find anything in the alley. Cecilia stepped into the Magical Goods Emporium while the guards were doing their investigation. She was sure the city guards had no idea what to even look for.

When she entered the emporium, a man greeted her with a very snooty attitude, as though he would get dirty just from speaking with others. "Oh. What can I help you with today?"

She looked down her nose at the man as if he were far beneath her, a slight smirk on her face. "You have a lot of nerve to be speaking to me that way." The man's haughty demeanor quickly retreated and was replaced with nervous caution.

The man tried again with poorly feigned respect , "I beg your pardon miss. How may I be of service?"

Cecilia rolled her eyes dramatically, as if showing reluctance to accept his assistance, but recognizing that he was the only option for help. "I am visiting relatives here in Parnul from the Kingdom of Merdal. I would like to see what kind of selection you have of a few different kinds of devices." She figured the Kingdom of Merdal would be close enough to be believable, but the man would probably have less current knowledge of the market there, so he wouldn't be able to figure out she was making it up.

The man's subdued caution began to subside as she could see he was attempting to figure out how much coin she was carrying. He let his eyes rove over her, pausing at her purse and and then again at her figure. He licked his lips in what she hoped was anticipation of large sales. "If you can tell me the kinds of things you are interested in, I can show you what we have."

She suppressed a shudder. This was exactly the type of high class scumbag that she liked to see taken down. She squared her shoulders, again taking command of the situation. "I am looking for quality personal wards, as well as wards or other devices that can be used to protect and monitor rooms or buildings." She turned away as if she was perusing his shelves, but then turned back. "Also, any kind of novelties that could be popular at home where they haven't seen such before might be good as well. Perhaps you have tools for long distance communication or something similar?"

She knew these items would be pricey, but that was exactly what she was looking for. Mostly, she wanted him to show her his most expensive items so she would know what to target. For the next twenty minutes, he showed her various devices, and she asked questions to draw out the information she needed. She took the time to evaluate what kind of security the place had, and getting a feel for how familiar he was with such protective devices would clue her in on what she had to work around

She found they had a newer security system which made it so some of the devices they sold wouldn't work unless the shop activated them. She already knew how to get around that. She noted that he kept a large safe, which was obviously enchanted for added protection. It probably contained money and activation tools. She eventually managed to make a clean exit, explaining she needed to return to her aunt's home to retrieve her funds for what she wanted.

Once she exited, she made note that the two guardsmen who were investigating the earlier disturbance had left, so she made her way over to the alley where the two thieves had disappeared. She could see the signs of how they managed their escape as soon as she entered the alley. The thieves were skilled enough to be useful, and the guards were completely clueless. Perfect, that meant that the thieves wouldn't be expecting her to track them down.

She used her spells, skills, and experience to discern where the thieves had gone, and what misdirection clues they had left. Then she tracked the paths they had left into some quieter and poorer areas of the city. She eventually found a place someone had been passing through into some abandoned building basements which had passage markers, detection traps, and even a magical silent detection ward. She didn't have tons of magic spells, but they helped her deal with wards and tracking and hiding her presence.

Soon, she found what she was confident the thieves had been using for their base of operations. It appeared it was only the two of them based on the sleeping arrangements and the amount of foot traffic. They weren't there at the moment, but it probably wouldn't be too long before they came back. She repurposed their traps and alarms to block them in and somewhat immobilize them once they returned. She was confident she could deal with them on her terms.

She set herself up with a possible route of escape in case things didn't turn out as she hoped. Then, she positioned herself like a spider in her web, waiting for her quarry to come to her. They must have had a busy day, since it took a couple of hours before they showed up. The first re-purposed ward let her know they were coming. She had made sure to arrange things to appear exactly the same as they had originally so they wouldn't suspect she was there. Then they came in through their normal entrance. At that point, their way out was blocked by one of the repurposed traps. Both thieves spun around to see their way out close and then were caught up in some netting she had found nearby.

They struggled fiercely for a few minutes. She estimated they were several years younger than her. Since they were fit young men, they were probably stronger than her. She let them struggle for a bit, and finally made her presence known. "There are easier ways to get out of that." Her voice seemed to come from everywhere at once, one of her special skills.

Both of them froze once they knew someone was present that potentially could be dangerous. "Who are you?" One of them asked nervously to the empty air.

"Just a fellow thief passing through who needs some information." she answered.

The one who spoke earlier licked his lips and looked over at his partner. "Um, we'd be ok helpin', depending on cost... and maybe any rewards that might be available."

She was mildly surprised yet pleased with their assertiveness. "Good, first, what are your names?"

The bold one spoke again, "I'm Smat, and this here's Scritch." She wondered if they had real names, but those would be good enough.

"Ok, Smat. Who's the top thief here in the city, and how are things structured?" She continued.

"That'd be Rolund. He's the guild boss. If you do anything here without payin' your dues, the guard'll find you quick."

"Where can I find Rolund?"

"He moves around, but has watchers in places. If we introduce you to 'em, they can take you to 'im." She could tell he was physically uncomfortable and wasn't surprised when he added, "Can ya let us out of 'ere?"

"Sure, that would be fine. Once you toss all your blades and weapons away from you. While you do that, tell me, does this guild have somewhere you can sell off items you acquire? What do you usually do?"

Smat was having issues reaching his weapons on his belt, but had tossed a couple darts onto the floor a little way away from them. Scritch had been trying to work his way through the netting with a small blade much of the time while trying to avoid attention. "Uh, yeah, Roland has a fence we sell at, but often we just sell stuff in a lower market. We got dibs on the upper market on even numbered days. That's cause we'd be some of the best."

Cecilia decided to defuse a potential problem ahead of time. "Scritch, you will get out of the net faster by following instructions, instead of trying to cut that net without proper leverage." He stopped and his shoulders drooped, then tossed the knife away. She then turned the conversation back to Smat. "Have you ever hit any of the merchant stores in the upper market, or do you just target people's pockets?"

"We filch some stuff sometimes, but we never try to break in. You gotta have magic skills for that. We don't touch the magic store or the alchemist, they got magic wards. We did get one of the magic ward stones from some lady that had bought one after she left the store, though." That explained the ward stone they had.

She finally arrived at a decision. "You need better training, and I am going to make you a deal. I will train you for three days, during which time, you will give me half of what you bring in. Will you accept?" They still hadn't seen her, as she had intended.

"Half?!? That's too much!" She expected Smat to feel the price was too high. She also noticed Scritch shaking his head subtly to give his answer to Smat. She needed to break down his resistance.

"If you pay attention and learn well, you will do better during those three days than you have ever done. Scritch, can you speak well?"

"N-n-n-n no." he stuttered.

"Sounds like you have a challenge. While it may be possible for you to someday overcome that, you seem to have some other skills that only need better training. You obviously have enough skill to escape the guards, and that red purse you picked up today looked to be a decent take, but you could do better. Oh, and you left way too much of a trail. I was able to follow you here without taking any detours." She inflected her voice so as to sound superior but without being condescending, "Scritch, would you like to have better skills?" She could tell he was surprised at how much she knew.

"H-h-h-h-h how d-d-d-d- did y-you?" he stopped without finishing his question, but she answered anyway.

"Because I have skills. Very high level skills. It takes a lot of time and practice to perfect them, but just knowing the basic skills would change things up for you a great deal. Scritch, would you like to learn some of those skills? How about you, Smat?"

Scritch nodded his head, and Smat answered "Yeah, of course. Roland hardly teaches us anything, and then we have t' pay up front. A whole lot."

"Will both of you swear by the Patron to serve me as my students for three days?" She paused to see their shock that she would invoke such a serious proposition. That was enough of a reaction to know it would work. "I swear by the Patron that if you do, I will teach you better skills. You will be required to introduce me to Rolund during that time." Swearing by the Patron Thief, who most thieves regarded as a kind of patron deity of thieves was taken very seriously. They held such oaths in very high regard.

Smat was pretty sold, "I swear by the Patron I will serve as your student for three days." Scritch had gone a little pale, but eventually seemed to make up his mind as well.

"I-I s-s-s-swear b-by th-th-the P-Patron," He paused as though trying to decide if he could finish, then continued, "t-t-to b-be your s-s-st-stud-d-dent f-f-fo th-th-three days." He breathed out heavily in relief when he finished.

"Very well. Let's get you out of those ropes. She released her hold spell that was keeping the ropes immobilized and they were able to get out quickly, then she stepped into their view."

"A-a L-L-Lady!" Scritch stammered when he saw her. Smat just sat there staring with his mouth open.

"Lesson number one. This, " she gestured to her clothes, "is a tool of the trade. Am I a lady, or am I a skilled thief? If you can tell by looking at me, I have already failed." They both stood a little more self conspicuously as she looked them over. "As you are working the upper market, you will want to get some better clothes. Grab and dash tactics can work, but the takes are smaller and puts you at greater risk more of the time. A better way to operate is to blend in and not even be noticed as a potential threat."

She looked them over again, deliberately appearing thoughtful and taking long enough to make them feel uncomfortable. "You will also need to learn how to stand, walk, and interact with others like a gentleman. Scritch, you have challenges speaking, so of course Smat will need to take on that role, but if you look like an average high class individual, who is minding his own business, they won't even realize you are there until you have made your move and faded into the crowd."

Cecilia had spent the hours while she was waiting for the thieves to return coming up with a plan. From what she had seen, she was pretty sure she knew their capabilities and potential well enough for the plan to work. She looked over them for a minute, like an investor shopping for a race horse, then said, "For the next two hours, you will learn how to act the part." And that is exactly what they did.

She knew they would not perfect or even become very proficient in what she would teach them, but it should be enough. She could tell their bodies were not used to standing, walking, and moving the way she had them practicing, and she could tell they were getting sore after less than an hour, but she made them go through the whole two hours.

Then she told them to take twenty minutes to stretch so they wouldn't be as sore. Unfortunately, they didn't really know how to stretch effectively, so twenty minutes soon became another hour as she taught them how to stretch and better condition their bodies. After that, she let them rest for fifteen minutes before they were to have a practice session to see what they remembered.

It didn't go great, but about as good as she expected. It would still work. They didn't have to be able to attend noble's parties and high end social events, just walk through crowds of higher end people without anyone noticing the riff raff around them.

Next, she helped them work through some tactics using social distraction, rather than physical distraction, to set up hits. Smat definitely needed to improve his speaking skills or it would not work. She figured he subconsciously knew how to speak properly, but doubted himself, so she trained him in using some basic phrases and pronunciations that would help him pull off the act.

It took several hours of him practicing before he got close enough to actually attempt using them, and Scritch had been practicing approaching her unobtrusively and then fading away into the crowd. He was going to need more work the next day. It was too late by that time to let them try on real targets, but they had made some progress.

Before they tried the next day, they would need haircuts and new clothes. She left them to rest, informing them that the next day would be very busy. Cecilia had previously found a room in the building above their hideout where she could sleep with a ward activated that would be secure enough. She smiled. Tomorrow was going to be fun.

Chapter Twelve

Cecilia

The next morning, she announced that before they could try to use any of their new skills, they needed to get better clothes and they would need haircuts. She decided to return to a somewhat lower scale market for them to acquire their clothes.

They were both worried that they weren't authorized to work that market, but she convinced them that since they weren't going after anyone's purses, it wouldn't be a problem. Once she identified the clothes she wanted them to acquire, she let them know what their target was, and left them to it. She had checked that there wasn't an active ward in the store, then occupied the storekeeper's attention while they snagged their new clothes and left.

It went very smoothly, and they met back up at a predetermined checkpoint. "Ok, before you put on your nice new clothes and make them dirty, you both need haircuts and baths." They both groaned, but didn't argue back. She took them both to a hairdresser she had identified earlier and used some of the funds she had confiscated from them earlier to have their hair cut in acceptable high class styles. Both of them tried to make requests, but she harshly overruled them. They couldn't hold on to any of their previous styles and make it work.

She checked the time and then led them to a bathhouse, where she ordered them to get clean. "And if I am not satisfied by how clean you are, I will drag you back in there and scrub you down myself, and I promise that you will not enjoy it." They both look somewhat terrified at the thought, and did a surprisingly decent job of cleaning up.

She had them dress in their new clothes and disposed of their old clothes. "Ok, now you both look and smell like gentlemen. Let's see if you can act like gentlemen." They had gone to another market district that was a bit more mixed. She had them escort her, then interact with other people, all while not making any hits on any purses or goods.

After 45 minutes of watching and offering a few key corrections, she was satisfied. "Ok, now, we are going to practice hits, but instead of taking purses, we are going to leave notes. The point is, we want to freak people out, but if you get caught, you get to pretend to be heroes for warning people of danger." They would make a game of it. She handed them each five notes that they had to get into the pocket of their marks next to their purses, with bonus points for getting the note into the actual purse.

She picked out marks for them, and had Smat run interference by engaging the marks in conversation while Scritch made the reverse hit. Scritch started off with two aborted attempts, while Smat tried to stay in character. After watching several attempts, she signaled them to fall back and regroup. Scritch needed some extra coaching on how to be more unobtrusive so he could brush by a mark while making it seem he was trying to avoid them. Smat needed some correction in his accent and a wider set of conversation pieces.

The whole thing wasn't going as well as she had hoped it would, but there was some promise. Secondly, she had used the different locations they visited all morning to find places that she could sell off things she picked up from her planned heist. She had identified several places that would work for what she needed. She had them meet her at an abandoned building near their hideout.

Once there, Cecilia reviewed what they needed to work on and had them practice on each other for several more hours while she corrected them and gave verbal instructions. She hoped they had improved enough, since she was running behind schedule. She had to remind herself that it wouldn't matter much to her if they failed to learn what she was teaching them. Still, after they showed improvement, she took them out into the high market.

It was not an even numbered day, so they weren't supposed to be doing any picks that day. However, since they were just practicing and delivering notes, they couldn't be accused of poaching, even if the other thieves were able to recognize them, which she doubted. She used the opportunity to evaluate the security for both her heist targets while keeping an eye on the boys. To her surprise, they performed adequately, perhaps even admirably. Still they had much room for improvement, but the change was highly significant from the previous attempt.

After they had finished delivering all their notes, she had them regroup at an upper level balcony nearby so they could watch if their efforts had any long term effects. They were amused when one of their marks discovered the note and flew into a panic. The mark was a young woman in a yellow dress, who eventually met up with another of their marks, a young man. They could only guess at the conversation, but soon the young man checked his own purse, which Scritch had actually been able to get the note inside of. They could hear his shouts of alarm from more than a hundred yards away.

A city guard soon approached to see what the disturbance was, which got more attention. Several other people began checking their own purses, a few finding notes and causing a greater commotion. Soon, another city guard joined the first, and Smat winced when he saw the guard. "That one is crafty. He catches more thieves than all the others together." The new guard began ordering people to disperse and go about their business.

A few minutes later, there was another commotion, with the crafty guard stepping out from seemingly nowhere and grabbing the hand of a scroungy young man, who in many regards resembled how Scritch and Smat had appeared when she first met them.

Scritch's eyes were wide as he pointed Smat's attention in that direction. Smat mumbled, "That's Lenny. They got Lenny. He's supposed to be the best." Lenny was immobilized and tied up, and when searched, several purses that were obviously not his were found in his possession. The crafty guard and another city guard beamed with pride as they escorted Lenny away. Then Scritch pointed out another person, this time a girl, who was obviously not high class racing out of the market. Smat explained, "That's Lenny's partner. She is probably going to Rolund to see if he can help. Rolund probably won't help though."

That the other pickpockets operating in the high market were stopped surprised her, but she actually thought it would benefit her pupils greatly. "I think that lines things up perfectly for us tomorrow. You will not operate like you normally have, instead, you will carry those notes. You will plant those notes on people who have smaller purses, but you will take the bigger ones. Before you go out and do any of that, however, you will meet me here and we will see if you can pick out the best marks. Once you have that clear, you will get to work. Now, it is time for another set of lessons. Come."

They followed her to one of the mid level markets, where she had them acquire some normal work clothes and some basic adventurer's gear. Then they returned to their hideouts where she had them change and carefully put away their finer clothes and change into the work clothes. She surveyed their new outfits and the stances. They stood awkwardly, obviously nervous about what new lessons she was about to teach them.

She knew she only had enough time to give them a taste of a higher vision, but she felt she would be amiss if she didn't do her best with her pupils. Then she began to teach them how to get past a variety of wards, alarms, and other methods of protection for businesses. It was time for them to expand their repertoire of targets and operations. After a long and grueling evening, they exhaustedly fell into their beds and she returned to the room she had previously used.

The next day, they joined her on the balcony again, where they talked about who would be a good likely target, and who would not. They could generally pick out some of the normal type marks that would typically get hit, but totally missed the highest rollers that moved through the markets. She explained to them what to watch for, and then sent them on their way, with instructions to regroup at the hideout in the evening.

While they had been observing and picking out ideal marks and such, she had noticed there were several curriers who served several of the higher end stores. Of special note is that they seemed to carry in goods, and sometimes carried away what might be coin. She decided to track them once the boys got started.

It didn't take long to figure out the curriers patterns. They came and went from the warehouse district, and if they were carrying coin, they often would stop by the banking district on the way back to the warehouse district, but not always. She was able to determine which warehouses served which stores, and which appeared to hold decent amounts of coin.

The two stores she had already been targeting didn't seem to use the curriers, but about half of the others did. From observation, she had learned that the gem cutter received deliveries by armed guards every other day, while the emporium got one daily, but didn't seem to send his coin anywhere except in payment for the deliveries. The guards who made the deliveries to the emporium made directly for some of the mage organizations where they had presumably gotten their goods and left the payments there.

That evening, on a whim, she broke into one of the warehouses, one that appeared to store the most coin. She had to be careful since there were armed guards with crossbows. There were a variety of wards protecting things, especially the big safe in the back office. The whole room was set to be a ward, which she guessed probably set off a very loud, and potentially dangerous alarm. She had picked up a lockpick set from Scritch, and since he really didn't use it, he didn't seem to mind.

She worked her way into the room, using her spells and skills to keep from triggering the wards, and managed to pick her way through a couple of layers of protection on the safe. She disarmed traps, disabled wards, and finally came to a magical combination lock. She opened it in 33 seconds, which while not bad, was definitely not her record.

Fortunately, there was a good amount of coin for her to take, as well as some very interesting records which she would have taken for later usage for bribes and blackmail if she was planning to stay in town very long. Then she left the safe open and made her way back to the hideout.

The boys were there celebrating when she arrived and they showed off how much they had made. Their celebration toned down a bit when she reminded them that they owed her half of what they made, but they paid her without complaining. Then she told them they would be learning how to do hits after hours on business, and then showed them her take for the day. It was more than twenty times what they had made, which was still about ten times what they normally made.

Their celebration immediately sobered and ended abruptly, and they both enthusiastically got ready for a new set of lessons. The lessons went late that night. The next morning, she instructed them to take her to meet Roland. They crossed through the city and ended up in a residential district on the edge of a smaller warehouse district. The boys identified one of the watchers and then approached as discreetly as they knew how.

"This here is a master thief from Merdal. She wants to run some operations in town and we told her she has to get approval from Roland." The watcher just nodded, and then waited for the boys to leave. Then the watcher signaled for her to follow. They wound through a few streets, and ended up going through a fence into the back of a small warehouse. Once they stopped at a door, where a big guard waited and looked at her impatiently. She made a secret sign to show her organizational level, and was let into an office that really only contained some stairs.

She took the stairs and came to a waiting room with a couple of doors where she waited for a few minutes. Finally, one of the doors opened and a rough looking girl perhaps a few years older than her stepped out. "Who is you, and whatcha want?" the girl drawled accusingly.

Cecilia responded as blankly as she could, "I am a thief from Merdal who is passing through your city. I was told I need to have permission from the local guild to run any operations here and that there are dues to pay. I also am curious if you have any special tools for sale or if you have anything set up to sell off hot items."

The girl's somewhat haughty attitude seemed to fade a bit. "Lemme check with the Boss if he'll see ya." She stepped back through the door and shut it. It took only a couple minutes before she opened the door back up. "He'll see ya. Follow me." She held the door open for Cecilia and then closed it once she was through, then led her down a long hallway and then seemingly at random picked one of the many doors along the wall. It opened to a large room with a cocky looking man sitting in a large chair like he thought he was a king on a throne.

"You want to work in my city, huh?" he brusquely asked. "You gotta have references."

She refused to bow down to this man. "You can ask Smat and Scritch what I have taught them in the last few days. They pulled in ten times the take that they normally get yesterday. But that isn't part of your normal process, is it?" She eyed him intently.

"We knew who they were when they were wanting a license, but I don't know you from anyone." he explained with a sly look, as if that should answer all her questions.

"How much for the license?"

"Gonna be a hundred gold" he said coldly, but she could tell he was just seeing how far he could push her.

"I'll pay five, which is more than you normally charge."

He looked at her dubiously, but she could tell he was willing to take it. They stared at each other for a half a minute before she explained more.

"My operations tend to be larger, but I hit and then I'm gone. The five gold will more than make up for your normal dues and concerns from increased scrutiny that happens after a large job, but since I will be gone and no one else will be doing anything like it, it will die down quickly."

"I don't like increased scrutiny." he said, "But, ok, that'll do. We'll get your license processed in a minute. You got any more questions?"

"Do you have a store for special equipment that can't be found elsewhere? My particular targets need some special considerations. Also, if I happen to come up with some very hot items, do you have a fence?"

"We have both, but we charge a surcharge for hot items. The hotter the item, the higher the surcharge."

"That's expected and understandable. Who do I pay my dues to?"

"Pay Janice. She will give you your license. If you need to access the fence, ask Bruno, the big guard at the warehouse office. He will show you where to go. Use your license to get in. Janice will take things from here. She can also help you with any special items you need, provided you pay upfront. We don't sell on credit." He picked up a strange stick sitting next to him and scraped it across the edge of his chair. It made a strange vibration sound. He seemed to be waiting for something and sat quietly.

While they waited, Roland then looked at her strangely, as though he was trying to figure something out. Half a minute later, the girl, presumably Janice, was back. Cecilia followed her out the door and down the hall to another door where the girl gave her a key with a number on it. Cecilia told Janice what items she needed, if they had it, and Janice retrieved them. It cost almost twenty gold, which was enough for a small house, but she would make it all back and many multiples more very shortly.

Janice then directed her back down to the waiting room and down the stairs. The guard, presumably Bruno, just looked at her passively, and then looked away. She decided she could show herself the way out and made her way back to the boy's hideout.

Chapter Thirteen

Nerian

As he rode through the main square of the small city he was passing through, Nerian noticed a commotion over to the side. A woman was yelling about something to the crowd, and there were a number of people who seemed angry about it. He normally would have ignored the whole thing, but he was sure he had heard the words 'Tower of Light' mixed in with everything else she was yelling. He brought up his horse behind the back of the crowd and called out using a crowd control spell he had learned, "What's going on here!"

The amplification of his voice, and his very official looking uniform for the Tower of Light brought most of the hubbub to a screeching halt. The woman looked up at him, as though unsure if she were in trouble or not. She was quite dirty, most of it appeared to simply be from travel, but she also had torn clothes that looked as though she had been through some serious physical altercations. The woman, under all the dirt, looked like she might be attractive and she seemed very fit, perhaps like a soldier, but wore no armor or uniform. She had hesitated as though she was working up the courage to address him. She called out. "Please sir, the people of this city are in danger. I have been trying to warn them, but they don't understand."

After hearing her words, Nerian wasn't sure he understood either. "What exactly are they in danger from?"

"The storm! A great storm is coming. It will be here in less than two weeks at the rate it is spreading. It is coming from a new dark tower that rose from the Pit. Lightning strikes from it near anywhere that people are, and causes monsters to rise from the ground. They will kill everyone!"

Nerian suspected the unfortunate lady was a bit off her rocker, but some of what she said caused some concern. One of the locals taunted her, "What are you talking about, a new dark tower from the pit? I fear you may have been reading histories while using bad medicine." Some of the people laughed at that, but Nerian felt bad about it. He wanted, no, needed to know what she was talking about, but was also a little concerned she might be crazy.

"I was there." The woman continued dramatically, "I was in Danlos, and the wizard's tower exploded and destroyed half the city. Then this huge new tower rose up out of the pit. It is thousands of feet tall. Smoke poured out of the top of it, and a dark cloud started to form."

Nerian was caught up on the first part. "Wait! What was that about the wizards tower? Are you talking about Dardanos' tower?"

The woman answered flatly, "Yes, it exploded. It is completely gone." She acted like it was common knowledge.

Nerian struggled to understand what all this meant. "What happened to Dardanos?" He noticed some people seemed to be taken aback by what must have seemed a casual reference to someone revered almost as a deity on this continent.

"I don't know. I assume he was destroyed with his tower. We didn't have time to search the rubble to see if there were any survivors. I didn't think much of it because I was trying to help some of the injured people, but the matron said we needed to flee to the Tower of Light before the cloud caught us, so we loaded on some wagons and tried to get away."

Nerian was still trying to understand everything she was saying. "Hold on! Who is this matron person?"

The woman was beginning to act a little frantic again. "The matron of the circus. I was a circus performer, and she told us to flee, but the storm caught us while we camped that night. Lightning was everywhere and these monsters formed right out of the ground where it hit. They killed everyone, but I got away on a horse. The storm is still expanding. I have been trying to warn people, but they won't listen. They have to get to the Tower of Light!"

Nerian was beginning to understand. If what she said was true, the second darkness had already started. He had failed his dying king's last command in yet another way. He had managed to push his self doubt down a bit during his voyage, but it came surging back. He wasn't sure what to do, but fleeing to the Tower of Light wouldn't help anyone. His voice was low, but still carried. "I am sorry to inform you, but the Tower of Light has also been destroyed."

The woman's face filled with horror. "What? No! ... No! It can't be. She said that is the only place we can be safe." She fell to the ground and began to sob. Nerian couldn't help but feel somewhat responsible.

One of the people in the crowd yelled out, "What are you talking about, and how would you even know."

Nerian tried to explain as his face darkened. "I was one of King Evander's Royal Knights at the Tower of Light. I was on my way to my shift when it exploded, along with the royal palace. I checked on the King and found that he was poisoned. Before he died, he told me to help Dardanos stop a second darkness. It looks like I am too late."

Somehow, this seemed to set off a panic in the crowd. People started yelling and screaming and running in various directions. Apparently, his news caused them to believe that what the crazy woman had been saying was real, and now they were panicking. Nerian decided he needed more information from the woman. He tied off his horse on a nearby post, and walked to the woman. He stooped to the ground next to her and put his hand on her shoulder. "I'm sorry," he said.

"I tried!" she sobbed. "I really thought we would be safe there!"

Nerian put his arm around her and held her while she cried. Once she finally started calming down, he spoke, "I wish I could give you answers. I wish I had answers, but right now I have only questions. Could we go someplace where we could talk a little more privately. I need to know what you saw and heard and experienced."

The woman looked at him like she didn't understand what he said. The understanding slowly dawned on her and she caught her breath and answered, "Ok." She pointed at a restaurant at the edge of the square. "I was there earlier. They have private booths."

As they walked to the restaurant, he asked her, "What is your name?"

She glanced up at him, "Micaela, sir."

"Micaela, sir. Well, it's nice to meet you, Micaela, sir." He tried not to wince at his awful joke.

The joke seemed to help lighten the heavy mood she was cocooned in. She wiped her face on her sleeve and corrected him. "Just Micaela. You?"

"My name is Nerian." She nodded, but didn't respond. As they walked, he tried to organize what he had heard, so he knew what to ask. She said she had been in Danlos when the tower exploded. She talked about a new dark tower that rose from the ground that created the cloud, or storm. He would need more clarity on that.

She had said something about lightning creating monsters or something like that. He would need to get more details. She had also said something about the storm coming in two weeks. How did she know that? Was it just a guess, or was it her fear talking? He would have to ask.

Once they were seated in a private booth in the restaurant and their food had been delivered, Nerian started by checking if Micaela had any questions first.

She asked, "You said the Tower of Light was destroyed, right. Can it or will it be rebuilt?"

He shook his head, "The one who knew how to build it was the king. King Evander was one of the three remaining Halidar. No one else knew how to build it. Dardanos was another Haldiar. Let's look at that for a minute. It's been about three weeks since the Tower of light was destroyed. Blown up like the whole tower was a big bomb. It totally decimated most of the city. When did Dardanos's tower get destroyed, and what was that like?"

Micaela's mouth dropped open before she refocused and answered. "It was destroyed about three weeks ago. More or less the same time. It exploded like a big bomb, like you said. About half the city was destroyed, and the tower wasn't even in the city itself."

Nerian rubbed his eyes for a minute. "Well, it sounds like whatever, whoever it was, did both towers. These were highly protected places, monitored by two of the most powerful magicians that there have ever been, and yet, both places were destroyed at the same time in the same way." They both took a minute to contemplate what that meant.

"Any other questions before I begin?"

"You said something about King Evander being poisoned. Shouldn't he have been able to heal himself or fight through that? Surely he has dealt with poisons before?"

"Yeah, I thought so too. Most of the people who were hit with it succumbed to the poison and died in seconds. The king took more than an hour to die, though, and for a good portion of that there had been powerful healers trying to combat the poison. What he told me is there was no cure. It is like he knew what it was. After that, he immediately ordered me to go help Dardanos to stop the dawn of the second darkness, but obviously, that was already happening at the same time. I don't think he thought it was possible for both towers and wizards to be destroyed at the same time."

Micaela bit her lip thoughtfully. "So, if he knew what the poison was, would we be able to narrow down who else knew about it? We can assume the other Halidar knew, but how did they get the King with it?"

Nerian's eyes narrowed. "You may be on to something. They flooded the administrative offices with poison gas, which means whoever did it were insiders or had help from insiders. At the same time, the throne room was almost completely destroyed by a giant chunk of stone that came from the exploding tower. It looked coincidental that it hit the throne room, but if that was the main attempt to kill the king, and the poison gas was the backup plan, that would match what I saw."

"And now you are here. How many other knights came with you?" She asked.

Narian felt very disturbed. "I was the only one uninjured enough to come. I was supposed to bring a whole squad."

She raised her eyebrows, "Do you think perhaps the king wanted those healthy enough to investigate to be removed from the situation?"

Nerian didn't like where this was going. "Wait, but, that would mean... Why would the king want his own death to not be investigated. Why..?" Fear jumped into his mind. *If the king wanted his death not to be investigated, did that mean he was in on it. Nobody could be more insider than the king!* He recoiled at his own thought, "No! No!, I .. I can't accept that."

Micaela seemed to not be following. "What can't you accept?"

"Why would the King want to be involved in his own death and destroy the tower he spent centuries building?" Nerian's mouth had become very dry. "Who else could have orchestrated it? No one else had the knowledge or access to be able to pull it off - would they?.."

She shook her head. "I don't know. Perhaps there is more involved. Maybe it was the king, but maybe he had been tricked or influenced in some way that got him to do it? I don't think that we can ever really know."

Nerian was very frustrated and huffed, "Great! Just great. Now I will always have doubts about the very person I have dedicated my life to. None of this makes sense." He growled in frustration and pounded the table. Then, he closed his eyes and breathed deeply to calm himself. "Ok, let's talk about this other new tower now. Tell me what you saw."

Micaela told him about climbing the hill, and the earthquake, then seeing that the wizard's tower was destroyed and the new tower rising out of the ground and the smoke and clouds coming out of it forming the storm. She explained their attempt to flee and being attacked by skeletons and how she escaped.

"There was no moon for most of the night. I used the lantern and rode through the night and the next day. It was slow riding at night, but faster than the skeletons and the storm. By the end of the next day, I was far enough ahead of the storm that I was able to take a short break and rest. Since then, I have done all I could to get ahead of the storm and warn people while making my way to the Tower of Light." She looked a little panicked again. "But the Tower of Light is gone, so now I don't know what to do."

Nerian sat there, just thinking, and Micaela watched him, like she was looking for answers. He wasn't sure if she was delusional, but apart from the fantastic nature of her tale, she didn't seem crazy. She seemed authentic and personable. Rational even. She could be helpful to have along once he figured out what they could do.

Eventually, he reached a decision. "I need to travel to where I can see the storm and measure some things. After that, we need a plan of what we are going to do. I traveled here after sailing to the port of Jasteros."

He paused to think about a more concise plan of action. "Jasteros is about five days from here by horse, maybe two weeks by foot. I recommend you travel there. I am willing to work with you to figure out a plan, but I need to go see the storm to be more clear with what we are dealing with. If you can go to Jasteros, stay in the Red Willow Inn. I will meet you there within two weeks. If I don't show up by that time, I probably got caught in the storm and won't be coming at all, but I am sure I will be there. Will you go there and wait?"

Micaela looked embarrassed, "Uh, I don't have money to stay in an Inn. I don't even have enough for this restaurant. When I was here earlier, I was looking for a handout."

Nerian wasn't totally surprised by her revelation. Considering what she had been through and the condition of her clothing, he wasn't really surprised. "Here," He reached into his coin purse and placed a stack of gold coins in her hand. "That should take care of any expenses you might need. You should probably get some new clothes too."

Micaela's mouth dropped open as she stared at the money and looked like she might pass out. Nerian asked, "Are you ok?"

She stammered, "That.. that's, .. I don't.. How.. I can't pay you back. I don't .."

He stood and put on his most regal persona, "I trust you will be a good steward of these royal funds, malady." Then he returned to his normal demeanor. "I have enough to cover these expenses and would like you to accompany me, at least for a while. Think about what our options are, and I will too. You are a survivor, and you have critical information, if we ever encounter anyone who can do something with it. Just take it and be grateful, and careful. People can be really greedy."

"Don't I know it." she mumbled. Nerian could see that she had experienced people's greed first hand. Then she looked up at him decisively. "I will wait for you at the Red Willow Inn for two weeks, get some new clothes, and be thinking about what our options are."

Nerian smiled, "Excellent. I will see you when I get there." With that he turned and left the private booth. He paid the restaurant and stepped outside, then retrieved his horse and rode out of town. He worked his horse hard for as long as it could go each day, and within about five days, he could see the storm in the distance. It was huge. He could see that it really would become a world covering darkness.

After another hour, he could see where the edge of the darkness was sweeping across the ground. It wasn't very fast, but fast enough that it would eventually make it everywhere. He got off his horse and set up a marker, and then measured a distance of half a mile and set up another. Both of them could be seen from the hill behind him. Then he climbed the hill and watched through his spyglass. He marked the time the storm reached the first marker, then again when it reached the second one.

He had seen only a few lightning strikes further into the distance, and couldn't make out clearly what emerged from where it hit, but something certainly had emerged. He shook his head grimly. He realized the storm was getting too close to his position for comfort and decided he had all the information he was going to get directly from the storm and rode away.

Once he had several miles of distance, he got out a notebook and did some calculations. Micaela was a little off, but not by that much. The town they met in had about three weeks before the storm got there. He decided to head out and stop by each town he passed and let them know how long they had before it arrived.

It really helped that he was a Royal Knight of the Tower of Light, since town leaders usually would meet him as soon as he asked. He used the meetings to rest his horse and rode through the night as often as the moonlight permitted. Once he had reached the town where he had met Micaela and warned the leadership there, he decided that he had to really push it if he didn't want to be late meeting Micaela. He got to Jasteros in the afternoon of the fourteenth day from when they parted. He went straight to the Inn, and hoped she would still be there. It took a while to get the information, but he was told she was still there.

When she came down the stairs to the main room of the inn, she said. "Wow, do you always like cutting it this close?" He looked up and was momentarily stunned. She was much prettier than he had surmised earlier. He paused as he realized that with her being clean, wearing a much nicer outfit, and both better fed and rested, her true beauty showed through.

He had been grinning to cover his lapse and leaned into it with a tease, "Not always, but I figured it would be more adventurous this way." Then much more genuinely continued, "I'm glad you are still here." His grin had turned into relief. He gestured for her to sit and she did.

"Ok, so, what is the plan?" She seemed eager to get moving.

He took a deep breath before trying to explain the idea he had come up with on his ride. "Well, I don't know if it would be of any use, but we could go seeking the last Halidar, Rhondalyn. She might know of a way to be safe from the storm, or even how to do something about it. Of course, that is assuming we can even find her, but I know where she is supposed to be."

He paused to gauge her reaction. When she didn't seem to react, he tried to explain a bit more of his thinking. "Even if we can't find her, it will take something like six to eight months before the storm reaches there, whereas it will get here in six to seven weeks. It is moving a little slower than you earlier estimated, but I have no way of knowing if it changes in speed much. Regardless, it gives us much more time before it gets to us there. Once it does, it will have covered the whole world, so there would be nowhere safe after that. That might be the safest place there is, anyway."

He could tell she was contemplating what he had said. After a while she asked. "How would we get there? And where exactly is that?"

Nerian realized he hadn't mentioned that detail. "On the continent of Isalor in the High Reach Mountains. That means we have to take a boat from Port Yadzul. Since we are already in a port, it would probably be faster, cheaper, and easier to take a boat from here to Port Yadzul rather than an overland coach. Then we would take a different type of boat across to Isalor from there."

She nodded her head, "I've never been on a boat. How do we go about it?"

He worked through a mental list. "First, I have to warn the city leaders, then I have to find a boat or ship that is going to Port Yadzul or that we can charter there. Then we get on the boat and sail there. Pretty straight forward."

That seemed to have resolved her concerns. "Ok, sounds good to me. What do you need me to do?"

"You can either come with me, or you can wait here. I think I should have everything arranged this evening, and we'll know how soon we'll sail."

She appeared pretty eager. "I'll come with you, then. Just waiting has gotten pretty boring and just increases the tension."

Warning the city leaders only took a brief while, and their reaction helped with finding a ship that would take them to Port Yadzul. The ship would leave in two days. There was only one cabin available on the ship, however.

As they left the port master's office, Micaela looked at Nerian with a great amount of seriousness, her mouth drawn tight, "So there is only a single cabin with a single bed. Let me make one thing clear. I'm not going to share a bed with you. Especially a small bed on a ship."

Nerian could understand her concern and spoke to reassure her, "I wouldn't ask you to. I'll sleep on the floor or we can sleep in shifts. Whenever one of us needs to change, the other can step outside the cabin. Is that acceptable?"

She looked a little shocked that he didn't argue back, but then smiled, "Yes. That should work fine." She turned and looked toward the city.

An awkward silence permeated the air for a few moments, and Nerian decided to change the subject. "So, we have two days until the ship sails. Any suggestions on what we should do?"

She looked over at him, more relaxed than before, "Um, not really. I would rather not just sit at the Inn the whole time."

He wanted to further reassure Micaela and he thought perhaps doing some shopping for supplies might help. He wasn't sure exactly what they would need, but he was confident they could figure it out. He suggested "Perhaps we can look around and figure out what supplies we will need on the ship, and afterward, once we get to Isalor. Would that be ok with you?"

Micaela looked up at him, uncertainty etched in her face. "Uh, I guess that would be ok." Not sure what else to say, Nerian took the lead and headed to the nearest merchant district. The conversations started off a little awkward, but within a short time, they both were able to relax more and things flowed more naturally. For two days they shopped, talked, ate, and waited.

Then, it was finally time for them to board the ship. They put their things in their cabin and then returned to the deck. As the ship left the port, they stood on deck watching Jasteros fade into the distance. The ship rocked with the waves and Micaela grasped the railing. She then turned her head towards Nerian and asked with an anxious face, "Do you think I'll get seasick?"

Chapter Fourteen

Cecilia

Cecilia only had two more things to take care of before she could execute her plan. First, she needed to set up her transportation. Second, she needed to wrap things up with Smat and Scritch. Despite their obnoxious youthfulness and lack of culture, they had grown on her in those three days. She decided to warn them about the Storm after she collected the last payment of what they owed her.

First, she worked her way to the far side of the city where the public for hire carriage station was. She certainly didn't have enough for the full ride, but she had enough for a deposit. It took a while since finding someone willing to travel many thousands of miles, which would be a journey of weeks or even months. Finally, they found someone. Not only that, but they had a few other people who were willing to join on the trip and split the cost.

Next, she returned to the hideout that Smat and Scritch had set up. It has a comfortable enough place to sleep, and they were the only ones who knew where it was. When she got there, they were eager to show what they had acquired while visiting various shops that day. They also had managed to pick up a few decent sized purses, since the leader of the odd day thief team had been arrested, they were free to work the high market, they just had to give the other team ten percent of their gains. Still, with what Cecilia had taught them, even after paying her half, they made much more than usual.

After they paid her, she pulled them to a corner to give them a warning. "I want to warn you. There is a great storm that is spreading from Sangar that brings monsters and will take over your mind. You can fight it a little bit. I did, but just enough to know to run from it. I don't know how far it will spread, but it resembles the legends of the Great Darkness. I am leaving as soon as I run my main heist and going as far from the storm as I can get. I won't tell you what to do, but I would recommend you consider moving away from here so you don't get caught in the storm."

"What's this storm like?" Smat asked.

"It blocks out much of the sun. It is dark under it, but dark in other ways than just lacking light. It is like you can't think clearly. Most of the thieves just started doing labor jobs like any poor person. So did the higher classes. It was like they couldn't think. I could see some of what was going on, but I just wanted to sleep, and that scared me, cause I'm never like that. I somehow decided to run from it. I stole a horse and just rode. The horse never even reacted like it had been stolen until we got out from under the storm. Then it started acting up. My mind cleared up as soon as I felt sunlight. It was strange. I have never felt so scared in my life."

"Others I have talked to talked about monsters like skeletons that come from the lightning strikes. I didn't run into any of those, but I did hear a strike behind me but just kept riding as fast as the horse would go.

I've taken a liking to you two boys. You're good students and have a great future, but not if you get caught in the storm. Just think it over, ok?

"O-o-o-oh kay" Scritch managed to get out.

Smat's face had gone pale, "I'll.. I'll.. We'll... Yeah, we'll think about it. Look, now you scared me so bad, I'm starting to stutter like him."

She glared at him. "Hey, be nice. I'm leaving now. It will be a long night and I have some preparations to do. Take care of yourselves." With that she left. She had to get everything in position. Prior to coming to the hideout, she had checked the targets. The gem cutter had just received what looked like a good sized order of gems, and the emporium seemed just about the same as always.

She went over her preparations. She had made sure to acquire enough bags to carry everything she'd need and acquire. She also had found a place where she could wait out the closing of the market while avoiding the rounds of the city guards. She prepared her newly purchased tools. She could break through a lot of wards with just her skills, but the ones she was up against that night were beyond just her skills and required special tools.

She decided to hit the gem shop first, even though he tended to work late. As she watched, she saw the smarmy owner of the emporium lock up his store and activate all the defenses. There was a couple he activated that she hadn't been able to detect before, but she hadn't seen him close his shop up before that. It wouldn't change her plans, however. She was sure there would be stronger wards on the safe than just the building anyway.

Eventually, the gem cutter locked his shop and activated its protections. Fortunately, there was nothing surprising there. She waited for the first patrol to come through, and then acted quickly. She quickly approached the shop and encountered the first ward. It was a tattler type that would notify someone if it was triggered. Next was a double shield ward, designed to catch a perpetrator between two shields. That one was tricky because to disable it, she had to be inside the outer shield, which made it possible to accidentally get caught in it even if she knew it was there.

Then she encountered the physical locks. One of them had a magically keyed ward embedded in it, but she was able to drain the energy from it quickly enough. Then she was in. Inside the shop, there were wards on all the individual cabinets. Tattlers were standard and some had doubles to catch someone who wasn't paying close enough attention. There were also attack wards of several varieties. She noted there were lightning, fire, ice, and poison traps. They even had different activation sequencers, but that didn't matter, as she was able to disable them all quickly.

She also removed multiple shield and trap wards. In the corner was a visual recorder ward device. She used one of her tools to clear its memory and set it to loop onto itself so it didn't record anything for four hours. She was able to work through the physical locks and found a few more wards to disable. Then she started clearing. The goods were small but extremely valuable. They also were heavy once enough were added to her bag, which is why it was triple reinforced.

Next was clearing out the safe. His safe had only the basics, and there was a decent amount of coin in it, but he did seem to have some bank receipts indicating he kept a lot of it in bank accounts. He also had some insurance documents. She smiled. No wonder he didn't have more than just the insurance required protections for his store. He was protected even if he got robbed. Well, he would be calling in his policy pretty soon.

Finally, she finished up with what she considered her calling card. She closed and locked everything up and reactivated the wards just as she had found them. Now it looked like no one had been there and the goods just disappeared. She verified that there were no tags or tracers attached to anything. She had found a couple earlier. She checked the time. The next patrol should be coming through in about 15 minutes. She returned to her hiding place and waited.

Once they passed by, she moved on to the Magical Goods Emporium. Potentially, the goods here were worth much more than the gems, but they also would be harder to sell and there was sure to be much more tricky and advanced magical protection. She started with using an additional advanced ward and magic detection device she had purchased. Depending on what it detected, she might not be able to hit the store, but fortunately she felt she could handle everything it found. She started canceling, disabling, and sometimes just draining wards and a few other spells that were protecting the store.

She found a lot of combinations of magical and physical locks, traps, and other gadgets meant to catch thieves such as herself. Very few of the thieves she knew could have cracked this one. It was a nice little challenge, but not too difficult. It took her almost twenty-five minutes to crack into the store and make sure everything was disabled.

She had to disable multiple recording devices, including some designed to catch and identify mages. Those ones recorded mana signatures, and were nearly impossible to wipe. Fortunately, one of her devices she had purchased simulated a mana free environment. She had two new heavy duty bags, and quickly filled one with items that were both on the smaller and more valuable side. She carefully avoided ones that would have unique signatures or identifiers.

She had been avoiding those that required activation up until then. In order to make those worth it, she needed to get the activation codes and totems from the safe. The safe could also have coin and other things that were highly valuable and portable. She double checked with her scanners, and found a few spells and triggers that activated when certain parts of the floor were walked on. The owner had been careless, since the safe parts of the floor had been worn down over time, so she knew where to walk.

Once she reached the safe, it took her a long time to work through all the protections. It was more challenging than she expected. There was even a portal spell that would swap the contents in the safe with another location if it was improperly accessed. She worked through that, and then managed to replicate the access spells she had sensed the owner used before.

Finally, she had made her way through everything and carefully opened the safe. There was another trigger that required a time delay when opening the safe, and another that sent out a notification every time the safe was open. She was able to intercept that signal with the final tool that she had bought, preventing the owner from even knowing the safe had been breached.

Inside were two large bags of gold coins, and everything she needed to activate the items she hadn't collected yet. She loaded the activators and returned to the main part of the store where she gathered all the activation required items that she now could make use of.

She decided to not leave her calling card, just to walk away and leave the front doors open. The guy was a creep, and if other people managed to steal more of his stuff, he deserved it. She then retreated to another location she had prepared so she could sort out what she was selling where. She had found five stores that she could sell things off to quickly when they opened in the morning. The rest either she would sell to the fence, or hold onto for selling later.

The stuff she was holding onto she loaded into special storage devices that she wore under her outer clothes, making it easy to keep it with her, while not appearing to have anything of great value. It would be ironic and stupid if she were to make herself a target for other thieves and lose what she had worked so hard to acquire. She was very close to three of the shops she was going to sell stuff at, so she closed her eyes and meditated until it started getting light.

The shops had been well chosen. They didn't question anything and just gave her the cash she needed. The other two were on the way to the area where Rolund's fence was located. One of them was the biggest purchaser and she had to wait for a runner from the bank with the funds she needed. She had waited calmly even though inside she was running just under a panic, with her fears telling her that the guards would be coming instead of the bank runner with the money. It seemed to take a little longer than she expected, but it all worked out. She then headed off to the warehouse where she could access Rolund's fence. When she got there, she found Bruno in exactly the same place with exactly the same expression. When she asked for the fence, he pointed down a wall and said "Third door."

She proceeded to the third door and used her license to enter. Behind a dark screen was a person, but she couldn't tell enough to even determine their gender. "Hi, I have some things I need to trade out."

A voice responded that was muffled, probably by magic, but she could still understand, "Temperature?"

"Maybe room temperature, or some just a bit warmer." she responded.

"Place the first lot on the counter and I will give you a bid." the fence directed.

She followed the directions, placing each lot on the counter and accepted the bids. She made to act like she wasn't sure about if she wanted to, but she knew she wouldn't be taking any of this with her and needed the cash since the cost of the carriage was very high. Once she had sold off everything she had planned on selling to the fence, she concealed the bulk of her funds and headed out. She was carrying about a quarter of her weight still between the coin and the goods she had kept.

She started heading toward the carriage yard to proceed with her trip when she sensed someone following her and fumed inside. Those dirty fools. She quickly found an alleyway and used some climbing tricks at the end of it to seemingly vanish. She stayed where she could discretely observe who was following her. She almost gasped when she recognized Rasdal, her former bodyguard that worked for her parents. Somehow she had been found out. This guy was seriously bad news.

She quickly worked her way into other parts of town using rooftops and alleyways. She set up several observation points to make sure she was no longer being followed. Once she was sure she was in the clear, she quickly made her way to the carriage station and got there with only twenty minutes to spare before her carriage left. She paid for the ride, grateful for the extra gold she got from the emporium safe, since she barely had enough from selling the other goods that she hadn't kept. She decided to stay mostly out of sight, just in case Rasdal or someone else came looking for her.

About three minutes before she was to board, Rasdal walked into the station yard. He walked around slowly carefully scanning everyone he could see. She had hidden where she could watch the whole thing using a reflection in a window. He passed by the carriage she was going to take and then the room she was hidden in, pausing once in a while. Once he was behind another carriage she quickly made her way to her carriage and got loaded. She positioned herself in a back corner, which while not typically comfortable, was perfect for her needs at that moment.

About two minutes later the last call for the carriage went out, and they took off. She used a small mirror to watch behind them. It didn't seem that he was watching that carriage and she was sure he wasn't following. It still left her feeling nervous. Every few minutes for most of that day, she would check again just to make sure. She hoped she would never see him again. At the end of the day, they stopped in another city. She was still nervous, but after staying the night in an inn and starting out the next day, she finally started to relax. It was going to be a long ride, but she felt confident that she would never have to deal with Rasdal or her parents again.

Chapter Fifteen

Ewan

THE AIR WAS COLD. Winter was fading and there was still a lot of snow on the ground. The ranger slowly navigated the path he was on, carefully taking in everything that was around him. He rarely ventured into the high mountains, especially this early in the season. Not that he was afraid, but there was little to gain from such a hike that couldn't be had much closer to the lodge.

The instructions had been very specific, though, so here he was, hiking into the Rockfield Valley. The snow was no longer as deep as it had been, making it possible for him to travel without difficulty. He had been here a few times before, but there was very little in this valley to make it worth the journey this early in the season. But it would be filled with rare herbs in a month or two, once spring had fully set in.

He progressed to the northeast side, and just as described, there were three pine trees growing in a row that had two trunks growing together from each of them. He never would have thought they symbolized anything, but the description matched too perfectly. He followed the small canyon as it climbed further into the mountains.

After about two and a half miles, the canyon had become steep and narrow on the sides. He found a small area on the right side that was fairly flat with a huge boulder sitting in the middle of it. He circled the boulder and found a little hunter's shack, partly built into a depression in the back of the boulder. The front of the shack had been finished enough and it had a door that was shut. The whole shack looked extremely old and weathered, but as he opened the door, he found that it was solidly built and the door didn't even squeak.

He entered and shut the door. There was a small cot, a small table, and two chairs. He put his pack down by the side of the cot, and sat at the table. He expected to have someone just appear out of nowhere the way the strange man had, but nothing happened. After a long time, he got tired. The man had said within a day, so the young ranger decided he would sleep since it was getting late. He laid down on the cot and soon fell asleep.

It was probably the smell that woke him more than anything else. He felt well rested, but someone was making what smelled to be an amazing breakfast. He looked around and realized he was not in the hunter's shack. He was on a very comfortable bed in a very solid and even luxurious bedroom. His pack was in exactly the position next to the bed that it had been in next to the cot in the shack, but he was most definitely not in the shack anymore.

He could see the door was slightly ajar, and could hear people moving in the next room. He cautiously approached the door to see who it was and where. There were a couple of people setting a table with a large breakfast. Behind them was an older woman who was looking directly at him and smiling. He felt very turned around in his head and looked over everything again. The bedroom, the bed, his pack, the table with breakfast and the older woman were all still there. He clearly did not know what was going on, but he felt distinctly that he was where he should be.

The woman extended a hand to him, "Welcome my young ranger. We have been expecting you. I hope you have adequately rested after your long hike."

He walked out of the room cautiously and looked around again, then answered, "Thank you I suppose. I am not really sure I know what's going on, but the breakfast looks and smells wonderful."

The woman beamed with joy, "Oh, I am glad you think so. Would you care to join me?" She swept her hand over the table at the generously provisioned spread. He realized as she was speaking that she wasn't as old as he had originally thought. He rarely felt so off about his own perceptions, and it was getting to him.

He nodded and swallowed, "Yes, that would be great."

She pulled out a chair and gestured to another as she sat. The people who had set the table had disappeared through a door.

The woman smiled, "I suppose introductions are in order. I am Rhondalyn. What is your name?"

The young ranger froze momentarily, and did a mental double-take. What? Rhondalyn? Can this be real? "Um, my name is Ewan." He paused for a bit, and then asked, "Are you the Rhondalyn who was one of the Halidar?"

"Oh, you have heard of me." she beamed, "That should make things easier."

As Ewan sat trying to think of what to say, her visage continued to slowly change. If he hadn't been paying attention, he would have missed it. At this point, Ewan was sure she was getting younger, which he knew wasn't possible. Her wrinkles had just about all faded away. Her skin glowed with the vigor of youth. She didn't look much older than him now.

He turned his mind back to the question at hand. He had been selected to come, but felt wholly inadequate, "Why me?" he paused. "And what is this about?"

"Ewan, what do you know about the First Darkness?" she asked, suddenly as serious as he had ever seen anyone.

He paused to collect his thoughts, "There was someone called Overlord Vlastorn, who built a great tower in a pit that went down to the core of the world, which then let out smoke or clouds or something that covered the world, causing the Great Darkness. You Halidar gathered together and defeated him and broke the tower and ended the darkness."

"That is closer than most would get." She ate some breakfast before she spoke again. "I have been renowned as being the greatest healer in the world, and while that has often been true, that is not the extent of my abilities. During the First Darkness, the more important work that I did was scrying. Seeing what was and what would be. Most of the other Halidar didn't know how I did it. I did not scry. I foresaw. That is my great secret. I am and have been the world's greatest seer in thousands of years. That still didn't allow me to stop the First Darkness ahead of time, and it hasn't stopped the Second Darkness from happening now."

Ewan was confused, "What do you mean Second Darkness? Now?" He waited and when she didn't answer he continued, "I haven't heard anything about a second darkness."

"No, you wouldn't have unless you can see what is happening on the other side of the world. The exact other side of the world." She emphasized the word 'exact'.

He noticed how she phrased it and decided to clarify, "I get the sense that is important beyond just the distance. What does this have to do with me?"

"There is only one way to stop the darknesses from becoming either a permanent horror or a frequently repeated one. In order for that to happen, a special group of people must be assembled and carry out one half of the greatest quest in history. You have two roles. First, you are to be one of that special group of people, but perhaps more importantly, you are going to recruit those individuals."

Ewan shook his head. "But I'm not all that special..."

"Of course you are. The youngest ranger ever, and the youngest elite ranger. If your age wasn't an issue, they would have already talked to you about becoming a master. Do you even know where the rangers came from? Do you know why they don't report to any one king?"

"They were founded independent of kings. They ... " He stopped and thought for a minute. "I don't know why."

"When I had the rangers started, it was to prepare for you." She looked at him as though challenging him to disbelieve her.

"What!?" Ewan's head swam. That made so little sense. "I.. That's.. " He looked at her in exasperation. "Me?"

"Yes, I saw you many hundreds of years ago, and I knew that a special organization needed to be there to nurture your abilities. I also knew that if the kings of Isalor got their grubby fingers in control of the rangers, it would fail in its purpose. They don't control it because I don't let them. We generally make it sound more diplomatic, but that's basically the reason."

Ewan's mind swam. He couldn't wrap his head around the concept that he was that special. Also, it did not match up with what he knew. "I thought the master's council ran the rangers."

"Of course they do, and they do a fine job of it. They just need guidance from time to time, which I provide." She seemed almost indignant.

Not feeling any less overwhelmed, he ventured a thought that perhaps what she was saying was true. "I.. I didn't know that. So, what do I need to do? How do I go about it?"

"The first thing you need to do is gather the core of the team. I cannot tell you their names, just like I didn't know your name, but you can see by the message delivered to you that I knew a great deal about you apart from that."

He still had a hard time thinking that the organization to which he dedicated his life had been created in order to nurture him. He thought back to when the messenger had delivered the summons to come and see Rhondalyn, "Yeah, that was a bit of a strange experience. So, who are these people? The ones I need to recruit."

She had a strange look about her as she started to speak. Her eyes glowed with an inner light and there was a powerful feeling in the room and it almost sounded as if her words were coming from a great distance. *"The people you need to find are five. One is a Royal Knight from the temple of light who is far from home who believes he has failed the mission given him by his king. A second is an acrobat, who witnessed the darkness for herself and is on a mission to warn the world. The third is a young noblewoman who would rather be known as a thief, but who cares about people too easily.*

The fourth is a jack of all trades who is the love child of a noble but who wants to be something more. The fifth is a young milkmaid who has traveled far to escape the darkness, but will travel much further than anyone else."

Her voice and appearance returned to normal and she looked very tired, "You will find them disembarking in Nexoro from ships traveling from Port Yadzul. Some of them will be hard to convince, but these will help." She pulled five glass stones from somewhere, just like the one that lit up when he touched it and placed them on the table. "Each one will only light for the right person. The stones cannot be deceived. By this you can know of a surety that you have found the right people."

He looked at the stone. "Do they do anything else besides shine?"

"For now, no, but later, yes.. Take these and use them to that end. Bring them back when you return with your new party. Have them remain on guard at all times." With that, she stood and gestured toward the room he had woken up in.

He took a last bite of breakfast and stood and followed her. She held the door open for him. "Will you fully commit to this task?"

He looked at her serious face. While he still doubted his own significance, something inside him knew it was all true. How could he not commit? "Yes, I will." As he spoke firmly, he felt a tremor rush through his soul, as if the world itself was attesting to his commitment.

She smiled, "Good. For many of you, this will be the adventure of a lifetime. It may also be very profitable. Ultimately, none of that matters, since if you fail, the world will be plunged into a darkness without end and freedom will be ended." She then retrieved a small package and handed it to him. "This might help you with what you need to do." Then shrugged her shoulders. "Once you find your team, return with them to the hunter's shack. You will understand more shortly." With that she shut the door.

Ewan stood staring at the door, which immediately became rock. He was back in the hunter's shack. His pack was still exactly where he left it the night before. The bed was a cot again. It was completely disorienting and comforting at the same time.

"Well," he said aloud to himself "I guess it is time to go find my team."

CHAPTER SIXTEEN

CHARLOTTE

CHARLOTTE COULD TELL SHE was getting closer to a city. She hoped it was Beaumont. Otherwise, it would mean she was lost. Her nerves were totally frazzled, but still with each step she made herself look around and pay attention to any sounds that seemed out of place. Fear drove her forward. There had been too many close calls in the last couple weeks.

She hoped she could replenish her food in Beaumont. It had lasted for a week and a half, since she had eaten sparingly, but eventually it had run out. She had been able to forage a few wild berries but she hadn't eaten enough for several days. Perhaps someone would be willing to give her a handout.

She didn't know how far ahead of the storm she had gotten, but it did seem to be slowing down a little bit. She reminded herself that slowing down was not the same thing as being stopped, and that she couldn't stay in Beaumont just hoping she would somehow be ok. One other thing she had noticed about the storm, when it reached somewhere that people lived, the lightning kicked up. Out in the wilds where no one lived or worked, there were rarely any lightning strikes. She figured that Beaumont would have a lot of lightning, and probably a lot of skeletons, so she didn't want to be there when it hit.

There were other refugees at the gate and around the city. The city guards had even set up a special line just for refugees, so things were fairly orderly and moved quickly enough. They didn't even ask her many questions. Where was she from? What was her name? What was her experience? What did she hope to do in Beaumont? That was it. She had expected a lot more. With a warning to not cause problems, she was allowed into the city.

Beaumont was bigger than anywhere she had been to before. From where she had entered the city, a major street ran from the gate through the middle of what looked to be a merchant district and on towards the middle of the city. In the far distance, she could make out another merchant district at some kind of cross street.

A bit further on, on a hill overlooking the center of the city she could see a magnificent castle. She wasn't sure why, but it seemed to draw her towards it. She made herself stop. The last thing she needed was more complications caused by nobility.

She redirected her attention to the area around her. She needed some food, but was out of supplies and money. She checked a few stands and shops if they had anything they could give a hungry refugee. One old woman running a run down bakery gave her a decent sized chunk of stale bread. It wasn't much, but far better than nothing.

She sat off the side of the road as she slowly ate the stale bread. It wasn't very good, but it was better than starving. When it was gone, she tried a few other stores to see if she could get something like meat or vegetables, but none that had any were willing to give them away. One did give her some water and allowed her to fill her canteen.

After failing to get better handouts, she decided it didn't serve much purpose to just linger there. She made her way to the central ring and then around to the road exiting the far side of the city. Once she exited the gates, she could see that the land on that side of the city was covered with farms.

That gave her an idea. She explored the farms for a bit and chanced upon one that looked to be a good sized dairy operation. She knew cows and milking, and she thought she might be able to earn a few coins or some supplies for the road. She didn't know how far ahead of the storm she was, but decided getting enough food to survive was as important as staying ahead of the storm.

The lady at the main house looked at her in a very distrustful way, but eventually agreed to talk to her husband who ran the farm. After waiting for a couple hours, she was given the opportunity to show she knew what she was doing. Once the man saw her skill and strength, he agreed to let her work for the day and the next two. She didn't want to stay that long, but she knew that she needed food. If she died of starvation, she would be just as dead as if monsters killed her.

She worked hard, and found that milking 50 cows was a lot more work than milking 10. She also helped prepare some new batches of cheese. She did try to warn them about the storm and what she had seen, but they dismissed her concerns and told them that Beaumont was strong and well defended and everything would be ok. In the end, she worked her time and was mostly paid in cheese and bread. They did give her a few coins to help her along when her supplies ran out and wished her luck.

She had slept at the farm the previous two nights, but was worried that she had delayed too long and headed out on the road before it got dark. The further she got before sleeping, the longer it would take before the Storm caught up. She made it quite a few miles before it got too dark to see, and found a little copse of trees to sleep in that night. The next 3 days were just more running and walking, eating as little as she could get away with, and not stopping to rest except in the very darkest parts of night.

On the afternoon of the fourth day, some people rode up behind her on horses. They were dirty and had a look about them that she had come to associate with those running from the storm. She called out to them and they slowed so they could hear what she wanted.

"Are you coming from Beaumont?" she asked.

"What's left of it." a man said.

"The storm got there, then. How bad was it?" She hoped they would answer.

"It was horrible. The lightning and monsters were everywhere. The castle was burning and then exploded. We got out and ahead of the storm. There were five of us, but..." he glanced at the others and shook his head," now there's only us three. The refugees that had come through had warned everyone, but it sounded so crazy, who could believe it? Are you one of them?" The man asked as he looked her over.

"Yeah, I have been running from the storm for almost three weeks now. I was hoping Beaumont would fare better than other places, but I guess not. I don't know what else to do besides just keeping going. I wish I had a horse like you." She smiled morosely, looking at his horse.

"Sorry lass, I would love to share, but this is all I have. I can share this with you, though." He pulled a bundle from his saddle bag and tossed it to her before he rode off. It turned out to be some biscuits that were so hard that she had to suck on them for quite a while before she could nibble on just the edge. It helped her extend her food several days.

She was again running out of food as she approached a small town called Mijople and hoped to find some more supplies or something there. From what she had learned from the horse riders, she was about three or four days ahead of the storm, and it had slowed down its advance to about the pace of a regular walk, which should help her stay ahead of it.

Realizing that her clothing was in terrible shape and she was absolutely filthy, she decided to try to wash up in the river that flowed past the town. She found a bend in the river where she felt she wouldn't be watched. She put down her pack on the bank and climbed in. She took off her clothes and scrubbed them on a big rock while she soaked in the water. Her clothes really wouldn't last much longer. They had been pretty worn and threadbare before all this started, and they were much worse now. She laid them out on a rock to dry as she scrubbed herself clean.

Afterward, though her clothes were still wet, she put them on and shivered. It was probably a good thing that his storm had not come in the middle of winter, or she would probably already be dead. She returned to the road and walked to the town. At the gates, there were a few other refugees that had congregated and were talking while they waited for the town guard to figure out how to handle things.

"Where are you from?" Charlotte asked a younger couple who were obviously together.

The man looked up with weariness, "We are from a town on the other side of Beaumont. I am Jans. This is my wife Asheena." he gestured to the woman.

"Where are you from, and how long have you been running from the storm?" Asheena asked as she looked at the condition of Charlotte's clothes. Charlotte was not sure if it was because they were so worn, or because they were not very dirty.

"I have been running for weeks now. I was a servant at the Manor of Ethalor in Merdal."

"That is a lot further than us. Do you know where it came from?" Jans asked.

"Some people who came through the Manor before the storm arrived said they had been running since the storm destroyed Sangar, so, that's a long way."

"Do you think it will stop?" Another refugee had overheard their conversation and interjected himself into it.

"Well, it did seem to be moving a lot faster at first, but I don't think it will stop anytime soon, or maybe not at all." Charlotte found it kind of weird that others were treating her like some kind of expert on the Storm.

A middle aged woman joined the conversation. From her appearance, she appeared to be from the higher classes, though probably not a noble, "From what I have heard and seen, it sounds a lot like the Great Darkness. Supposedly it ended up covering the whole world before the Halidar defeated it."

"How far is the furthest you can get from here?" an older teenage boy asked. "Is there a point where you can't get any further away?"

The upper class woman answered, "If this is like the original darkness and it came from Sangar, which it sounds like it may have" she said, gesturing to Charlotte, "then the furthest you can get are the high mountains on the continent of Isalor. That is where the Halidar Rhondalyn is said to have gone. Maybe she chose that place for more than just its remoteness."

The explanation picked at Charlotte's curiosity, "How do you know all that?" asked Charlotte, "I'm Charlotte, by the way."

The woman gestured to herself, "I'm Elanor. I was a teacher at the noble's school in Beaumont. I was fortunate to be returning to the city when the storm got there, so I could see the destruction and get away. What is your story?"

"I hid while skeletons attacked the cattle I took care of. I managed to get away and I ran, but was followed by one of them. I had some provisions, and once I got ahead, I just kept running. The skeleton mostly kept up and never slowed until about four hours later, when it just fell down and turned to dust."

About that time, one of the town guards on duty approached their group. He was younger, maybe late twenties, but weathered enough to look like he knew his job. He also seemed to be tired of dealing with people like them. "Ok, so you lot are refugees, is that right?"

They all mumbled agreement and he continued, "Mijople really isn't set up to handle refugees, but we won't turn you away. I am Edmund, by the way. I don't really have anything I can give you to help you out, but I can tell you that if you are respectful and don't steal nothin', things will go a lot better for you in town."

"Sir?" Charlotte spoke up. "You have to warn the town's people. The storm is coming, and it brings monsters and destruction."

"See, now that is one of them things. I can tell you mean well, miss, but if you go talking like that in town, it is going to cause problems, and then you and I are going to have problems. Please don't cause problems."

"Is there anything we can do to earn some coin to buy supplies?" The teenage boy asked.

"You can ask around, but the town is small and pretty self suffi-cient, so there probably won't be a lot. How long do you all think you will be in Mijople?"

Charlotte still wanted to make her point, "Won't be more than a couple of days, sir. The storm will be here after that, and we don't want to get caught up in it. I'll try not to mention it to people if they don't ask about it, though."

Charlotte could tell the guard was exasperated by her continued mention of the Storm. He turned a little red as he ordered, "You see that you don't missy. I'm already taking a disliking to you."

"Sorry, I'm just being honest. We'll be polite and watch what we say. Can we go now?" She just wanted to get out of there.

His face turned from a little red to very red, but he kept his feelings under control, "Yes, go ahead, but I'll be watching."

The whole group of refugees hung together and walked towards the entrance until they had entered the town, then started breaking off as they went about their business. Charlotte was unsure what to do, and watched the different people. There was a man walking close to her who certainly looked like a local. She called out to him, "Excuse me sir, I have been walking for weeks and am hungry and out of coin. Do you know anywhere that would be willing to help me out?"

The man certainly looked uncomfortable at her question. "Uh, I don't know anyone. Sorry." He quickly changed direction to move away from her.

Figures! She thought. She started walking down the street toward what looked like a tavern and most of the businesses. She had no idea where to look for help. She also was worried that she somehow had to warn the town's people without causing problems and getting in trouble with the guard. She saw a man coming out of a mercantile and decided to try again. "Excuse me sir."

He turned to her and asked. "Yes? How can I help you?"

She decided to go for broke. "I am one of the refugees who have come to Mijople. Do you know of anywhere that might help a young hungry girl in dire need?"

He looked concerned for a minute, then said, "Well, you can ask the people here in town, but if they don't know you, they might be slow to help. You could ask that young man over there coming out of the tavern. He was once in almost as bad a place and seems to have done ok since then." She looked over at the tavern and saw a very handsome yet kind looking young man shut the door behind him. He was probably a few years older than her. The handsome young man noticed the man she was talking to pointing her in his direction, so he approached.

"Hey Paulino, how's it going? And who's this?"

"Uh, a hungry refugee looking for help, apparently." Paulino seemed to be anxious to leave.

As Paulino turned to leave, the young man called, "Ok, see you later Paulino." Then he turned to Charlotte and smiled his handsome smile, "A refugee huh? Is this about that storm thing?" she nodded before he continued. "I can probably help you out in exchange for some information. My name is Finn."

CHAPTER SEVENTEEN

CECILIA

AFTER MORE THAN TWO weeks of traveling, Cecilia was finally settling into the routine of traveling. She had become acquainted with the other passengers and they talked about all sorts of things as they traveled. She had just about completely purged any concern about Rasdal from her mind, and was far enough from Parnul and Blahn that she wasn't concerned about selling any of the goods she had carried with her.

They had been through the Kingdom of Rinash, where the Beaumont family had a fair number of dealings, but nothing had happened there. Then they made it past that to the Kingdom of Kornech. She did her best to keep a low profile there. At one point in the past, she had been told she was to marry the lecherous old widowed king of Kornech. She was really glad she had avoided that situation.

She wasn't sure that the people of Kornech had ever even been notified of her being a runaway, but she didn't want to take any chances. After a tense five days crossing the kingdom, nothing had happened. She was relieved, and after that she had stopped keeping track of how many other kingdoms and cities they had traversed, but it had been a lot. Every two or three days they passed through another city and she was sure no one this far from Blahn would have even heard of her family, not to mention her.

They had been traveling for about six hours that morning, and it was about time to figure out something for lunch. Then the wagon master, Walter, announced, "We will be making a brief stop for about two hours in Risvale, which is coming up ahead. We are in the Kingdom of Ushbor, which can be more strict about some things like loitering than some others. I recommend you find a nice lunch and then return to the carriage station and wait things out there."

Cecilia thought she might take a brief stroll to stretch her legs, then pick up lunch. The town was nice enough, and the stroll was rejuvenating. She was sitting near the back door in a small cafe that was adjacent to the station, just finishing up her lunch. She thought about what she wanted to do, since she had enough funds that she didn't really need to run any new heists for a long time.

Suddenly, someone grabbed her arm and covered her mouth so she could not scream and dragged her out the back door to the cafe. She squirmed as much as she could and tried to twist and see who had her, but their grip was like iron and she couldn't even see who they were.

They pulled her into a dark room and shut the door. They released her and threw her to the floor. She rolled and flipped around to guard against her attacker and when she came to her feet, she saw that it was Rasdal. "What?!? You?!? What are you doing here?"

"You pathetic little brat. I should break both your legs to keep you from running more. Do you know how much trouble you have caused me?" He obviously didn't care about what she said.

"Not as much as you have caused me! I had to throw my entire life away and start all over because of you." Her fear had totally converted to fury at this point.

"No, you hussy, you are just too unhinged and need to be taught your place. I am taking you back to Beaumont, and I think you will find that your adventures are over. They may even be able to salvage your marriage to the King of Kornech. He did marry someone else, but has been widowed again." He grinned malevolently. His arrogance was as strong as it had ever been.

Cecilia refused to back down. "I will never go back to that horrible place. I will never serve as a bargaining chip for my parent's political ambitions, and I will never do anything you tell me." Her mind scrambled to figure out a way for her to get out of the room, but the only exit was behind him.

"Oh, you are going, even if you insist on doing it the hard way. Of course, I kind of prefer it that way." He pulled a mace from his belt and began to advance on her.

Would he really strike her? Wasn't he supposed to protect her? Well, that hadn't really stopped him before. She didn't have a weapon, but then, it probably wouldn't do much good against such a monster. She turned and ran at the side wall and he quickly pursued, but when she reached the wall, she ran up it at an angle and flipped back over his head. He hadn't expected that at all and was completely taken by surprise. She used the opportunity to escape through the door. She turned and fled down the street. She needed to get away and think.

She saw an alleyway and sprinted into it, and could hear him exiting the room in time to see her enter the alley. She raced to the end and vaulted up the dead end and dove over the edge of the roof before he could enter the alley. She could hear him breathing hard and cursing down below. He then let out a great roar of frustration and she could hear him stomp out of the alley and head back toward the carriage station.

He obviously knows what carriage I am taking, and he was able to catch up. He knows where I am going. If I want to escape him, I need to do something he won't expect. She thought about her bags on the carriage. She had already changed into some more comfortable travel clothes rather than the fancy dress she had been using at the beginning of the journey. Perhaps she could get her bags still, but she needed a different way out of there.

While more than a thousand miles from where she started, it was still a long way to Port Yadzul. She knew she needed to continue moving away from the Storm, and now with Rasdal pursuing her, she realized she needed to get off the continent. She made a snap decision that she would journey to Isalor. Maybe he would follow, but perhaps he wouldn't take the chance if he didn't know where she went.

Cecilia carefully worked her way down from the rooftops, making sure she was not seen. She ventured out to the edge of town and eventually found some horses grazing in a corral. She looked around and didn't see anyone. She did see the saddles and tackle for riding the horses however, and smiled. She picked a strong young horse and tried to get it to come to her. It seemed pretty friendly and came right over. She soon had it saddled and out of the corral. Then she rode out past the edge of town down the road where the carriage would pass.

When it finally appeared in the distance, she remounted the horse, who she decided to call thunder based on the way his hooves furiously struck the ground while running. She soon matched speed with the carriage and flagged them down. It took them a minute to recognize her but once she made it clear she needed her bags they stopped for just a minute. One of her bags was still on the carriage, but the others had been unloaded at the station when she hadn't returned for the rest of the journey. They had missed the one bag that was still there.

She took her bag and headed back to town. She expected that Rasdal would still be there with her other bags. She would just have to steal them back, after all she was a master thief.

She tied thunder up outside of town in a thicket and snuck in as it was getting dark. As she expected, Rasdal had her stuff. He seemed super confident that she would be returning. Had he gone through her things? It didn't matter, it was just clothing and stolen goods. She could always steal more, however, it would simplify things greatly to have her money back, the bulk of which was in those bags. She watched him from a distance until he finally grabbed her bags and made his way to an Inn.

Hmm, I suppose he will use everything as bait. She thought. I will just have to show him that I am more than he suspects I am.

She observed the Inn and figured out which part of the rooms he would be in. She also figured out that he had paid the innkeeper to keep an eye out for her and to let him know if she showed up. That was ok, she could work around that. She left the area and found a nice residential neighborhood.

She soon found a home where the occupants weren't present, but it obviously had a woman living there. She broke in and used the woman's makeup and clothes to change her appearance. She changed how she looked from young, blond, fit, and attractive to old, brown haired, heavy, and somewhat plain looking. Her tall stature for a woman seemed to shrink down to be a bit on the shorter side and she now walked with a limp.

She made her way back to the inn, and entered the main public room. She could see that Rasdal had come down and was sitting in the corner watching everyone while he ate. She worked her way over to the bar and ordered their cheapest meal, then took her place at the table nearest Rasdal.

He had glanced at her, but she had not even acted like she knew he was there, and he certainly didn't seem to recognize her for who she was. Once she ate her meager meal, she returned to the bar and rented a room. She haltingly made her way up the stairs and found her assigned room. She checked the doors to the other rooms that she thought could be his and found that two of them had wards and alarms on them.

She disabled the wards on one of the doors and peeked inside. It obviously wasn't his room. She then re-enabled the ward as she left. She then double checked his presence in the public room downstairs. The room she thought was his was not close to where he was sitting, and he didn't look like he would be getting up very soon. She smiled and went to his door and disabled his wards. Then she checked for physical traps, of which there were two. She disabled them and proceeded to enter the room.

She checked out his room. There were really nasty traps on the windows that were intended to maim anyone breaking in. She shook her head and carefully searched. In a trapped dresser drawer she found her bags. She carefully checked them just to make sure there was nothing that would trap or warn him in the bags themselves. She used the scanners she had picked up in Parnul and found he had added some simple tracking devices to her bags, which she decided to use to send him on a wild goose chase. Then she took the bags and left.

She went back to her room and then locked the door with a bar that could only be set from inside. Then she went out the window and climbed down the back of the inn. She made her way out of town, and once she reached the thicket, she changed back into her rogue clothes, since they made the best riding clothes that she had. Then she rode thunder back toward the previous town she had been through.

It didn't take long to find a wagon camped along the side of the road. She hid the tracking devices on the wagon and then headed out across the wilds toward where she knew the closest border was for that kingdom. She didn't remember what the kingdom on the other side was, but she would be taking a different route to Port Yadzul.

Chapter Eighteen

Finn

Finn looked at the girl before him. She was at least several years younger than him. She had a messy unkempt braid of light brown hair with reddish highlights, but what stood out most was that she was very thin. Not that she was tiny. She wasn't, but she looked like she hadn't eaten in a long while. Her skin was far too weathered for a girl her age, and he wondered what all she had been through.

He had just introduced himself and expected her to respond in kind, but she looked at him almost like she didn't understand a word he said. Then she shook her head like she was waking up, "Oh, yeah. Yes, I am a refugee from the Storm. Just like everyone else around here will soon be if they live."

"Where did you come from?" He had heard rumors that Beaumont had been destroyed by the storm and he wondered if she was from there.

She took a long breath, then explained, "I was working as a servant at the Manor of Ethalor in Merdal. Some young men had run through the pastures and said they had been running from the Storm since it destroyed

Sangar. They said everyone needed to run, and then they ran. Then the storm hit and I ran when everything was destroyed." Just describing it seemed to make her more tired.

That still didn't answer what he wanted to know, "Wow, that is awful. Did you go through Beaumont?"

"Yes." She seemed almost deflated with her answer.

"Did it get hit by the storm while you were there?"

Her shoulders slumped further, "No. I was told by some people on horses that it was destroyed about three days after I left. I also talked to some other refugees that saw it."

It was obvious that everything she had been through was taking a toll on her. Still, he needed to know more information. Perhaps it would be better if he got her some food and they could talk while she ate. "Would you like some food?"

"What?" She looked at him like she didn't know the words he spoke.

"Food?" he gestured like he was eating and grinned.

Her face reddened slightly, but she grinned with relief, "That'd be nice. Thank you."

He led her back across the street to the tavern. When he got there, that man behind the counter called out, "Ho there Finn. Who'd that be that ye got there."

He smiled and nodded, "Hi Bojerus. This is one of the refugees from the storm that we have been hearing about. She came in on foot and is very hungry. Can you please feed her?"

Bojerus smiled at the girl and then glanced exasperatedly at Finn. "I can't just give food to every hungry person who comes along."

Finn looked up confidently. "I know, but can you do this one as a favor for me?"

"Yes," Bojerus had already been dishing up food for her behind the counter and handed it across. Finn just smiled at him and took the food.

He turned to the girl, "Let's go sit over there where it's quieter." He gestured to a table far to the back. "By the way, what is your name?"

"Charlotte." she answered, looking a little overwhelmed and apprehensive.

He put her food on the table and pulled the chair out for her to sit down. "Thank you." She nodded and sat.

"Go ahead and eat and we can talk after." Finn moved to the seat across from her. He did his best to not closely watch her as she ate since he didn't want her to feel self conscious. More quickly than he expected, she was done.

Charlotte looked straight at him across the table. Despite being younger than him, she looked at him with what seemed like a challenge. "So, what information do you want?"

He would rise to this challenge. "First, I want to know everything you know about the storm. I want to know about your travels, and what you have learned from others. Let's start with that."

He could see she was thinking about it, and then something in her seemed to accept the idea and she began to talk. She told him about working in Ethalor, how she had gotten there, and then about the people crossing the pastures and them telling her about the storm. Then she told about the larder and her supplies, and then the storm hitting the manor and hiding in the cow pen. When she told him about the skeletons, he asked for clarifications, but then let her continue. She told about how she escaped and how the skeleton disintegrated after a time.

He made special note of the lightning seemingly targeting people, and that the skeletons seemed to appear when the lightning struck. She also described getting ahead of the storm, and that it slowed down a little as it grew. She told about her experience in Beaumont and leaving, and then the discussions with the horse riders and the other refugees at the gate. She also told him about the guard's warning to not talk about the storm unless asked.

When she was done, she had been talking for a long time. He went and got her some water from the bar. As she drank, he asked, "What are your plans now?"

"Just keep running, I guess. That woman at the gate talked about the Halidar Rhondalyn being on Isalor for a reason and maybe I could be safe from the storm there, but I have no idea how long it would take to get there." He could see the hope rise and fade as she talked. "If I had a faster way to travel maybe, or money to pay for things. But I don't. All I have are these worn out clothes."

Finn looked at her in thought, recognizing that she would have been close in size to his mother, maybe with a little larger frame, but as thin as she was, there might be an easy solution. "I might have a way to help with that. I still have my mother's old clothes from before she died, if you want to see if they will fit you. Are you interested?"

She looked at him strangely, as if not sure what he had said. "Seriously? I mean, if you really are ok with that."

"Sure, why not. It isn't as if I could wear them, and I never really got around to selling them. Didn't even think about it, actually." He stood and offered her his hand to help her stand. She took it with a smile and stood and then followed him out.

They walked through town and he led her to his small cottage. It had a loft where he had slept when he was younger but that now held everything he hadn't gotten rid of after his mother died. He took boxes of things down, and showed her the clothes she could search through. She started going through them, and went into the one bedroom to try them on.

While she tried things on, Finn sat at his kitchen table and thought about things. If the storm was really going to reach Mijople, then it didn't make sense to stay there. He was already planning on leaving eventually, but he hadn't decided on exactly when. He should try to convince people to leave, but he didn't know how he would do that. If they were to leave, where would they go, and what provisions were needed. He supposed that a wagon would be helpful, and for that, he would need to recruit assistance from people. He made a mental list of who he could talk to.

After a while, Charlotte came out wearing a new outfit that Finn vaguely remembered his mom wearing long ago. It fit differently enough on Charlotte that it almost looked like different clothing. It still looked good. As he looked her over, her cheeks flushed, and she shifted a little uncomfortably. "It looks good," he observed. "Is that the only outfit you want? There are plenty more, and I'm not hauling them with and if the Storm destroys everything, they will just be lost."

"I don't want to be greedy, and doubt my old bag could carry more than one change of clothes." She looked back wistfully at the clothes strewn about his room.

"How about this? I have an extra pack that would hold quite a few outfits. You can have it. Go pick out the several of the most durable outfits that will fit you, and keep that one, which looks nice, but probably wouldn't endure a lot of wear and tear. Then we'll figure out the best way to get out of town and far enough ahead of the storm that we won't have to worry about it anymore."

Charlotte seemed to be in awe about something. "You're willing to come with me?"

"Well, perhaps the other way around. I don't really want to run and walk all the way to the other end of the continent while staying just a couple days ahead of the storm. If we are going to do this, I think we want to do it in the best way we can. That means horses or wagons, with supplies and resources. We probably need more people."

"But I am not supposed to talk about the storm if people don't ask." she protested.

"That doesn't apply to me. I have good relations with most of the people in town. They know me and most trust me. I don't know how many will listen, but it would be foolish not to try. Go pick more outfits, and I will grab my packs and load some things up." She went back to the room and started going through the clothes again. He got out his two large travel packs and a smaller one, and began to pack things up that he felt would be important to keep. He packed some clothes, pulled his bedding from the room, packed up what food he had, and started gathering a few tools.

After she picked out another outfit, she closed the door and changed again. When she came out, he looked her over and said, "That looks a lot more durable. What about shoes or boots? Will her shoes fit you?" He had noticed that she hadn't really looked at the shoes too much, but Charlotte's current boots were not in good shape.

She nodded and started going through what was there. She tried on some boots and seemed happy with them. "These are at least as comfortable as my other boots and in much better shape. They don't feel too small."

Finn looked them over. "Great, they are yours. Just let me finish packing things up." Eventually, he stopped and looked at her as if trying to make a difficult decision.

After pondering for a bit and then taking a big breath, he announced, "And... we are going to need as much coin as we can get. Let's start with this, just don't call attention to it when we are out in public." He then walked over to a cabinet at the back of the cottage and banged on the side of it before pulling open what appeared to be a hidden compartment. He pulled out a large leather shoulder bag. Then after setting the bag on the table, pulled off his shirt and put on the shoulder bag, then put his shirt back on so that it covered the bag completely.

She looked at him ponderously, but without asking her question. He smiled. "I have saved almost everything I have earned for the last 4 years since my mom died. Most of my basic needs are met by freebies from the places I do odd jobs for. I never spend anything I don't absolutely have to, but having coin won't do me much good if I'm dead."

"How much do you have?" she asked curiously.

"At this point, I would rather not say, but enough that it should help us on our journey. We need to talk about what our plan is."

She looked a little irritated, but considering her youth, she probably wasn't used to being trusted with much information. She thought for a second, "Ok, what about the plan? Do you have an idea for one?"

"I thought what you said about going to Isalor and trying to find Rhondalyn was a good idea. If she can do anything, then perhaps we could be safe there. If not, it probably wouldn't be worse than just dying somewhere else when the storm reaches wherever it is we decide to stop, and it would be the last place the storm would reach. What are your thoughts?"

She looked at him as if trying to decide if she could trust him. "Why? Why me?" She stopped but held up a hand, "If you have all that coin, you could just go ahead on your own. Why would you just take me along?"

"You have already survived against the storm for a whole kingdom and then some. We are right on the edge of Blahn, and you won't give up. I don't know who I can get to join with me, but they won't know the storm. I don't know the storm. You do. I will be relying on your experience and determination. I do expect you to do your part and help out and speak up when you feel or think something is important."

"I can do that. I've gotten in trouble ever since I was young cause I can't keep my mouth shut." She put the spare sets of clothes in the bag he had given her and turned to him, "So, what do we do now?"

"Well, now we need a wagon or horses. Depending on who goes with us, a wagon might be better. I know just the person to talk to, who I'm supposed to be meeting with right now anyway. Let's go see Staynor."

Finn walked through the streets towards Staynor's warehouse office, greeting people as he went. He had missed his normal round and the town guard barracks, so he would have to warn them. Charlotte did her best to keep up. When they reached the warehouse office, Finn knocked twice and then just walked in. Staynor looked up from his desk where he was shuffling papers and preparing orders.

"Good evening Finn. I don't have much for you to do today." Staynor called out from his desk, then gestured toward Charlotte. "Who is this young lady?

"This is Charlotte. She's one of the refugees from the Storm. It's real, Staynor. We have been hearing rumors for a week and a half, and now we have people here who have had to battle through it."

"How can you be sure? Just because someone thinks they saw something doesn't make it accurate."

"Lightning that attacks only where people are. Skeletons that rise from the lightning strikes and then crumble back to the ground after they have destroyed things for four hours. They are strong enough to kill cattle, While the spread has slightly slowed, it follows the same pattern as the Great Darkness." Finn was getting louder, trying to make his point. "It's back, Staynor, and it's coming for us next. Based on speed and trajectories, this town will be destroyed in about four days."

"Are you sure you are not overreacting?" The old man still didn't seem convinced. "Who saw these things?"

"I did!" Charlotte spoke up. "I was the milkmaid at Ethalor. When the storm hit, first there was the lightning. Then, skeletons attacked and started breaking things. I hid in a tiny alcove at the back of the cow pen in the barn, with the doors barred with a heavy bar. Three of them smashed the door to pieces. They didn't open the gates to the pens, they smashed them apart." Charlotte was pretty animated at this point. It seemed she was fed up with people not believing her. She continued.

"After the bull fought the skeletons, one skeleton was still moving, but was damaged. I was able to keep ahead of it until it crumbled to dust four hours later. After that, I thought I was safe, but the storm caught up. The skeletons don't attack with weapons, but they don't need to. They strike with fists that can smash rock. The edges of their fists are sharp enough to cut through a bull's hide."

Staynor held up his hands to soothe her fervor. "It seems you have had quite the ordeal. What about the other claims? Did Beaumont survive? How do you know when it will get here?"

Charlotte took a deep breath. "I left Beaumont about three days before it reached there. No one would listen. They all thought they were safe. About four days out from Beaumont, some riders passed me. I called out to them and asked them what happened. They said that Beaumont was destroyed. The castle had exploded. It's all gone. At the pace I have been going, I usually have been able to gain about a third of a day for every day I walk. That means you have about four days until it gets here. From what I have been able to tell, almost everyone who stays dies. You have to believe me! I'm telling the truth!" Charlotte was pleading. Finn almost expected her to get down on her knees and beg.

"What do you want me to do?" Staynor asked somberly.

Finn picked it up here. "Three things. We want you to rig up your wagons. Then, help us get as many provisions as we can on them, and then get as many people as we can fit on them to join us. We don't want to force anyone, but we want to save as many as will join us."

"What about my business?" Staynor asked, gesturing around him at the warehouse.

Finn was incensed. "Have you not heard a thing?" he almost yelled. "There will be no business, no suppliers, no customers. Nothing to buy and nothing to sell, cause everyone who doesn't leave will be dead." Finn ran his hand through his hair and turned in a circle in frustration. "Even before Charlotte got here, I have been collecting information on this, ever since we were in Beaumont ten days ago. I have asked as many refugees about it as I could, just trying to see what was consistent. It is the same story all across the board!"

His voice lowered to just more than a whisper. "This is the end of Mijople and the wonderful community we have here. This has happened before. It's been 800 years, and now it's happening again. Please help us save some of the people here. We can't save everyone, but we can save some, at least. Please?"

CHAPTER NINETEEN

FINN

FINN WATCHED NERVOUSLY AS Staynor rubbed his chin for a bit like he was thinking things through. "Well, you did say you wanted to travel, and I did recommend you go far from here. At least your stepmother's people won't be trying to poison you. And if Beaumont has been destroyed, then so has Horshon." He turned toward them with a little more focus. "I've been paying attention too. That is why I'm not gone anywhere right now. I had to be sure what to do." The old man suddenly got a questioning look on his face. "Do you have anywhere in mind to go, or are you thinking of taking up a wanderer's lifestyle?"

Finn glanced at Charlotte. "Based on something Charlotte heard, we think there might be someplace that could be safe. On the continent of Isalor. Where the Halidar Rhondalyn went."

Staynor pursed his lips like he didn't agree. "You wouldn't rather try your luck going to the Tower of Light on Chibor?"

Finn's eyes blazed again at Staynor's obstinance. "The Tower of Light was supposed to prevent this. That is what all the books and histories say. If it has failed, it wouldn't be safe there either. Rhondalyn never said what she was going to do, but she picked a place as far from the source as she could, on the exact opposite side of the world. It has to be more than just running away to be a hermit. She would have a purpose."

Charlotte joined in, "Finn suggested that we travel overland to Port Yadzul, and try to find a boat from there. Not everyone has to go that far, but we want to. We don't know if we can do anything, but we feel that is our best shot."

Staynor seemed to accept that. "Are there specific individuals you would like to reach out to first?"

"Hmm," Finn thought for a minute "I would like to start with the people I work with. Perhaps Paulino, since he introduced me to Charlotte."

Charlotte raised her hand to interject, "Could we check on a couple of the other refugees and see if they are still in town? At least one of them was really knowledgeable, and there was a nice couple that I think would be helpful."

"Sure, I think that would be fine. Now, how soon do we think we need to head out? If the storm is supposed to be here in four days, we should probably leave no later than three days from now. Two would probably be preferable. I have two wagons, but by their nature, the one is faster than the other, but the slower one will carry much more weight."

Finn started forming a picture in his head, "Let's start talking to people this evening, and also trying to get a line on whatever supplies are available. We can start setting up the wagons tomorrow, but only hitch the teams the next day when we leave."

Staynor looked pleased at Finn's suggestion. "I think that is probably about the right approach. Go with Charlotte and see if you can find the refugees she mentioned, then visit your employers. Try not to be too disappointed if not everyone wants to go." Finn nodded and he and Charlotte rushed out the door.

The first place Finn went was back to the tavern. If anyone knew where the other refugees went, it would be Bojerus. "Hey, Bojerus." He said as he entered, with Charlotte following close behind.

The tavern keeper looked over at him warily, his eyes quickly flicking to Charlotte and then back. "Ho there, Finn. Back so soon? Can't give away any more food, ya know."

"Oh, we aren't here for that." Finn waved his hand in dismissal of Bojerus's concern. "We are looking for a couple of the other refugees. A younger couple and an older higher class woman. Do you know anything about them?"

Bojerus pursed his lips in thought, "Um, a younger couple came in, but didn't want to spend coin on food. The high class lady did. She left about an hour and a half ago. I've heard there is an area on the north side of town where the refugees have set up a temporary camp. The older lady looked like she was all cleaned up and hadn't been sleeping on the ground. She might be staying in a house or an Inn or something, but she don't have a room here."

"Ok, thanks Bojerus. We will probably be back to pay for dinner in a while." Finn emphasized 'pay' to make his point.

"Sure thing, Finn. Hope you find em." Bojerus waved as they left.

They walked to the north side of town and asked a few people if they knew where the refugees were camped out. It took longer than he thought it would, but eventually they found it. There weren't that many people there, but he hoped some of the ones they were looking for would be found. He turned to Charlotte, "Do you want to ask around for them? I don't know who exactly we are looking for."

"Sure," Charlotte looked less than excited about the prospect, but she didn't hesitate to move forward and start asking around. She soon found a lead, but they weren't there. Before they left, she raised her voice so most of the refugees could hear her. "In two days, there will be a group of people leaving together. You can head out earlier if you like, but if you want to be part of a larger group, you can join. Meet in the town square around noon."

As they walked away to follow the lead, Finn said "I don't remember picking the town square and noon as the specifics of the plan. Did you just make that up?"

"Yeah, I realized we needed to give them something they could act on, and it seemed like a reasonable time and location. Now we can tell everyone else we talk to the same thing. At least we don't have to convince these people to flee, they're already doing that."

They crossed the town to where they had been told they might find the couple. Apparently the couple had arranged to sleep in a room in someone's house in exchange for working in their garden. The couple were outside doing just that when Finn and Charlotte arrived. Charlotte took the lead again. "Hi there. Remember me?"

Jens responded, "Oh, yeah, the girl from the gate. How can we help you?"

"Well, I was wondering what your plans are from here." Charlotte said.

Jans shrugged, "Just keep running, I guess. The storm is still coming. We have a couple days where we can work and rest and earn some supplies, but we want to be long gone before the storm gets here."

"There will be a group leaving together in two days. I would love to have you along. All the details are still being worked out, but we should have a wagon or two for supplies and such."

Asheena spoke up with a cautious look on her face. "How did you manage to arrange that?"

Charlotte gestured to Finn. "This is Finn. He is a local, but has been watching and learning about the Storm for a couple weeks. He has contacts with people who are somewhat aware of what is going on and know the only chance is to leave before it gets here."

Finn spoke up. "Charlotte spoke highly of you two as competent people who would be good to have along, so we tracked you down. I hope you join us. Meet at the town square in two days at noon if you want to join."

Jens and Asheena looked at each other, and Jens said. "We'll think about it. If we decide to join, we will be there."

They were about to leave when Charlotte turned back and asked, "Oh, by the way, you wouldn't happen to know where Eleanor went, do you? You know, the refined lady we talked with at the gates?"

Asheena glanced at Jens, who shrugged one shoulder, "She was talking with some people down that street when we went past earlier today."

"Thank you. We will check over there." Charlotte raised her hand in farewell.

Finn and Charlotte walked over to the road Asheena had indicated and started down it. As they did, Finn called out to a woman who was outside her house, sweeping her porch. "Hi Rostella, would you happen to have seen a woman, one of the refugees, who might be staying with someone in this area? She is a little older and perhaps higher class."

Rostella stopped sweeping, "What's she look like?"

Charlotte answered, "Probably in her late 40s or early 50s, about two inches shorter than me, thin and fit, slight graying in her brown hair, pulled into a metal hair net. Has a refined air about her. Smaller gray eyes, but very alert."

Rostella looked kind of shocked at the specifics of the description Charlotte gave, but answered, "Yeah, I think I saw someone like that talking with Matilda down the road. Not sure if she is staying there or not, but you can ask."

Finn stepped forward a bit. "Rostella, have you heard what people are saying about the storm that is coming?"

She looked around like she didn't want people to hear what she said. "They're sayin' it be another darkness and it will destroy everything. Others think they are making it up. I don't know what to think."

Finn looked at her, and then Charlotte, then back at Rostella, "Charlotte here has been running from the storm since Merdal. She went through Beaumont only three days before it was destroyed by the storm. Based on its speed, we estimate it will destroy our town in four days."

Rostella looked horrified, "What should we do?"

"Figure out what you absolutely can't afford to leave behind and pack it up with what supplies you can carry. Meet at the town square at noon in two days. Probably get the word out."

In a full panic, Rostella stammered, "I... I don't know if I can do that. Are we sure it is coming?"

"Unfortunately, yes." Charlotte spoke up. "We have a lot to do and people to talk to, but do as Finn suggested and we will see you in two days if you want to survive." With that, she turned and started walking down the street. Rostella stood on her porch with tears in her eyes and Finn turned to follow Charlotte.

When they reached Matilda's house, Finn took the lead and walked up to the door and knocked. They could hear people talking briefly, then the door opened, revealing Matilda, an elderly woman. She spoke, "Hello, Finn. What can I do for you this evening?"

Finn answered, "We are trying to find a woman named Eleanor, one of the refugees from the storm that is coming. We were told she might be staying here? Is she?" He paused, trying to give a hopeful look, "If she is, can we talk to her?"

Matilda looked a little flustered and unsure how she should answer, glancing behind her. Then a voice came from deeper into the house. "Did I hear that someone wants to talk with me?" Eleanor appeared behind Matilda, and Finn noticed that there was a vague similarity in their appearance. Once she reached the door and saw Charlotte, she said, "Oh, you're the girl from the gate. How can I help you?"

Charlotte smiled hopefully, "Finn and some others from the town are organizing a group of people who want to evacuate ahead of the storm. I had mentioned how knowledgeable you are, and we thought it would be good to see if you wanted to join, or at least share what you know that would be helpful."

Matilda raised a questioning eyebrow, "Who all is involved in this? Aren't you going to get yourself in trouble with the guard?" Matilda gave her a stern look, and Charlotte stepped back meekly.

Finn took over, seeing the woman had intimidated Charlotte, "There are a number of people involved. We already have two wagon teams committed, and there may be others. We are not the only ones talking to people. Charlotte has not been speaking about the storm to anyone who hasn't asked or already been talking about it, but I don't think Edmund's going to raise too much of a fuss. If people stay, they will die. It's as simple as that." Finn looked deeper at her. "How long are you planning to stay before you leave town, and would you be willing to talk to some of the town leaders about what you know?"

Charlotte then had built her courage back up, "And if you don't already have plans, would you consider joining our group?" She smiled as big of a hopeful smile as she could.

Eleanor looked at them for a few seconds before answering. "I was planning to leave with my cousin here as soon as we had things ready. Probably late tomorrow or the next day. I would be willing to speak to people, but I don't want to stay longer than I have to. Staying ahead of the storm is going to be hard enough for us old people without delaying any longer than we need."

Finn looked at Charlotte and back at Eleanor, unsure what to say, "Um, I will have to get back to you about timing. I know there are some people meeting in the town square in two days at noon. There will probably be some people wanting to talk before that. Can I get back to you?"

Eleanor nodded, "Sure, that would be fine, just keep in mind that I can't delay my departure."

"Ok." Finn responded. "I will come back as soon as I know more." Then he turned and left with Charlotte in tow. When they had walked a fair distance away he said, "You didn't tell me she was so intimidating."

"She wasn't intimidating at the gate. I had no idea she would be like that." They walked for a while, then Charlotte asked, "Where are we going now? We found the refugees we were looking for."

Finn answered, "We need to go back to the tavern and I need to talk to all the people that I do work for. I am hoping we can get them all to join. I suppose if we could get everyone in town to leave, that would be best, but I don't know if we could keep everyone in a single group." Charlotte didn't answer and they walked in silence for a while. Soon they reached the tavern. Once they entered, Finn walked to the counter and slapped some large copper coins down on it. "Two dinner platters please," he said to Bojerus with a big grin. "Can we eat at the bar and chat with you while we eat?"

"Sure. Is this about the talk of running away from the storm?" Bojerus asked. "Don't know that I want to abandon everything I spent my whole life building." He put their platters down on the bar where they could sit on stools.

Finn took a bite and answered. "Well, that's the thing, Bo. If you stay, you lose everything. If you prepare the best you can and leave, you get a chance to keep a little bit. Not really great choices, but dying is a pretty poor option."

"Don't sound like there is a good choice in there, anywhere." Bojerus was evidently not happy.

"No, there really isn't, unless you are just tired of living." Finn smiled grimly. "I don't know what it will all look like, but they could probably use someone who can cook well and make limited supplies last. It's not a tavern, but still better than dead. We have been telling folks to pack up and meet in the town square at noon in two days."

"Well, I heard something about two days, but there wasn't a time attached." Bojerus responded. "I will probably be there, but I still got a lot to figure out. You already talk to all your other bosses?"

"No, just Staynor. He was going to talk to some other people, but we were tracking down those other refugees we asked about." Finn was starting to get full, since he often only ate a full meal once a day. He still forced himself to continue. He might be wishing to be stuffed full in not very long.

"Well, you probably started with the best person. If anyone can get some crazy evacuation organized, it would be Staynor." He looked at both of them as they ate their meals. "You look about done, Finn. How's the food, miss?"

Charlotte almost choked in surprise at being addressed, but was able to clear her mouth before answering. "It's very good, sir."

"You see that, Finn? She has manners. You could work on that some." Bojerus teased with a wink, "I would have thought you would have more with some of that fancy tutoring you had when you were young." The comment caught Charlotte off guard, and she looked at Finn questioningly.

"Yeah, well, that is in the past. I'm just me now, with nothing to prove and no one to impress." He stood up. "We should be going. I still have my other bosses to talk to. I'll check in if you need help tomorrow. Hopefully it's helping you pack up."

With that comment, Bojerus got a distant look in his eyes. "Yeah... Yeah, packing up... I'll see you when you check in."

Finn and Charlotte left. First he headed out to the hunter's lodge out the north gates, where he left a message for Gesh. He figured his cousin would be okay with picking up and leaving since he did that frequently anyway.

Chapter Twenty

Finn

After leaving the hunter's lodge, they stopped by the Barracks. Finn could tell that Charlotte was nervous being around the guards. He stepped in and saw Captain Hallin. "Captain, I wasn't able to check in earlier, and I don't know that I will be able to do that much in the future with the storm coming and all." Finn figured he might as well jump into the thick of it.

"Yeah, all you panicky people." Captain Hallin shook his head. "Staynor stopped by earlier. We sent a couple guards out on horses to check the conditions of the storm. We don't want to panic, but we don't want to doom ourselves by not acting either."

"Who'd you send?" Finn was curious.

"Since Edmund didn't believe what's been going around, I sent him, and then I sent Joben with him, since he believed all of it. I figure one of them is going to come back with their story all changed. I agreed with Staynor to let word get out for people to meet in two days.

Finn hoped the timing would work out. "Do you think they will be back before noon on that day?"

"Ah, probably not, but shortly after." The captain looked at Finn a little suspiciously. "Why?"

Finn frowned, "I have been talking to people and telling them to meet in the town square at noon, but it would be best if we had clear answers before that."

"Well, be that as it may, not much we can do about it now. You can probably talk with Staynor and the other council members and figure out a way to make it work. They do that sort of thing all the time and people usually don't catch on that they're winging it."

Finn was surprised, "Really? They wing it. It never looks that way."

"See, that's exactly what I mean." Hallin grinned.

"Ok, well, I guess I'll go talk with my other bosses and let them know." Finn gestured farewell as they left. After they were out in the street he said thoughtfully, "Maybe we should check back in with Staynor about the time people should meet before we talk to anyone else."

"I guess that would be good." Charlotte was beginning to look pretty tired.

They caught up with Staynor at the edge of the market and didn't have to go all the way to his warehouse. "Staynor!" Finn yelled down the street to get his attention. Staynor looked up and then headed their way. When he got there, Finn explained what they wanted. "We have been telling people to meet at noon in two days, but then Captain Hallin said the riders wouldn't be back by that time. What should we do?"

"Oh, that will be fine." Staynor smiled, "We will be able to explain things to people and then the riders should be back before too long, just to verify what we have already said. There will be less panic that way. Good job!"

"Uh, ok. You're welcome." Finn grinned.

"Who else were you going to check in with?" Staynor asked.

"Just Ganslow and Isan. Maybe others I know well on my way home to sleep. I think Charlotte will sleep in my loft tonight." He turned to Charlotte. "Are you ok with that?"

She nodded and smiled, "That should be fine. We'll finally be able to put these bags down. Especially since we won't be leaving for at least two days." She was visibly exhausted, but he could see she wouldn't back down.

Finn turned back to Staynor, "Should I check in with you tomorrow morning?"

"Yes, first check the council chambers. We are in emergency mode right now, so my warehouse is going to have to wait a bit. If I am not there, check the tavern before you check the warehouse."

"Ok, will do. Thanks." Finn and Charlotte then headed to the blacksmith's forge.

Ganslow was not working at that hour, but since he lived right next door, Finn just knocked. Ganslow invited them in with a twinkle in his eye, "Finn, who might this young lady be."

Finn realized Ganslow was insinuating a relationship and wanted to make things clear, "Oh, this is Charlotte, and there's nothing going on like that. She is one of the refugees from the storm. That's what we wanted to talk to you about. Has anyone told you the storm should be here in four days?"

"I had heard something like that. News goes fast in a small town like this, you know."

Finn continued, "Yeah, so, I want to encourage you to pack up as much as you can of your smithy and head out with the group that is leaving in two days. There is a meeting in the town square at noon on that day."

"Do you know what you're askin'? Smithies aren't easy to move and pack up. I need a heavy duty way to haul it." Ganslow was obviously taken back by the suggestion.

"Yes, I know. That is why we would prioritize space on Staynor's heavy wagon for you. You would be critical in keeping the group from town moving and preventing or fixing breakdowns. You and Isan would have to work together, of course, but you already do that often enough."

"How dangerous is this storm?" Finn could see that Ganslow had gotten serious.

Finn turned to Charlotte, "Tell him about your manor and Beaumont."

Charlotte explained how the Manor was destroyed and her experience with the skeletons, and then what she had been told about the castle in Beaumont exploding. Ganslow's face became grimmer and grimmer as she talked. When she finished he said, "None of that sounds good at all."

Finn said, "To verify everything, two of the town guards were sent out to observe the storm and determine when we can expect it to arrive. Presently, our best estimate is in four days."

Ganslow grimaced darkly. "I don't see that there's much choice. I'll talk with Staynor about makin' sure there's a workable space on the big wagon. Wouldn't do much good to have to unload the whole thing every time somethin' needs fixin'. Can ya check back midday tomorrow to see what help I might need packin' things up?"

"Sure, I'll do that. See you then."

The last person Finn wanted to visit was Isan, the carpenter. Isan also invited Finn in. He also had a gleam in his eye upon noticing Charlotte, but didn't say anything about it. "What can I help you with at this late hour, Finn?"

"Have you heard about the Storm that's coming?" Finn figured it would be best to just get it over with since Isan was a very direct person.

"I heard a bit, but don't feel like I know enough. Heard someone say that anyone who gets caught in it dies. Sounds pretty extreme, but I haven't talked to anyone who witnessed anything directly."

Finn did his best to give a tired smile. "That's why I have Charlotte along with me. She is one of the refugees in town, and has had a fair amount of experience with it. Do you want her to tell you her story?"

Isan shook his head. "No, just answer this. How dangerous is this thing? How serious is the threat of death?"

Charlotte looked relieved that she didn't have to tell the whole story another time that day. "The only ones who I know who have lived have fled. A few of us got caught in it, but we were able to get away and out in front of it and keep ahead. I have almost been killed several times, and I have seen enough death to last me forever."

"Any chance to survive at all?"

She shook her head. "Not that I know of. The manor where I worked and the castle in Beaumont and the city were completely destroyed. I don't know how anyone here could survive when they couldn't."

Isan frowned, "Yeah, that sounds pretty serious. Now what?"

Finn was glad that Isan was pragmatic. "Figure out what tools you will need to help support a group of wagons, along with what Ganslow puts together, and we will make sure Staynor reserves enough space on the heavy wagon for it. There will be a meeting in the town square at noon in two days, but you probably want to have things figured out before then. You will need enough supplies and tools to keep things going, but space is limited. I'll be checking in with Ganslow about helping him pack up tomorrow afternoon. Did you want me to check in here as well?"

Isan's eyes took on a distant look, "Yeah, that would probably be helpful. I'll see you tomorrow then."

Finn and Charlotte then left. When they got to his cottage, they put their bags by the door and Charlotte climbed up into the loft and immediately fell asleep. Finn sat at the table for a bit to try to organize his thoughts, then he went to bed.

The next morning, Finn was up at his regular time, but Charlotte was still asleep. He followed his impulse to let her sleep and set out fairly early to see if he could catch Gesh at the hunter's lodge. To his surprise, all three hunters were there discussing the storm and what their roles needed to be. When they were done, he got to talk to Gesh, and told him about everyone meeting, but Gesh had already heard that.

Finn explained that they already have multiple wagons lined up so that they could better support all those that were fleeing the storm together.

"It won't work." Gesh said flatly.

"What?!" Finn was shocked. "What do you mean?"

"Having everyone in a single large group. It won't work. The size of the group will be too unmanageable, and it would slow everyone down enough that they would eventually get caught in the storm and they will all die." Gesh said matter of factly.

"What would work?" Finn didn't want to believe what Gesh was saying.

"You should break it up into groups. There should be a group that goes fast and explores the lay of the land and prepares the trail for the others. Then a couple of balanced groups with both strong and weak people each that run in the middle, and then the slowest group should be the support group with things like wagon repair and such. If someone has a problem, the slow group will catch up to them and be able to support them. The slow group should help stragglers from the middle groups catch up to their original groups and catch any that fall through the cracks. If someone can't keep up with the support group, they will be on their own and probably caught by the storm.

Each group should have someone to handle food, another to deal with health issues, and another to deal with logistics and supplies. Oh, and probably a hunter in each group, but we only have three of us, so, one in front that will leave extra supplies for the middle groups, one with the middle, and one with the support group."

"How did you come up with this?" Finn was in awe.

"I don't know. I just watch people and see how they work together, or don't as often is the case."

"Can you come explain that to Staynor, please?" Finn asked.

"Sure, we are not going out hunting until we know what the plan is better." Gesh accompanied Finn to the council building, but Staynor wasn't there. Instead, he was in the tavern, having breakfast. Finn was sure Staynor had not slept at all that night. He looked tired and cranky. Finn tried to explain what Gesh was saying, but turned it over to Gesh, and then went to check in on Charlotte. She was still asleep, so he left her a note.

That made him ponder if she knew how to read, and how well. As he walked to his next destination, he tried to make sense of his thoughts and feelings about the girl. She wasn't bad looking. Even pretty, in a simple sort of way. She seemed intelligent enough. He had been more attracted to Isolde, the barmaid at the tavern in Beaumont, than he was to Charlotte, Isolde had definitely been interested, but he felt her interest was flimsy at best. Charlotte, on the other hand, was as steady as anyone he had ever met. He still wasn't sure if he liked her. He had caught her gazing at him a few times that made him think she had a crush on him, but he wasn't sure if he felt the same way about her.

He reached Isan's shop before he reached a conclusion. Isan welcomed him in and Finn helped him sort out what raw materials would be needed to support the wagons. The sorting took almost two hours. Once he was done, he went back to check on Charlotte again and found her awake. She joined him at the tavern, where they helped Bojerus organize storage for food that would end up on the wagons.

Finn told them about Gesh's idea of splitting everyone into groups, so they factored that in their organizing of the food. They both ended up eating a large lunch after that. Then, he went to check on what help Ganslow needed while Charlotte went to see if Staynor had anything he wanted her to do. Ganslow had already talked with Staynor and was getting things rigged up on the heavy wagon.

After helping for a short while, Finn left and felt a little thrown off and unsure what to do next. His routine had been disrupted in a way he wasn't used to. He eventually caught up with Charlotte and Staynor.

Charlotte was organizing plans for livestock, and figuring what support supplies they would need for them.

Staynor called Finn over. "Finn, here is a list of people who have wagons and carts that we want to get to contribute to the evacuation. The whole council is on board with it, so this is now official. If someone doesn't want to join, we won't make them, but we have authorized funds to purchase wagons or carts if people who don't want to join are willing to sell them. I want you to visit as many as you can before dinner time and let me know who is joining and who is selling."

"Ok," Finn left to fulfill his task. He was amazed at how many people had some kind of wagon or cart. He hadn't realized there were that many in town. He talked with people all afternoon, and after dinner, several more people were assigned to help him. Eventually, they ended up with 37 horse or ox drawn wagons, and a bit more than 200 carts, though he was reluctant to actually think of some of them as carts.

Charlotte had been helping with planning distribution of supplies amongst the various teams. She explained the plan that had finally been agreed upon to him as they walked back to his cottage. There would be a fast wagon scouting and preparation team. A middle wagon group that would go next who would set up and take down camps for the middle groups, and the heavy support group.

The draft horses and heavy oxen wagons would be assigned to the heavy support group. There would also be runners on fast horses that would support each section. The scouts would have a couple, the middle wagon group would have a couple, and the support group would have some. The runners were responsible for scouting, communication, tracking, and helping smaller groups who had issues to get caught back up with their assigned group.

As Charlotte explained it all, Finn wondered where he should go. He still had to worry that his step-mother's agents might still want to poison him. He didn't know who the agents were, so he didn't know which group would be safest. He figured he could talk to Staynor the next morning. He wasn't sure, but figured there was a good chance that he wouldn't be sleeping in his cottage ever again after that night, and so he didn't sleep as well as he would have liked.

The next morning, he went to ask Staynor for advice. One of the surprising discoveries from recruiting wagons was that Matilda had a good wagon with strong horses, and they were going to be leaving ahead of all the groups and travel on their own. Staynor had spoken with Eleanor extensively and arranged for Finn and Charlotte to travel with them. When he found out, they had less than two hours to go before they headed out.

Finn rushed back to the cottage to get Charlotte. "Hey, we have to go. Staynor arranged for us to travel with Matilda and Eleanor, and they are leaving early. We have just over an hour to get all our stuff and join them at Matilda's house."

"What, when did that happen?" Charlotte jumped up in near panic.

"I just found out." Finn rushed through everything again. He was already living out of his bags, so he just made sure it all was packed. He looked around the cottage, but couldn't think of anything else he needed. Emotion flooded into him as he realized he might never see his cottage again. He thought back to all the experiences he had there with his mother, and living there alone since. When he realized his eyes were filling with tears, he quickly wiped his face and forced himself to breath deep before he turned toward Charlotte.

Charlotte was already waiting for him, so finally he shut the door and they were off. Eleanor already had their wagon ready to go. It was more like an open carriage, which surprised Finn. They loaded their bags where directed and climbed on. Finn was instructed to drive the wagon, and he figured that was part of how Staynor had convinced them to take them along. Charlotte sat next to him on the drivers seat. As they drove out of town, she remarked, "I guess we may never know what the scouts decided when they went to look at the storm."

"That's true." Finn replied. A minute later, he realized he had questions to ask. He called to Eleanor, since it was obvious that she had assumed command of their group. "Hey, Eleanor, where are we going? Is there a plan?"

He looked back to see her with a devious smile. "We are going to Port Yadzul. How else would we get to Isalor?"

Chapter Twenty-One

Cecilia

Cecilia arrived in Port Yadzul in the Kingdom of Fraisza a full four weeks later. It had been a grueling journey, but she was there. She checked in at the carriage yard, and was delighted to learn that she had beaten the carriage there. That probably gave her some buffer room. She found an inn by the wharf, and then contemplated what steps she needed to take next.

She asked around and found some people who were willing to buy Thunder. She returned to the inn, and after double checking her room, she went to the adjoining tavern. It was late, but she didn't wait to start asking around to find a boat to Isalor. The first person she asked was the bartender.

"Isalor, eh? I don't know nothin, but ask that group playing cards who they know." He pointed to a group in one of the front corners of the room. They had ignored her earlier when she was asking around, but perhaps they would give her a minute with the bartender's recommendation.

She waited until they finished a hand and approached. "Excuse me. The bartender said to talk to you folk about what boats might be available to get to Isalor."

The man dealing the cards didn't even look at her but answered, "You want information, you gotta play."

She grabbed a chair from the table behind her and pushed her way to the table. "Fine, what's it cost to buy in?"

Another of the men, this one chewing on a small stick, answered, "A silver per round. Have to stay for a minimum of ten rounds."

She fished out a silver and threw it into the pot. "What's the rules of the game?"

A couple of the other gamblers laughed subtly as the dealer started to explain. Surprisingly, she did ok at the game despite not paying too close attention to it. Instead, she asked about ships to Isalor. The men were not very forthcoming with the info, but it trickled out. She figured it was part of their way to make sure she stayed the whole ten rounds. She was confident it would cost her the full ten silver to get the information, but after eight rounds, she was only down two silver, having won the last two rounds.

During her tenth round, they mentioned that the Grudge Merchant had just arrived. She wasn't sure who the grudge merchant was, but eventually it became clear that it was a ship. It would probably be making another trip in two days if it kept to the normal schedule. There wouldn't be another ship heading out for at least a week.

They warned her about the captain. The captain was a crusty old man known to frequent one of the other taverns in the area. He had a mermaid tattoo that he liked to show off. He also never took passengers.

He occasionally would let someone work as a crew member, but he was a hard man to please and ran a tight ship. They finally told her his name was Captain Yermont.

Once the last of her ten rounds was complete, she thanked the men and left. After getting directions to the other tavern, she went in and looked for a ship captain with a large mermaid tattoo. She soon learned that he wasn't there, since they were still unloading, but he might be there the next night.

She returned to her inn, and thought about what would be involved in becoming a crew member for the trip across. She asked around the pier the next day, and some of the dock workers gave her some pointers and wished her luck. She had made a point to identify the rough merchant ship earlier that day, and decided if it was going the right direction, it would do. She found him in the other tavern that night. She approached him cautiously. "Excuse me. Are you Captain Yermont?"

He answered without looking, "Aye, whose askin'?" He turned to her and eyed her up and down, then grumbled with finality. "Don't take passengers."

"I am willing to work. I just need to get to Isalor." she responded with courage.

"Sure ye do. Still don't take passengers." He grumbled to himself as she stood defiantly. Finally he asked, "What kind of work can ye do?" He didn't look like he thought much of her.

"I can lift my own weight and carry it for hours. I know knots and have excellent balance. I am not above scrubbing decks and cooking food. I might not be a gourmet chef, but I can make decent chow." She hoped that would be enough, cause she didn't think he would likely appreciate many of her other skills. She also didn't mention spells, because she had learned that if she said she could do some magic, it often put people off. Only the really wealthy and the super talented had the talent or the time and resources to learn magic, and it made others wary.

"Hmm, well, come by the ship tomorrow at sunrise, if me foreman thinks ye work well enough, I can take ye on. Just the one way?"

"Aye captain." she responded with a salute and a grin.

He scowled at her salute, "Ahh, get outta here. Be there at sunrise." He turned back to his drink. The conversation was over.

The next morning at sunrise, she was standing at the peer at the base of the gangplank. The captain was there within seconds of the sun rising. "Ok girlie, get up here."

She walked up the plank and snapped a salute to the captain. "What do you want me to do first, Captain?"

He grumbled and then called out over her shoulder, "Seeley, I gotcha some fresh meat. Wants to work across. Lemme know whatcha think." Then he turned and headed back somewhere else.

The next thing she knew a huge man was standing in front of her. When he spoke, it was like the depths of the world were speaking to her. "And a gurl, too. Well missy, get to work and let's see whats you can do. Start with that load a crates right there on the pier."

"Yessir!" She immediately went down to the crates and tried to pick one up. It was heavier than it looked. She refocused and lifted it. They were really heavy, but she thought she could manage them. She realized was going to be pretty sore afterward though. She carried it up the gangplank and onto the ship. She looked at Seeley to her side. "Where do you want them?"

The way he grinned at her, she was sure she was doing something wrong, but was determined to not let it get to her. "Into the hold, about the middle next to the red crates." He kept watching her with his big grin as she worked out how to get the crate into the hold. There was a ladder into the hold, as well as several short sets of staircases that led to the other parts of the ship and eventually made it down into the hold. The crate would not fit down the passageways, so she was stuck using the ladder.

She realized trying to carry a crate down the ladder would only end in disaster. She looked around and saw some loose rope which gave her an idea. She grabbed the rope and tied it around the crate and then used it to lower the crate down into the hold. Once it was down, she untied the rope and then moved the crate around into the right place.

Seeley's grin kept getting bigger as he watched, and it was evident that she hadn't done it right and he thought it was funny. Trying to keep her cool, she turned to him, "I can see by your expression that I am not doing it right. Can you please tell me the right way to do it?"

His grin broke into a full laugh, and he nodded while laughing. She waited as patiently as she could until he stopped laughing. "Use the pier winch to load the whole stack, then swing them over the hold and lower them down." He pointed to each location as he explained the process. Since she had already moved one crate, she only had seven in the first stack.

It took her a few minutes, and she quickly learned to ask if she wasn't completely sure she was doing it right. She found Seeley to be cheerful and willing to give clear directions, once she asked for them. Once she moved the whole stack into the hold, she had to shift each crate to the right spot and restack them.

She thought she earned bonus points when she asked about the proper way to secure the stacks, and Seeley explained and demonstrated the process. It was all hard work, but she was determined and would not quit. At one point, she was lowering down a very heavy stack of crates, and Seeley jumped down into the hold, grabbed the base of the whole stack, and quickly maneuvered it into place.

Cecilia was dumbfounded. She was sure that the stack weighed at least ten times what she did. Seeley had to be stronger than anyone she had ever met, including Rasdal. She descended into the hold and looked at him intensely. He noticed her looking at him and flashed a smile. "Uh, I work out a bit." All she could do was shake her head in disbelief.

The day continued. Several teams of men helped with the loading. At one point, Seeley had her do a visual verification of the cargo where she checked it against a list. Then they secured the load. They had a couple more smaller shipments of goods that they needed to load, but there was some time spent waiting for those to arrive.

While they waited, they would go up top and he showed her how to perform the basic operations of the ship. She learned which knots to use at various places and what different orders meant. During those times she was up top, she kept a careful eye out to make sure Rasdal hadn't caught up with her.

By the time the sun was getting low, she was drenched in sweat, and thoroughly exhausted, but they still hadn't given her a verdict. Finally she caught sight of the Captain giving Seeley a questioning look. Seeley just nodded. "Well miss, we be pulling out in 45 minutes. Ya have a ride to Isalor. Do ya have bags?"

"Yes Captain. I can be back in twenty minutes."

"Seeley will show ya where to put your bags."

She ran for the Inn and once there grabbed her bags, still being careful to check for Rasdal everywhere she went. Back at the ship, Seeley showed her where in the hold she could put her bags and what bunk she would be sharing with another crew member. It was a small crew of fourteen people, with her it made fifteen. The captain and Seeley had staterooms. Everyone else was supposed to share a bunk, of which they had eight, so while one was resting, the other was up working. There were four of them that didn't normally have to share, but with her along, one of those four was forced to share with her. The one she shared with was the cook.

She was up on deck when they pulled out to sea. They were several hundred yards out when she looked back at the docks and saw Rasdal run down the pier. She could just see enough detail to make out the absolute hatred on his face. She glared back at him as his form grew smaller and smaller. It didn't matter if he followed her. She didn't plan on being around the port on Isalor for him to find even if he did follow her.

CHAPTER TWENTY-TWO

EWAN

STANDING ABOVE THE SEAWALL overlooking the waterfront in Nexoro, Ewan watched as the ship slowly worked its way into the dock along the pier. Just a half hour before, he had been notified by the Harbormaster that a passenger ship from Port Yadzul on the continent of Arden was due to dock at any time, and there would be a fast cargo ship from there that would arrive later the next day and then nothing else for about a week. He had used all his authority as a Ranger to coerce the Harbormaster to agree to send him notifications of ships coming in from Port Yadzul.

He really didn't have a lot to go on. When he had left Rhondalyn's little hunting shack, he thought he had a clear idea of what to do, but when he arrived in Nexoro, he quickly discovered his instructions were much more vague and difficult to accomplish than he expected. There had been five ships arrive from Port Yadzul in the four days he had been there. In three of the cases, there had been passengers from the ships that potentially matched with one of the profiles that he had been given.

He had quickly figured out that if the potential match had someone waiting for them or if they showed familiarity with Nexoro that they probably weren't who he was looking for. He also had realized that people who knew right where they were going or that ignored most of what was going on around them were not them either. The people he was looking for would most likely look around a lot to get their bearings, would most likely not be tied to a larger group of people who didn't match the profile.

Ewan decided that four of the five people that he was looking for would have certain similarities. One was a royal guard. Another was a trapeze artist. There was also a jack of all trades who was a laborer, and a thief who was also a noble. All four of those would probably be strong and agile. They would move with strength and skill and would be nimble. They would also be highly observant. All these things would show in how they walked, held themselves, and how they looked around at things. As he watched people getting off the ship, he watched for these traits. He also watched for any other characteristics that might reveal if they were who he was looking for.

As they left, there were two people who moved fairly well, and he supposed the young man could be a jack of all trades, and a woman might be the acrobat so he wrote down their descriptions in his notebook. The young man greeted a young woman with a kiss. She had been waiting at the gate of the pier, so that probably ruled him out. He would still follow up. The potential acrobat didn't even really look where she was going and navigated with ease, indicating a lot of familiarity with Nexoro. That made him ninety percent sure she was not it.

Pretty soon, all the passengers had left the ship, and he would have to follow up on the young man. He had noted the direction the young man went, as well as the confident young woman that came after. He was able to track the young man fairly easily, and found him at a lumber yard, working. It only took a few minutes to ascertain that the young man was a local who had just returned from visiting Port Yadzul. The confident young woman turned out to be an employee of the city government and had been working on renewing trade agreements, meaning neither were who he was looking for.

The next day, he was again waiting where he could see the cargo ship come in. There were no passengers aboard the Grudge Merchant, which he thought was an awful name for a ship. They docked and the crew quickly went about unloading. The ship supposedly made more runs back and forth to Port Yadzul than any other ship. Among the crew, he noticed an attractive young woman. The young woman moved like a cat, with precision and strength, but with a noble bearing. He suspected she could move very quickly and seemed to have a lot of agility. Her balance getting off the ship showed a high degree of experience as well.

Once the ship was unloaded, the woman went back aboard and then returned carrying a couple of adventurer style travel bags, and dressed like a rogue. She looked around carefully, taking everything into account, like she was categorizing everything she saw. She had a couple of daggers on her belt, and it appeared she had a number of other weapons or tools that were hidden in her clothes. Also, there didn't seem to be anyone she was looking for, or waiting for her.

This was the seventh ship that had come in while he had been there, but this woman was the first that he was more than fifty percent sure could be one of the candidates. Ewan moved quickly to reach the pier gate before she did. When she came through the gate, he approached and had to force himself not to trip up. She was more than just attractive, but outright beautiful. "Excuse me miss. I was wondering if I could speak to you for just a couple of minutes, right over here." He indicated a place along the side that would be out of people's way, but very much still public.

She kind of drew back warily, and he could see her eyes evaluating him intently. When she didn't agree immediately, he added, "In exchange for answering a few simple questions, I can give you information about the city and help you find what you are looking for."

She pursed her lips like she was still trying to decide. Then said "Ok, if your questions are not too inappropriate or invasive, I will answer, unless I don't like the question. If that's the case, the discussion will be over."

Ewan nodded and smiled, "I can work with that. Ok, first question, what is your name, just so I know what to call you."

She hesitated just a moment, then said "You can call me Cecilia."

"Great. My name is Ewan. I have been tasked by Halidar Rhondalyn to find some specific people, and you match one of the descriptions quite closely. I don't want to pry, but if she is looking for you, it generally is a good thing. Next question. Did you grow up as a Noble, or with nobility?"

He could tell that the question made her feel uncomfortable and she looked at him a moment before giving him a calculated answer, "I was around enough of the Nobility to know to be wary of them."

That was enough of an answer to match the profile. Then he said, "Ok, that will do. Next, I noticed that you have very developed observation skills and a lot of strength and agility. Where did you learn those, and what would you call your profession?"

Her expression went hard and he could tell he had lost her. "This conversation is over." she said with finality.

At that point, he was sure she was the thief who had been a noble. As she turned to leave, he quickly interjected, "Please, just one more thing. I need you to just touch five stones with your finger .."

She angrily pushed him aside and stormed off, "Leave me alone!"

He stood there thoughtfully watching her go. He could tell she was paying attention to the fact that he was still watching her, and it bothered her. She soon reached a street and went down it. He could just see her as she turned into the first alleyway that she passed. Once she was out of sight, he grinned. He gave her seven minutes to move on. Then he went to the alleyway. He utilized his skills and immediately knew exactly where she went. He tracked where she went, and paid attention to what he could tell she had done there.

He was now certain she was the thief. And a beautiful one at that. He mentally rebuked himself for the thought. This was an assignment, and she was a thief, although he wasn't here to apprehend her, but rather recruit her. She would probably be the hardest on the entire group to convince. Well, he thought, perhaps it is best to start with the hardest.

He noted where she had waited to watch her back train to see if he was following. Then, he tracked where she had gone through a couple of different market squares. He noted where she stopped and where she went next. It always amazed him how his tracking skills could tell him so much after the fact. She had looked at quite a number of shops in the markets. She had gone into several of them. At least three times, she had actually gone to talk with the store clerk. Twice, she had done so almost directly. In another store, she had looked around at their goods in detail before doing so.

He used his status as a Ranger to get the shopkeepers to tell him about what she did. In one, she had sold some gems. In another, she sold some small but expensive magic items. In the third, she had purchased a few miscellaneous items, but the main thing she had picked up was some food. He continued to track her, and found she had doubled back on a couple of places, one in particular. He evaluated her patterns and decided that there was a good chance that she would be making a hit on that shop. It used magic wards as well as physical protections, so he thought that was interesting.

Finally, he tracked her to a couple of Inns, and found where she was staying. He found out which room she was in, and made a point to keep an eye on her for the next while. He still had to check back in with the harbormaster every day or so to monitor any incoming ships from Port Yadzul, but his main focus became Cecilia. He wondered if that was actually her name.

He carefully watched her from the shadows for the next several days. When he was sure she was getting ready to break into that store, he made sure she had left the market square and went to her targeted store and identified himself as a ranger. "There is a skilled thief that is going to rob your store. I want you to quietly remove any small high value items and relocate them someplace secure. I want her to still break in, but I want to make sure that what she is hoping to steal is not here."

"What!?" The storekeeper was shocked, but they did not question his judgment as a Ranger. He worked with the storekeeper to smuggle his high value goods and cash out to a safe location without making it obvious that it had all been moved. He had to make sure Cecilia was not watching the store while he helped the merchant set things up and move valuables out.

He continued to keep an eye on her when he could as she assembled her equipment and prepared. He didn't want to spook her when she came in, so he made sure everything was set up exactly as she would expect it. After he was sure everything was set and that she was ready to make the hit, he looked around double checking the preparation. He imagined her face and reaction, then smiled and chuckled a little.

He let the storekeeper know it was all set, then took his place where he would wait for her. The storekeeper went through his normal routine in locking up his store, while Ewan waited in concealment. He had seen enough high end thieves in his time as a ranger, and he was sure she would strike that night. He made himself sit completely still and went through various martial forms in his mind.

He knew he might be waiting for hours before she struck, or, she might show up any minute. His meditation had to be coupled with extreme awareness so she didn't slip in without him being alerted. Finally, after waiting for a couple hours, he sensed that something was happening with the wards around the building.

Chapter Twenty-Three

Cecilia

Cecilia watched her target closely. The storekeeper locked up his store like usual. Then he headed off with his head down. She waited a couple hours for several sets of city guards to make their rounds through the square, then moved in. It took her a little while to work through the wards and magical alarms.

The style used in Nexoro was a bit different than she was used to, but it all went down just fine eventually. She had been concerned that it would take her too long and the guards would come back, but she got it all done in time. She made sure there was nothing that would alert any guards when they came by. Then she double checked to make sure she hadn't missed any additional wards, alarms, or traps, and made her way inside.

Once she was inside the store, she breathed a lot easier. Getting in and out were almost always the riskiest parts of any operation. She looked around carefully, making sure nothing was out of place. What she had decided to target was some overpriced jewelry that were mass produced enough to not have maker's marks on them. The store also carried some magical devices that used a different type of configuration than what she was used to.

She moved to the cases that held her first targets, but they were gone. Hmm, not good. Why would they move the jewelry? She thought to herself. Next she moved toward the magical devices, but there they had a sign that instructed customers to talk to the clerk behind the counter. That was a second change that didn't make sense. She didn't like it.

Figuring that they would have moved the devices to the safe, and that was the biggest reason she had targeted that store, she decided to do the safe next. That was one of the things she liked most about this target. They had a big high end safe and it seemed they rarely kept anything in the bank. They should have a ton of coin in there.

As she had noticed with the main wards for the store, the wards on the safe were a bit different from what she was used to. She still got through them ok, even if it took a little more time than she would have liked. Once the wards were down, she quickly made it through the mechanical locks and opened it up. When she opened the safe, it was empty. She just stared at it. How could this be? What's going on?

A voice suddenly came from behind her. "You're really good at that." She froze for a second, then spun and saw the annoying man from the pier leaning against the counter. He was just out of reach if she were to lunge at him. He had a smile on his face and she could tell he had total confidence in the situation. She tried her best to not show any panic, but wasn't sure she succeeded.

What was going on? Had they somehow found out that she was coming? How could he be here, in the middle of an operation. The wards should have gone off when he came in. She was certain he hadn't been there when she came in. He hadn't made any noise either. She realized she was in major trouble. She had never been caught doing a heist before.

This man had somehow just appeared out of nowhere. He obviously was not an amateur. She hadn't had anyone sneak up on her undetected since she had first started learning the trade. He was obviously dangerous in the extreme, and had caught her red handed, only, there wasn't anything to steal.

How had he set her up? How did she not see this setup?

He smiled warmly at her, like he thought he knew her. "Tomorrow, I will contact you with instructions to meet me. You will want to agree to it." He almost looked like he was going to burst into laughter, like he was playing a hilarious joke. Part of her wanted to give in, but another part of her rebelled at the thought of admitting defeat.

She just stood there staring at him, trying to figure out what to do. What could she even do? Again, he smiled, then turned and jumped over the counter without making a sound or even disturbing the dust. And then he was gone. Completely gone without a trace. What!? How could he just disappear? Cecilia was in even more of a panic. She had never imagined she could feel that far out of her depth with the level of her skills. Suddenly, she was feeling like a novice again.

The man had caught her red handed, and could easily take total control, or arrest her, or something, but then he just left after saying he would contact her. None of it made any sense. Her mind raced as she tried to figure a way out of the situation. She didn't know enough about the man to know what to do. Strangely, she felt her best option might be to meet with him, just to see what he wanted.

Since there was nothing of value she could easily get from the shop, she closed up the safe and reactivated the wards. As she waited for the guards to pass outside, she couldn't take her mind off the man. Hadn't he said something about the Halidar at the pier? Her mind raced to understand, but she only came up with more questions.

Once the guards passed, she left, reactivated the store wards. Then she silently made her way back to her inn. She couldn't shake the feeling that she was a pawn in someone's game. It was late, nearly the next morning before she arrived back at her room. She had to fight the impulse to flee immediately. There was a note that had been placed under the door. It said, "At 10am, go downstairs and ask the innkeeper where his private meeting room is. He will show you. Don't be late, or early."

She stood with her mouth agape. He knows my inn well enough to reserve the meeting space? Ahead of time? She felt paranoia like she never had before, but then thought that perhaps she should have been feeling much more paranoid earlier. Maybe she had grown too complacent. Now she had somehow gotten herself into something much bigger than her, and she felt totally clueless as to what she should do. None of it made sense. If he had been a guard or officer, he would have arrested her, but he just disappeared.

She went to bed to try to catch a little sleep before their meeting. She wasn't sure what the point was, though, because all she did was toss and turn. She couldn't stop thinking about the man. How could he have even been there? How could he disappear like that? Why was he so infuriatingly good looking? She wanted to wipe his smug grin right off his handsome face.

At two minutes before 10am, she went downstairs. She looked around and then went to the innkeeper. "Where is your private meeting room?"

The innkeeper looked up at her somewhat with surprise, and then turned and said "Come with me." He showed her a room in the back and stood aside so she could open the door and enter.

When she entered the room, the mysterious man was seated at a table waiting patiently. What was his name again? Evan, or something like that. She reluctantly closed the door and then took the seat he gestured to. She didn't want to be the first to speak, so she just waited. The first question out of his mouth just about made her want to scream and run from the room, but she controlled herself.

"What do you know about the darkness, and what experience have you had with it?" he asked.

"How do you know all th.. " She cut herself off. She wasn't going to let him control her emotions. She would just answer the question. "I was in Merdal, and it came through. All the thieves in the guild stayed hidden while it went through the city. Much of the city was destroyed, but there were still some people there. The others around me started acting strange, and I felt like I could barely think. They walked off and started just picking stuff up and cleaning things. They didn't respond when I asked what they were doing. I figured I had to get out of the darkness. All I could think about was being in the sunshine again. When I finally got out into the light, it was like waking up. I made sure to get away from it and stay away from it after that."

"Interesting." He then pulled out five clear gems from a thick pouch. Or, perhaps they were glass. She could sense the magic in them from across the table. Part of her desperately wanted to steal them and run away, but a bigger part wanted to run away from them as fast as possible. "Will you please touch these stones with your finger, one at a time."

She touched the first stone. It just felt hard. Nothing else happened. The same thing happened with the second and third stones. On the fourth stone, just as she was about to touch it, she felt like there was energy in the air around it. She forced herself to go forward and touch it. When she did, it lit up brighter than the sun. She jerked her hand back and the light began to fade. Quickly, the man grabbed the stone and put it in a different pocket of the thick pouch that cut off the light completely, then put the other four stones back where they came from.

He reached into a pocket and pulled out a strange device, then pushed a button and mumbled, "Dang, I should have done this earlier." She felt a magic lock trigger on the doors and a barrier around the room snap into place. They were strong enough that it would have taken her a while to get through them. She wanted to flee, but obviously, he wouldn't go away. She felt trapped.

Then he spoke up. "Can you sit while I explain some things?"

She realized she had jumped up and reluctantly nodded and sat again. "Rhondalyn instructed me to find five people. She didn't know their names, but did know a lot about them. One of them is a Noble who would rather be known as a thief. She described some of what she had seen in her visions about them, and gave me these stones. Each one is attuned to one of the people I am supposed to find. Obviously, that one is attuned to you. No one else in the world can trigger it. There is another one that Rhondalyn has that only works for me.

We are foretold to be part of some great quest to stop the second darkness. She will train us and equip us. I don't know everything about what she wants, just that part of my job is to find the others. I'm from Isalor, and none of the others are, so perhaps that is why she picked me. Anyway, I have to find the others. They will all be coming on ships from Port Yadzul, like you did. Will you agree to help me find, identify, and convince the others to join us and go see Rhondalyn? If you do, I can try to make it worth your while."

"Like, what, you can pay me?" She raised her eyebrow in distrust.

He reached out and set a stack of gold coins on the table. "Oh, I am sure Rhondalyn could probably provide much more, but I was thinking of something perhaps a little more hands-on. I can teach you better tracking and stealth skills while we wait. Interested?"

She hadn't expected that. It seemed like this guy knew her better than she knew herself. There was no way she could turn down training like that, especially after he had run circles around her ever since she had arrived. He obviously could out track her, and she had no idea he was there in the store, in her inn, or anywhere else. He was obviously much more of a master of these skills than she was.

It didn't hurt that he was gorgeous too. She caught herself and promised that she would not let a handsome man ever get in the way of what she really wanted. The last thing she needed was emotional entanglement. Still, it looked like she was going to be working with him for at least a little while. She committed to seeing this through, at least until they met with Rhondalyn.

Chapter Twenty-Four

Finn

As the wagon they had traveled in slowed, Finn felt himself start to calm. It had been a long trip. He had driven the wagon for a month and a half and basically been the porter for Eleanor and Matilda. Matilda had required additional assistance due to her age. Charlotte had spent much of the trip being a nursemaid for Matilda, while Eleanor had certainly taken charge of everything. Fortunately, she also had paid for just about everything, which meant that Finn still had most of his savings..

They were next to an inn on a hill in the city of Port Yadzul, overlooking the harbor. There were multiple piers along the harbor with ships pulled into the dock loading or unloading or waiting to do so. Finn spoke up "How do we go about finding a ship to Isalor?"

Eleanor started, "Oh, um, about that. I have realized that with Matilda's health and age, we need to give her time to recover before we subject her to an ocean voyage. I am told they can be quite arduous."

The news came as a total shock to Finn, "How much time to recover do you think she will need?" He glanced at Charlotte who was taking care of Matilda. She shrugged indicating she had no knowledge of the plans.

Eleanor responded flatly. It was evident the prospect didn't make her happy, but she seemed resigned to it. "Probably at least several weeks, if not a couple months."

Finn looked back and forth at her and Charlotte, then at the ships in the harbor. Finally he was able to articulate what he was feeling. "I feel like I have to go sooner than that. I don't know why, but I need to get there."

Eleanor suddenly looked more tired than before. She smiled weakly. "I can understand that. I won't ask you to delay for our benefit."

Looking back at Charlotte, he asked, "What about Charlotte?"

Eleanor looked at Charlotte too, then at Matilda, then back at Finn before answering. "I would appreciate it if she stayed to help me with Matilda, but that would be up to her." She turned to Charlotte, "How do you feel about it, dear?"

Charlotte seemed torn by indecision. After more than a minute of consternation, she answered, "I need to do what I feel is right. While I would like to be able to stay and help take care of Matilda, I feel like I need to go to Isalor as soon as possible too. I would like to go with Finn, but I don't know if I have enough to pay for passage."

Finn smiled broadly, "I always assumed I would be paying for you anyway, so we should probably be good. I am glad you are coming." He looked down before continuing. "I am sorry Eleanor. I appreciate all you have done for us. I would have liked to continue this journey together."

"Oh, Finn. I appreciate all you two have done for me and my cousin. We will miss you, but we'll get along. If you feel you should go, then you should go." She looked at them with tenderness, "I can't tell you what might happen either way, but I've learned in my life that listening to your own soul will lead you right more often than anything else. I won't ever blame you for being true to yourself."

Charlotte seemed touched, "Thank you Eleanor."

Finn nodded in agreement. "Yes, thank you. I hope everything works out well for both of you. Who knows, perhaps we will meet again in Isalor."

"Perhaps." Eleanor looked like her eyes were starting to moisten. "You two should get going and see if you can find a ship. I think they should have a harbor master that might be able to help you out, or you can ask people there along the waterfront or at the piers."

Finn picked up his bags and Charlotte followed his example. As they headed down the hill, he called back and waved, "Thank you, again. Goodbye."

Eleanor waved and then watched them as they walked away. They worked their way down the hill toward the harbor. As they got further into the city, Finn said to Charlotte, "So why exactly did you decide to come with me?"

She looked apprehensive and perhaps a little defiant at his question, "I really do feel like I have to keep going. Maybe it's just habit. I don't know. I also feel like whatever I am going to do, I would rather do it with a young person I trust rather than a couple old ladies who mostly just order me around. I had enough of that at the Manor."

Finn wasn't sure what to make of that. He had asked because he wanted to be sure she really did want to come along. It seemed that she did. "Well, I can't promise that I will be much better company, but I will be straight up with you and try not to order you around too much."

Charlotte replied with a straight face. "Gee, thanks. You make it sound so inviting." She then heaved a big sigh. "I can work with that. What should we do next?"

Finn looked around at the harbor and the ships. He had no idea where to start, but Eleanor had mentioned something about a harbor master, so that might be a good place to start. "I guess we start at the harbor master." He headed down the road expecting Charlotte to keep up with him, and she did.

After they got closer to the harbor, he called out to one of the locals. "Excuse me. Can you tell us where the harbor master's office is?"

The man who had just set down the load he was carrying turned and gestured down the waterfront. "That small building there that stands out on its own with the double doors. That's the one."

"Thank you sir," Finn called and they headed toward the indicated building. When they got there, there was a sign on the door indicating that the Harbor Master would return in a couple hours. Finn sighed. "I guess we can talk to other people by the docks to see if anyone knows where we can find a ship to Isalor."

The waterfront included a long wharf that had eight piers jutting out from it with a large distance between each. Only smaller boats docked at the wharf, and the larger ships docked along the piers. Each of the piers had a large gate which was used to limit access to the pier and provide order. Piers that mainly served passenger ships were restricted without acceptable documentation, and the guards at each gate would refuse entry without it.

As they walked along the wharf, going from one pier to the next, they saw that a recently docked ship on the next pier was dislodging passengers. Several groups of people who had disembarked were approaching the gate. Charlotte pointed at one of the groups, a somewhat younger couple who would be passing through the gate about the same time that they reached it. "They look kind of nice. Let's ask them."

Finn followed where she pointed and saw a tall and well built man in a white and gold soldier uniform escorting an attractive woman. She held his arm as they walked and talked. They both seemed fairly happy and they were pointing around at different things in the harbor.

When they reached the gate, the couple was just coming through. Finn called out, "Excuse me, sir. Would you happen to know if there are any passenger carrying ships that will be heading out to Isalor soon?"

The man looked over, somewhat surprised at their approach. "I'm sorry, I don't. In fact, we are looking for the same thing, but have just disembarked after a journey from Jasteros. We have never been here before. Have you asked the guards at the gates?"

Finn felt his face flush, "Uh, No. I.. I didn't think of that."

The man grinned widely at him. "I'm Nerian. What's your name?"

"Uh, I'm Finn." Then he realized he should probably introduce Charlotte as well. "And this is Charlotte."

Charlotte eyed him, leaving him unsure if he should have spoken for her or not. Nerian, as the man had called himself, had noticed. He turned to the woman with him as she spoke, "I'm Micaela." Micaela gave Finn a look that he thought might have been some kind of disapproval.

As he thought about it, and since Micaela had introduced herself, but he hadn't allowed Charlotte the same respect, he realized it may have looked bad. He turned to Charlotte, "Sorry, I should have let you introduce yourself."

She waved him off, "Don't worry about it. We need to focus on finding a ship."

Nerian interrupted, "Since we are looking for the same thing, perhaps we can all look together. Let me ask that guard." He walked off, leaving Micaela with them and went to talk to the guard. Micaela leaned in close to Charlotte and whispered something Finn couldn't hear, and Charlotte whispered back. It made Finn feel conspicuous, but he decided to pay attention to what Nerian was doing instead.

The guard looked irritated, but kept looking at the insignia on Nerian's uniform. Nerian said something, and the guard answered back. The exchange went another two rounds and then Nerian turned back toward them.

Nerian looked a little less happy when he returned. "The guards are not allowed to answer questions, but even if they were, he said he had no idea and that we would have to ask the Harbor Master."

Charlotte answered. "Oh, we were just there, and a sign said they won't be back for a couple of hours." She pointed toward the harbor master's office.

Nerian frowned slightly when she said that. "Well, I guess we will have to wait."

Finn tried to explain that was what they were trying to do. "That is why we are asking people at the pier gates if they know of ships sailing to Isalor. We thought we might find out something while we waited."

"I take it you haven't found any?"

Finn grinned "No, you were the first people we asked."

Nerian ignored the grin, then looked toward the Harbor Master's office. "Well, I suppose we can wait for the Harbor Master and his people to return." Then he started off toward the harbor master's office without another word. Finn sullenly followed. He hated waiting.

The waiting seemed to take forever. Micaela and Charlotte sat off to the side quietly talking, but Nerian seemed to have no interest in talking. Eventually, several people approached as a group. They all had somewhat somber looks on their faces. One of them took out a key and opened the office and the others filed in. They shut the door behind them and Finn heard the lock click. He had expected to be let right in, but was not. Soon, another man approached in fancier clothing. It was similar to what the other people had worn, but much nicer.

Nerian stood and bowed slightly. "Harbor Master." he greeted the man. The man nodded his head as he passed. He unlocked the door with a key and entered, again locking the door behind him.

Finn wondered how Nerian would know that man was the harbor master. He looked at Nerian questioningly, but Nerian just smiled back. A few minutes later, there was movement heard inside the building. Nerian stood, "This should be us, finally."

Just as he said that, someone took the "returning later" sign down and unlocked the door. Finn was amazed and couldn't hold his question back any more. "How did you know? I thought you said you hadn't ever been here before."

Nerian looked at Finn like he was evaluating him, "I paid attention to the details and was able to deduce what was going on. It wouldn't accomplish anything by acting rushed and pressuring others and might have potentially made things worse. You seem like a smart kid, but you lack experience. Give it time. It will come. In the meantime, we are here right now with similar goals. I will help you along if I can."

Finn wasn't sure what to feel about that loaded statement. "Oh. Thank you for the help." was the only thing he could think to say that felt right. Just then, the door opened, and Nerian turned to enter. Finn and the girls followed him. A half dozen others who had congregated behind them also entered.

When they got into the office, there were several booths that had workers behind them where passage and shipping orders could be purchased or processed, but each of them still had a little gate on their booth closed. The Harbor Master stood at the head of the room, checking his watch. Everyone stood around waiting for something, but Finn wasn't sure what.

At some point, the Harbor Master called out, "May I have your attention, everyone. Please." Instantly, everyone was silent and paying attention. "As a general announcement, due to the increased demand for people trying to obtain passage to Isalor and the other continents, the council has issued the following: Any ships adding routes to Isalor that qualify as ocean capable ships will be given a routing bonus. Additionally, surcharges for passage are increased to 4 times the price of passage. Shipments of raw materials incoming to Port Yadzul will also be given priority docking and a discounted pier fee." If you have further questions, my staff can help you."

Immediately, he turned and exited the main public area through a door at the back. Finn tried to understand what he had just heard, and what that meant for them. "What does that mean for us?" he asked Nerian and Micaela.

Micaela answered, "Things just got a lot more expensive, that's what."

Finn was worried, "Is there a way for us to find a different way to Isalor that doesn't cost so much? How much are we talking about?"

Nerian didn't seem worried at all as glanced over at Finn, "We won't know until we find a ship that is going there. Then we ask. Once we know, we can work out the details."

The workers behind the counters started opening the little gates on their booths. Nerian approached the nearest one. "We are looking for the next ship to Isalor. When will it leave, and what will it cost?"

The person behind the counter checked some different charts arrayed around his booth, and answered. The next ship to Isalor will be the Silent Star. It will arrive tomorrow evening and then leave again the next morning. The passage with the new fees will be 128 silver per stateroom and another 64 per additional person, maximum of two passengers per room. It only has 8 cabins and they will fill up fast, but it is a fast ship with an excellent safety record. How many rooms would you like?"

"Oh, No!" uttered Finn under his breath when he heard the prices. Apparently Micaela heard him and raised her eyebrow at him. He leaned in close and whispered, "I don't know if I have enough. It's taken me years to save that much."

She whispered to him, "Do what you can and we'll see how things go." Finn couldn't help but feel extremely nervous. He opened his coin purse and started counting. Nerian seemed strangely unaware of the drama unfolding behind him. Both Charlotte and Micaela watched as he totaled his funds.

When he had totaled everything, he stared and then felt around in his coin purse, trying to see if he had missed anything. He whispered back to Micaela. "I only have about 95 and a half silver. What should I do?"

She looked around and then placed a gold coin in his hand. "This should make up for it. Book your passage."

Relief and then guilt flooded into Finn, "I can't just take your money. I can't pay you back." He looked at her like she was crazy.

"Don't worry about it. Do what you need to do. Besides, it isn't even mine. I just found it not long ago." She looked away as if terribly interested in something across the room.

Finn didn't know what to do, but the pressure was getting to him. Just then, Nerian turned to him, "Finn, do you want to book passage?" The pressure he felt seemed to double again.

Charlotte, Nerian, and the clerk were all looking at him while Micaela seemed to not even be aware of his existence at that moment. With nothing else he felt he could do. He counted out what he had and paid for the passage. That left him with only 3 and a half silver to his name. He felt lightheaded and overwhelmed right then. Micaela then put her hand on his shoulder. He worried about what she would now demand of him. She simply whispered in his ear, "You did the right thing."

They didn't say anything else until they were out of the office and heading toward the nearest market area. Still trying to wrap his head around everything, he asked, "How much will it cost to get a room at the Inn for tonight and tomorrow?"

Nerian replied nonchalantly, "Oh, probably between two to four silver a night."

Finn stopped in his tracks, causing Charlotte to bump into him. Everyone stopped and looked at him. His mouth felt dry. He stammered as I tried to speak, "I.. I.. I don't have enough." He turned to Charlotte,

"Charlotte, I'm sorry, but, I can't get us a room. I don't have any idea what we will do when we get to Isalor. I, I just .."

Charlotte smiled at him. "I was broke and starving and dressed in just rags when I met you. We'll figure things out."

Right then, Micaela said, "Nerian." with a strange lilt to her voice.

Nerian looked a little bothered, then swept his hand to the side. "Fine. You two can stay with us. We will get a room for the guys and one for the girls, will that work?" His last question seemed directed to Micaela.

She smiled and looked him straight in the eyes. "That will work nicely. Thank you."

There was a lull for about fifteen seconds where they looked back and forth while no one said or did anything, like they were all waiting for someone else to move. Finally, Charlotte said, "So, where do we stay until the ship is ready?"

Narian looked around and pointed, "I think I saw an inn or tavern somewhere over that way." He started off before anyone could respond and they all jumped to follow him.

Chapter Twenty-Five

Finn

The place that Nerian had seen turned out to be a combination inn and tavern, with two separate public rooms. One for tavern patrons, and the other reserved for those staying in the Inn. The rooms were decent, and Finn ended up sharing with Nerian, while Charlotte shared with Micaela.

The rooms came with breakfast and dinner, and so the four of them sat together waiting for their meals that evening. Finn looked around at the other patrons of the Inn sitting in the reserved dining space. There was a short hallway that led to the main tavern room and occasionally, there was a lot of noise from there, but enough was blocked out that a normal volume conversation could be held fairly easily.

Micaela opened up the conversation, "Now that we have passage to Isalor and a place to stay and food to eat, let's get to know each other better, shall we?" She looked around and saw that everyone was ok with it, she continued. "I am, or was, a circus trapeze performer. Our circus was a traveling circus based out of Danlos. I was there when Dardanos's Wizard Tower was destroyed, and saw the huge new dark tower rise and start creating the storm. The circus matron told us all to flee, but the storm caught us while we were camping that night and I think everyone else was killed. I escaped and was trying to get to the Tower of Light and trying to warn people when I met Nerian."

Nerian picked up from there, "I was a Royal Knight at the Tower of Light. I was on my way to my shift when the Tower of Light and most of the city there was destroyed. I tried to rescue King Evander, one of the Halidar from the rubble of the palace and did find him alive, but he had been poisoned with something that had no antidote. Before he died, he ordered me to travel to Dardanos's Wizard Tower and help him prevent a second darkness."

"I had no idea that both towers had been destroyed at the same time. After I met Micaela, I journeyed to the edge of the storm and took some measurements to determine how fast it was moving, then rejoined Micaela in Jasteros, where we took a ship to Port Yadzul, where we met you." He looked back and forth at Finn and Charlotte like he expected them to pick up from there.

Charlotte took her turn. "I was a servant, a milkmaid, at Ethalor Manor in Merdal. The storm came and I ran from skeletons while they attacked the cows. One of the skeletons followed, but couldn't catch me because it was damaged. It disintegrated about four hours later, chasing me the whole time until then."

"I made my way to Beaumont, and tried to warn people about the storm, but I don't think anyone listened. I worked to earn some supplies and continued onward. The storm destroyed Beaumont about three or four days later. The next town is where I met Finn and a woman, another refugee, named Eleanor. She knew a lot about history, and had a lot of reasons that the only hope was Rhondalyn." She then looked over at Finn.

Finn figured it was his turn then, "Before I met Charlotte, I worked as sort of a general laborer and helper for a bunch of different crafters and merchants in our town. I was an illegitimate son of the Baron of Horshon, but didn't really know him. I was told that his wife, the duchess, had both him and my mother poisoned and they both got sick and died in a short amount of time. Before that, we had a lot, but afterward, I had to work hard."

"Anyway, I was helping a traveling trader from our town on a trip to Beaumont when I first heard about the storm. There was a bard there that told about the first darkness and pointed out similarities to what was rumored to be happening. Not too long after that trip, I met Charlotte. She had seen the storm and everything herself. She also was able to give an estimate of when it would get to our town.

After talking with all the people I knew, we got the town to evacuate. Strangely enough, we ended up not going with the people from the town, but with Eleanor and her cousin Matilda who were coming here. She planned to sail to Isalor to seek Rhondalyn. When we got here, her cousin needed to recover from the trip before she tried to sail across the ocean, so we moved on to find passage on a ship to Isalor, and that was when we met you."

The mood while everyone was telling their stories was intense, but as they got to the end, it had lightened quite a bit. Finn was curious, "So, why are you seeking Rhondalyn?"

Nerian answered, "My king was one of the Halidar. He died. It appears that Dardanos tower was destroyed, and possibly him with it. It was obvious that the destruction of his tower and the rising of the new tower were linked together. It is probably a long shot, but that leaves Rhondalyn as the only remaining person in the world that was there to fight the first darkness, and since this second darkness seems to be following the patterns of the first, we hope she can help us know what to do. If we can find her. If she's even still alive."

Charlotte nodded, "Yeah, I guess that is the same for us. Eleanor had all sorts of reasons and theories about why Rhondalyn would have the answers we need, but like you said. If she is alive, and if we can find her."

As Charlotte was speaking, Finn had glanced around at the people near them. Sitting at a table not far away was a large dark haired man with fine quality, but utilitarian clothing. Finn wasn't sure, but it seemed like that man might be listening in on their conversation. Either that, or he was really deep in his own thoughts. The man was mostly facing away from them, but had his head cocked just a little bit like he was trying to hear them better. Every once in a while he would lift his tea cup and take a sip.

Charlotte interrupted his musing, "Finn, are you ok? You seem distracted." Her sudden question caused him to jump.

He made one last glance over at the man, and then said "No, I.. I think I must be tired. Maybe imagining things. I think I need to get some sleep."

Nerian spoke, "Ok, that sounds like a good idea. We can work on gathering supplies tomorrow like we discussed." Finn figured he had missed that part. The man had gotten up and left while Nerian spoke. Finn still couldn't be sure if the man was listening in, but he still felt uneasy about the whole thing. He followed the others up the stairs to sleep.

The next morning, Micaela had made lists of things to get, and Nerian had given them enough coin to cover the expenses. He and Charlotte walked about, picking up food and the other things on their lists. Their previously depleted bags soon began to bulge. They picked up more bags to hold the remainder of the supplies on their list. When they joined back up at the Inn, Finn couldn't help but wonder if they had over prepared, but didn't say anything. He and Nerian later went to the docks to verify the Silent Star had arrived and the departure time. They all went to bed early that night since the ship was leaving at sunup.

On the day of departure, while still in the predawn hours, they made their way down to the pier their ship was docked against. After being let onto the pier by the guards, they made their way to the gangway. At the top, the captain and bosun greeted the new arrivals. "Ahoy there. I be ship Captain Drogo. This here be Bosun Jostor. If ye need anything, talk to him or First Mate Rheshak, who be supervisin' cargo loadin' over there." He pointed off to the other end of the ship where an extra tall sailor with a jacket was directing others in loading cargo.

After checking their tickets, Bosun Jostor directed them to a set of stairs. "Yer berths be the second and third rooms on the right. Please stay off the main deck until we have left the dock, and stay off the upper deck throughout the voyage unless invited by the Captain."

As they were walking across the main deck toward the stairs, Finn looked back at the gangway, and saw the same man that he thought might have been listening to them at dinner two nights before. The man was just acting like a normal passenger, but it still sent a chill up Finn's back. He would be keeping an eye out for the man during their eight day journey.

They made their way to their rooms, which were much smaller than the rooms they had in the Inn. They also had small cots that they had to sleep on in a bunk fashion. There was a little porthole window above Finn's eye level, but just about perfect height for Nerian. Finn had never really felt jealous of anyone before, and he did his best to tamp down his feelings. After all, Nerian had treated them very well, but it seemed everything about the man was nearly perfect. Nerian laid on his bunk while Finn stood on his tiptoes trying to see out the porthole. Eventually he gave up and sat on the bench built into the wall opposite the bunks.

After what seemed like forever, the ship finally got underway, and they were able to go up to the main deck. The ship was just leaving the harbor and they watched Port Yadzul slowly fade into the distance and disappear over the horizon. Charlotte and Micaela had joined them, and they made small talk while they watched. Finn noticed that the man from the restaurant was fairly close to them along the rails of the ship. He decided he would call him Mr Creepy. It wasn't long before he noticed that Charlotte looked like she wasn't feeling well.

"Charlotte, are you feeling ill?" he asked.

"Uh, yeah, that really came on fast." Her face was quickly taking on a green tint.

Nerian was concerned, "You might want to lay down. If you are sick, use a bucket to prevent making a big mess."

Finn went over to one of the crewmen, "One of our party members is sick. Do you have a bucket she can use?"

The crewman looked up at him, then directly at Charlotte. Apparently it was easy to tell who was seasick. "Aye, let me fetch one." The crew man ran off and returned shortly with a bucket. "Ere ye go."

"Thank you Mr. .." Finn prompted for his name.

"Trefaris. You can call me Mr. Trefaris." The man smiled quickly and went back to his work. Finn turned away and gave the bucket over to Charlotte, who immediately needed to use it. Micaela spent much of the next couple of days nursing Charlotte's health. Finn realized that it was probably a good thing that Eleanor hadn't brought Matilda on the ship with her already struggling from the long wagon trip.

As he stood at the railing, looking out over the rolling sea, he heard someone come up to him. He turned as Mr Trefaris asked, "How be the little miss?"

"She's still sick, but I think she is starting to get used to it."

"Aye, that be good to hear. You know what they say about sea sickness?" Mr Trefaris asked with a glint in his eye.

Finn's curiosity was picked, "Not really, what do they say?

Mr. Trefaris grinned, "First, ye get so sick, ye thinks ye's gonna die. Then ye's gets so sick, ye fear ye won't." He laughed at his own joke and returned to his work. Right then, Finn could hear someone else laughing quietly. He spun around to find Mr. Creepy looking out to sea and quietly laughing. He hadn't even noticed him there earlier.

Finn was incensed. Something inside him insisted he confront the man, "Excuse me sir, are you spying on me?"

The man was a little taken aback, but answered, "No, but it is a small ship and I have excellent hearing, so it's hard to not overhear. I do hope your friend is feeling better soon."

Finn just stood and stared as the man walked away. He didn't know what to think, but the man obviously had been paying attention to them.

He decided to go talk to his friends. Then he stopped. Is that what they were? He wasn't sure.

He was confident Charlotte was his friend, but he thought she might have a crush on him, and that made him uncomfortable. Finn didn't really know what he was looking for, or if he was even looking. For now, he would just think of Charlotte as a friend. As for the others, he wasn't sure about Nerian. He seemed emotionally distant from everyone except Micaela. She certainly was friendly, in a big sister sort of way. He wasn't exactly clear about Nerian and Micaela's relationship either. At times they seemed like there was mutual interest there, but others they were just members of the same travel party.

When he got to the rooms, he asked Nerian if he could join him in the girl's room. He needed to talk with them about something. They both entered the other room when Micaela opened the door and once the door was closed behind them, he started. "There's a guy on the ship that's been spying on us. Or, at least listening in on our conversations."

Micaela looked at him with concern, "Finn, the ship isn't that big. It would be easy to accuse anyone on the ship of spying. Unless we find him in our rooms, we can only assume he is just another passenger on a small cramped ship."

"It isn't just on the ship. When we were eating dinner the first night in the Inn, he was at the next table with his head turned enough to listen to what we were saying."

Nerian looked concerned, "Are you sure it is the same man?"

"Absolutely!" Finn thought he should add more details. "He also was close to us when we were all on deck as we left the harbor, and just now when I was talking to Mr. Trefaris, he was listening in when Mr.

Trefaris made a joke. When I saw the man laughing, I knew he had been eavesdropping. I confronted him, and he said he overheard because it's a small ship and he has excellent hearing, but he is always close by whenever we are on deck."

"What does he look like?" Micaela was beginning to look uneasy.

"He is tall and trim. Probably close to Nerian's height, but with a much thinner build. He has dark hair and looks like he might be around 40 years old. He moves about as smooth as you and Nerian."

Nerian cleared his throat, "I hadn't noticed him, but we will keep an eye on him for the next couple of days. We aren't doing anything that we have to worry about keeping secret, so it may not matter. We should probably stay together, but if he has bad intentions, I don't think that he would try anything while we are on the ship. Can we agree to that?"

Finn was a little disappointed, and wanted to do something more, but didn't know what. As he looked around, he could see both the girls nodding in agreement. He reluctantly agreed, "Ok, I can agree to that." He knew disappointment was evident in his voice, but he meant what he said.

The rest of the journey was mostly uneventful. The strange man still showed up close to them, but not so close that they could definitively say he was targeting them. Eventually, the journey neared its completion when the port of Nexory came into view. It seemed like a very orderly city from a distance. As they reached the mouth of the harbor, First mate Rheshak called out, "All passengers return to their rooms until we dock. ALL CREW ON DECK!"

The group returned to their cabins while the crew rushed around the deck complying with orders. It didn't take long for the ship to dock.

Finn heard the ship clunk against the pier, and just minutes after, the call went out to disembark. They had packed all of their belongings already, so they adjourned to the deck.

As they stood on deck waiting for their opportunity to descend the gangway, Finn looked out over the city. There weren't as many piers as in Port Yadzul, but the piers were much wider. He noticed a man and a woman that seemed to be watching his group, and he wondered what the next mess was that they were going to get into. As they reached the top of the gangway and started his descent, he looked back and noticed Mr. Creepy arriving on deck from his cabin. He hoped that his fears were imaginary and that he wouldn't be seeing the man anymore.

When they got to the gate at the head of the pier, the man and woman he had noticed earlier approached them. The man was dressed in high quality leather armor and carried a great bow on his back, while the woman looked like some kind of upper class adventurer. The man spoke, "Excuse me, I was wondering if I could ask you a few questions. I promise to be brief."

Finn, Micaela, and Charlotte all looked at Nerian, who after glancing at their expressions replied, "As long as it is brief. How can we help you?"

The man directed them over to a spot a little further away from the pier where they would not be in the way of people and goods being unloaded from the ship. He introduced himself. "I am a Ranger of Isalor. My name is Ewan, and this is Cecilia. We have been sent to find a group of people that fits your description." He turned to Nerian, "Are you a Royal Knight of the Tower of Light?"

Nerian looked uncomfortable, but answered, "Um, yes."

Ewan then pointed to Micaela and raised an eyebrow, "Circus performer?" She looked a bit shocked, but still nodded affirmatively. Then he looked at Charlotte, "Milkmaid?"

She was totally in awe, but looked scared, "How could you...?" She left her question unfinished, but it was evident he was correct.

Finally, he turned to Finn and smiled, "Son of a Duke and jack of all trades." It wasn't really a question, but Finn's face couldn't hide his response. The man continued, "Wonderful! We are all here. Will you please come with me so we can discuss some details in private? Rhondalyn would like to see you."

Chapter Twenty-Six

Robert

As he walked toward the gangway to disembark from the ship, Robert kept an eye on the odd group that he had been watching during the trip. He first encountered them while eating dinner at an Inn in Port Yadzul two days before the ship sailed. He at first thought they were just a strange mismatched group, but they sat near enough to him that he could easily overhear many of the things they said as they ate dinner. It was interesting enough that he used his enhanced senses to listen in better.

He wasn't sure if he was really surprised, but they were seeking Rhondalyn. From their conversation, it didn't seem like any of them actually knew her, but each of them knew enough. He suspected the Royal Knight from the Tower of Light might know more than he let on, but perhaps not. He decided he would keep an eye out for them just in case he ran into them again.

Two days later, much to his surprise, they were ahead of him getting on the same ship he would be traveling on. Since it was a small ship, and they were the only ones who had caught his attention, he tried to stay close enough to listen in. Embarrassingly, he had been found out by the boy when he overheard a joke from a crewman and laughed.

After that, the whole group seemed to be paying more attention to him, and he tried to keep his distance a little more. He had started using his clothes' obfuscation features to get close to them. He still listened in on them using the enhanced senses from the amulet he received, but there were some things he couldn't hear clearly. Worse yet, it seemed their conversations became totally guarded. He figured it wasn't all that important as they didn't seem to know where to go to reach Rhondalyn anyway.

As he walked down the gangway, he noticed the group being met by another man and a woman. They pulled them off to the side and had a few words that he couldn't hear, but he activated his enhanced senses as he approached them. To his surprise and delight, what he heard was the man saying, "Rhondalyn would like to see you."

He did his best to mute his reaction and kept walking past them activating his clothing's obfuscation once he got far enough ahead.. Since they most likely had to follow the same route he did, he figured he would let them catch up to him for a change instead of following them around. He walked up the gradually sloping road to where a cluster of Inns, taverns, and shops were located.

He stepped into one of the Inns behind some other people from the same ship, then activated the full stealth capabilities of his outfit and slipped back outside. The group he was watching was headed into the largest inn of the cluster, directly across from where he was. He quickly summoned the comm-scryer from the ring, which he had to be quick to catch, since it didn't actually land in his hand. He turned it on and tagged the back of the head of the boy just as he went into the inn.

He looked around and tried to decide the best course of action. Ultimately, he needed to know more, and needed to stay in range of the tagged boy for that to happen. It seemed the man in leathers actually knew Rhondalyn, and she knew of this group he had been observing. Robert quickly made his way across the square and slipped down the alley next to the Inn they had entered. He didn't want to enter since it increased the chances of him being discovered.

The comm-scryer could make it through many wards, but often with a reduced amount of signal. He went as close as he could to the part of the building where he suspected any private meeting rooms might be and the turned on the receiver part of the device. There was an image and some static laden sound, but nothing clear. He realized the image was of a wall, likely behind the boy as he sat. Robert recalibrated the comm-scryer to adjust what it was sending.

The image went completely blank, and as he adjusted it, the sound began to be clear enough to understand. He could hear a man's voice, who he thought was probably the man in leathers.

".. able to identify each of us through visions. Here are the ultimate arbiters to verify that you are who she has seen, but finding all four of you together with such distinctive identifiers just about clinches it for me, however, her instructions are clear. I will ask that each of you hold each one of these stones in your hands, one at a time. If it lights up, that is the identifier for you. It won't light up for any other person. If you have held each stone and none of them lights up, then you are not who she foresaw, and I will have to dismiss you."

"Shall we have the ladies start first?"

A girl's voice spoke up. "I'll go." There was some amount of movement in the room. Something clunked on the table.

A smooth sounding woman's voice spoke, "Nope, try the next one."

Another woman's voice with a higher pitch asked "How clearly will they light up?" There was a thunk of something hard being placed on a table.

The leather clad man's voice spoke again. "Oh, you will have no question when they light up." That was followed by another thunk. A male voice said, "Last one."

Suddenly there were several cries of surprise, followed by the first woman's voice. "Congratulations. Welcome to the team."

This pattern continued for a while, and the other three were each welcomed to the team. Robert wished he could see what was happening, but getting sound was the best he could do at the moment. Then the man spoke again. "I have been instructed to guide you to a place high in the mountains where Rhondalyn will meet with us. I don't know everything she wants from us, but she was very specific that each of us six are to be part of something important to deal with the second darkness. I have no idea what exactly."

"I suppose before we adjourn to our rooms, we should take a little more time to introduce ourselves. I will go first."

Robert made note of who each of the six were. The leather clad man was a Ranger of Isalor named Ewan. The first woman, named Cecilia, who had been waiting with Ewan was a former noble from Beaumont and now a professional thief. The other woman was a circus trapeze artist named Micaela, who had been there when Dardanos's Wizards tower had been destroyed.

The big man, named Nerian, was a Royal Knight from the Tower of Light. He reported its destruction and that Evander was now dead. The young man who he had tagged was an illegitimate son of the former Duke of Horshon and a jack of all trades who was named Finn. Lastly, the girl was a milkmaid servant from Ethalor named Charlotte.

"What a strange group of people to stand against the darkness?" Robert thought to himself. The Royal Knight was probably formidable, and perhaps the ranger and thief, but the others didn't make sense at all. "What in the world is Rhondalyn up to?" Two other things that bothered him were the destruction of the Tower of Light and Evander's death. Surely his master wouldn't be involved in that, but nothing else made sense. He decided to reserve judgement, but would certainly be paying attention as things developed.

By the sound of things, they had a meal that they were sharing as they finished up their discussion. Ewan was saying, "Rhondalyn said she would explain more about the stones later, and that for now, I should hold them. We have several weeks of walking to get where we are going."

Nerian offered to hire a coach or buy horses to shorten the trip, but Ewan told him it would probably only save them a day or two, since where they were going was impassable for a carriage, and exceedingly difficult for horses. Nerian still insisted that he hire a coach for that two day gain. After that, the group returned to small talk and discussion of basic provision and supplies needed for their trip. Robert recognized the discussion was over and decided he would be following them from a distance to find Rhondalyn.

He put away his comm-scryer and retrieved the tail tracker. He made sure his stealth was still fully operational and made his way into the Inn.

He got to where he could see what he figured was the door to the room he thought they were in. He waited only a short time until it opened, and he was able to tag the milkmaid so he would be able to follow them.

Then he quietly stepped outside the inn and disabled all but the passive cloaking on his clothes. Since he was following the group, he would need to get his own supplies and probably some kind of horse for the leg they were using a carriage.

Chapter Twenty-Seven

Charlotte

THE CARRIAGE BUMPED HARD over the increasingly rough road. Charlotte held her head where she had banged into the side of the cabin. She had no idea how many times that had happened. She had never ridden in a carriage before she left the manor, and really struggled to see why the rich liked them. She looked across at the ranger Ewan. "How long until we get out and walk."

He looked mercifully at her, "Still another couple hours I'm afraid. Is your head ok?"

"I'll survive." She grumbled. She didn't like that she was so much younger than everyone else. They often treated her like a child, and she hated it. She refused to show weakness if she could help it.

"I'm glad to hear that." Ewan smiled as the carriage bumped hard again, but this time Charlotte managed to keep from banging her head.

The ride continued for a couple more hours, bumping and banging along while the occupants were bruised and jostled inside. Finally, the driver pulled it over, and the doors slowly opened. Even though she hadn't been the closest to the door, Charlotte took no time exiting the hated carriage and was one of the first ones out. A feeling of extreme relief to be done with the painful ride swept over her. She watched the others climb out with obvious soreness. Evidently, she was not the only one who was happy to be back on her feet. The only ones who seemed unaffected were Ewan and Nerian. Even Cecilia seemed to have some soreness, which somewhat surprised Charlotte. Cecilia seemed like she was in as good of shape as the other two and always moved as gracefully as a cat.

Ewan and Nerian assisted the driver in unloading their packs, and then Ewan called everyone together. "Ok, from here on out, the trail can get pretty rough. We will go through a couple of other crossroads, and there is some threat of brigands on the trail, so we need to keep as quiet as possible. We will make camp each day, and everyone will need to take a turn on watch. Nerian and I will share the watch with each of you until we are sure you have learned how to do it right."

Charlotte watched Cecilia out of the corner of her eye. To her, Cecilia was close to as strong and skilled as the knight and the ranger, and certainly fit the part of a rogue. With Ewan's comments, she could see her cringe. Cecilia didn't say anything, but it looked like she didn't appreciate the idea of being babysat by the two professionals.

Ewan continued, "We have a long way to go before we make camp. We will take a break and rest in about two hours. Any questions?" He looked around and nobody seemed to have anything to say. "Ok, let's get going."

Everyone hefted their packs. The new pack Charlotte had to carry was much larger and heavier that what she had originally started with. She thought back on how far she had traveled, and how much had changed in a short amount of time. She supposed that things would likely continue to change. She had met Finn, and really liked him. Micaela felt like the big sister she had never had, and now they had been joined by Ewan and Cecilia. She still was getting to know them, but they seemed like good people to have on her side.

She thought about the storm, and that somehow, this small group was supposed to do something about it. She certainly didn't know what they would be expected to do, or even what they could do. The whole concept felt infinitely bigger than her. Still, the instructions they received had been very specific. It didn't make sense to her that a milkmaid from a small province would be important enough to draw the interest of one of the Halidar. She knew that Rhondalyn knew about her, and wondered why she had attracted the ancient archmage's attention.

She ended up walking behind Finn, making her fourth in line. Ewan led, and Narian brought up the rear. Ewan set an aggressive yet steady pace, but not quite so fast that she couldn't keep up. Several times, she found herself falling behind and had to hustle to catch up. She was beginning to feel like she couldn't keep going when Ewan halted and signaled them toward some rocks at the side of the trail. The trail led through a mature pine forest along rocky hillsides, with enough breaks in the trees to provide for heavy but patchy underbrush.

Ewan motioned for them to stay quiet while he scouted around to make sure they were in the clear. While she waited, she worried about keeping up at this pace. It was brutal and she strangely found herself missing riding in the carriage. She would never have believed that she would miss it so soon.

They all sat and rested while they waited for him to return. After about ten minutes Ewan returned. "It appears we are in the clear." he spoke quietly. "How is everyone holding up?" He looked around at the group, then stopped on Charlotte, "Charlotte, I noticed you falling behind a few times. How are you feeling?"

Charlotte swallowed. She didn't want to be the cause of slowing them down. "I.. I can keep going, but I need to rest a bit more. I think."

"Ok, will twenty minutes be enough? If we wait longer than that, you will probably get muscle cramps."

"Yeah, I think that will be good. How far are we going to try going today?"

"Just one more leg. Maybe a bit further, but there is a good place to camp, and no good alternatives before then." He paused, then suggested, "You may want to try to meditate to improve your recovery. It sometimes helps."

Charlotte was grateful for the extra rest, but felt irritated that she had been singled out. Still, she was going to do her best to use the twenty minutes the best way she could. She didn't know much about meditation, but decided to use the suggestion. She sat on the ground and focused on her breathing and tried to clear her mind from all her worries.

After a minute, she was already feeling improved, and she increased her focus on her recovery. While she made efforts at meditation, she noticed a strange feeling inside her. Somehow, there was some indistinct part of her that felt full of energy. While her muscles were weary and weak, the strange sense of energy and vitality seemed to counter her weariness.

She struggled to tell where the source of energy was located in her body, but could only partly narrow it down. It wasn't in her limbs, but seemed to be at least partly in both her core and her head. She continued to pay attention to it as she tried to meditate, and she noticed that tiny motes of energy would wind their way through parts of her body and then dissolve or dissipate when they reached a place where she was especially sore or tired. The soreness and tiredness was noticeably reduced in a small area afterward.

She continued until Ewan nudged her leg. "It's time to get going." Twenty minutes went by way too fast. She wished she knew what she had been experiencing. Very little conversation happened while they waited. Charlotte wasn't sure if everyone stayed quiet because of exhaustion or out of caution. They soon moved out in the same order they were before. Charlotte noticed that it seemed just a little slower or easier than before, and she didn't start having difficulty keeping up until they had been going for over two hours.

At the point that she began to feel exhausted again, Ewan led them off the trail into a hidden little clearing. He again motioned for them to stay there while he scouted out the surroundings. He didn't return for twenty minutes this time. Once he returned, he directed her and Finn to dig a deep fire pit, while the others set up tents and prepared a meal.

Setting up camp was more difficult than she expected. Ewan made them go back twice and dig the fire pit deeper before he was satisfied. Once all the other work was done, they waited while Ewan made food. Finn somehow convinced him to let him help, but Ewan wouldn't let the others help. While they waited, Charlotte noticed that Cecilia kept looking at her. She wasn't sure what to make of it. Eventually, Cecilia got up and walked over to sit next to her.

"Hi," Charlotte decided to be proactive in starting whatever conversation was going to happen. She wasn't sure what Cecilia wanted, but her intensity made Charlotte nervous.

Cecilia looked over, and Charlotte tried to figure out what her look meant, "I think I heard that you went through Beaumont. Is that correct?"

Charlotte continued to try and figure out what Cecilia wanted, but came up with nothing, so she just went with light and simple. "Uh, yeah, I did. About four days before I got to Finn's town. He lived in Mijople. Anyway, what do you want to know about it?"

Cecilia seemed nervous or uncertain, which was out of character. "What were things like when you were there?"

Charlotte thought back. "It was a big city. Probably the biggest I had been to at that point. There were a lot of refugees trying to get in. The people were proud and when I tried to warn them about the darkness, they either mocked me or dismissed what I said. They were very confident that they would be fine in Beaumont. One place gave me some stale bread, and then I passed through to the other side of the city where I did some work for a dairy farm for some supplies, and left as soon as I had been paid."

Cecilia's troubled countenance was unsettling, "So, you weren't there when the darkness got there?"

Charlotte decided to just state things as directly as she could, "No, but some horse riders caught up with me four days later and they talked about what happened. They said the castle had exploded and the whole city was destroyed. I don't know how much they may have exaggerated, but I did talk with a couple other people later who verified their story." As Charlotte talked, she could see a certain dark look pass over Cecilia's face.

Cecilia began breathing hard like she was panicking. Then she burst into tears. It drew the attention of the others in the camp. As she recognized the attention she was getting, she cryingly stumbled through an explanation, ""I'm sorry! ... I don't even know why I'm crying. ... I hated it there. ... They never loved me and I never wanted to go back. Why am I even crying?" She continued to cry for a while, but was able to keep the sound of her sobs reduced.

Charlotte had no idea what to do, but she wanted to comfort Cecilia, so she reached over and put her hand on her back. "I don't know what you are feeling, but we are here for you."

Cecilia had buried her face in her hands. When Charlotte's hand touched her back, she curled into herself and wept harder. Charlotte had no idea what was going on. She looked over as she felt Finn sit down next to her. He whispered, "What did you say to her?"

She whispered back, still expecting Cecilia to hear her, "Nothing! I just told her what I saw and heard about Beaumont. I don't know what this is all about."

"Hmm," Finn was obviously perplexed. The two just sat together while Charlotte tried to comfort Cecilia. The crying didn't make sense, and she obviously didn't have enough perspective to understand why it impacted Cecilia that way. After a few minutes, Ewan announced the food was ready. He looked over at the group with a confused look as he made the announcement. Finn got up, "I'll bring you some." He returned a short time later with food for both Charlotte and Cecilia.

"Thank you," Charlotte murmured. Cecilia must have been very hungry because she stopped crying and accepted the food with a nod and began eating in silence. No one spoke as they all ate.

Ewan finished first, and watched as everyone else ate without speaking. Finally, as Cecilia finished her food, Ewan asked, "Cecilia, are you ok?"

The rogue looked uneasy as she looked around at everyone. "Yeah. I'll ... I'll be ok. I just... I learned what happened to Beaumont, which is where I grew up." She paused, but when no one else spoke, she continued. "I didn't think it would affect me much. I guess learning that my parent's castle exploded and that they and my siblings are probably dead, it hit me harder than I expected. I suddenly felt like everything in my past was concluded whether I wanted it to be or not. I can't go back anymore, even if I wanted to. The choice was taken from me. I haven't cried hard since long before I ran away years ago. I'm sorry."

Ewan nodded, "It's ok. Each of us will probably have to deal with stuff from our own pasts in the coming days, and some of that could be painful. I don't condemn you for having feelings. If anything, it shows depth of character."

"Um... Thank you," Cecilia answered quietly. She turned away and Charlotte could tell she wanted to be by herself, so she left her alone.

Charlotte scooted a little closer to Finn, hoping to trigger a change in conversation. "How did things go for you today?" she asked. He looked up, apparently not expecting the question.

"Oh, uh. It went ok. I have done a lot of hunting and traveling in the past so this wasn't all that different, other than setting up camp. Never had to worry about camp security before."

She smiled, thinking about their task in setting up camp. "We did get the fire pit dug eventually." He smiled somewhat weakly.

"Yeah.." he began but then was interrupted by Nerian.

"Finn," the big man called out. "We have first watch. Come on."

Finn turned to her and shrugged apologetically. "Sorry, I have to go." She watched him head off, Nerian already instructing him. As she watched, she thought about the day and anticipated what the next several days would be like. She felt a bit uneasy, but wasn't sure why. She also tried to sort out how she felt about Finn. They hadn't really had any conversations about each other's feelings, and despite him being very good looking and always treating her with complete respect, she wasn't sure if what she felt for him was realistic. She did like him to an extent, but it didn't seem that he was interested in anything more than being friends.

The more she thought about it, the more she felt confused. She was also exhausted and finally decided to head to bed. She got up and walked to her tent. As she climbed into bed, she could tell things were settling down inside.

Chapter Twenty-Eight

Robert

It hadn't taken a long time to catch up with the group, but it was a constant effort to stay unobserved, especially by that pesky ranger. Robert watched the group through his long range flying scryer. He didn't dare get too close with the magically generated remote sensor, called the gnat. He was sure that at least two of the group could sense close proximity scrying, so he made sure the gnat stayed at a far distance. The group had settled down for the night, with two on watch. He could tell that the royal guard was training the boy. The guard probably had a way to sense close scrying, so he maintained its distance.

Robert hadn't been able to detect anything magical in the environment around them yet with the analyzer, but he couldn't get close enough to check for smaller low power devices in close proximity to them, but from what he had overheard earlier, they were still weeks away from their destination, and he probably wouldn't have to start worrying about more advanced magics until they got much closer.

Out of curiosity, Robert tried to look ahead on the trail they were following. As he looked, he could see a large camp about a day ahead of the group where their trail crossed the first road that they would come to. It was a much larger camp, but with some kind of wards keeping him from getting too close.

From what he could tell, it looked like it could be a brigand camp. *Hmm, we can't have those brigands keeping the group from getting to Rhondalyn. That would make it much harder to find her.* He thought. He scried the area around the brigands. He was able to see where they observed the trail and road in each direction, as well as see that they had set up multiple ambush sites on each route.

There didn't seem to be any way around what he thought of as the brigands so he would have to do something about them. Unfortunately, the trail they followed was in a narrow canyon with no way to pass the little group that he was tailing without risking detection by that pesky ranger. *I will just have to follow a little closer when they start getting close. My horse can't go much further on this trail, anyway.*

Robert activated camp and proximity wards and began compressed meditation, allowing him to fully rejuvenate and be fully rested in half the time that sleeping would take. He also made sure to keep a small degree of awareness of the world around him in case something triggered his wards. He was up well before dawn and began a slow careful approach toward the group, making sure to stay unobserved. Occasionally, he would stop and distance scry them, looking down on them from high in the sky.

The group was up fairly early, and headed out almost immediately, eating old trail rations for breakfast as they started. They kept to the same order, with the knight still bringing up the rear. He seemed skilled at observation, but not nearly so frustratingly good as the ranger. Robert figured he could get fairly close to them before they reached the ambush point. He couldn't stop the ambush, but he wanted to be there in case it was something the group couldn't handle. Without more information on their skills and those of the brigands, it was nearly impossible to predict how it would go.

They had taken their second break only about two miles from the ambush point, and as usual, the ranger had gone to check everything. Robert had barely evaded detection. He used the break to check the brigands with his gnat and noticed a place where he might be able to get the drop on one of the groups of ambushing brigands.

They were well set up and obviously aware they had victims about to fall into their trap. The brigands looked and acted like they had been professional soldiers in the past and more recently had taken to banditry. From what he could tell, the brigands didn't plan on leaving their victims alive. He was definitely going to have to do something about them.

He hoped the ranger would be able to keep the whole group from getting killed right off. As soon as the group started moving again, Robert double-timed it to catch up before they were ambushed. He needed to be close in order to stop the first group of ambushing brigands while staying unobserved, but he had to time it just right, and still needed a fair amount of luck for things to go just right.

Robert caught up and was close enough to the group that he occasionally could see the knight at the rear through the trees and around rocks. He activated his stealth features on his clothes to keep the chances of being discovered low. They were about a quarter mile away from the ambush site when he left the trail and raced to get into a position on the cliffs above one of the groups of brigands. He got there and quickly threw a container of knockout gas into the middle of the brigands and started down the cliff behind them. There were four of them, and three quickly went down.

The fourth began to panic, looking around for the cause of his comrades going down. After looking around and not seeing anything, a hard angry look appeared on his face, and he turned back to where he would see the approaching victims once they passed the retreat cutoff. As soon as he could see the first of them, he raised his crossbow. It appeared to be a heavy duty model. Once the last of the group appeared, he fired at the knight, who was the last one to appear. The bolt was of a type to piece armor, which it did, though not as well it was supposed to.

The knight dropped to the ground with a shout of alarm and pain, and the group took what shelter they could. The two other groups of brigands that were waiting to begin the ambush had not expected this one to attack so early, and Robert could see that they were thrown off their plan. Robert could hear some of them cursing from the other groups.

The brigand had shot a few more bolts at the little group while Robert moved into position on a ledge behind him. He was getting ready to shoot again as Robert made a diving roll from the ledge and stopped behind the irate brigand. He rolled and came up, pricking the neck of the brigand's neck with the paralysis dagger, instantly paralyzing him.

Robert could hear the ranger yelling, "Finn! Guard the women!" Robert looked through a small gap in the rocks that allowed the brigands to see their victims. The boy moved to a position where he could protect the women, but it was obvious that he didn't know what he was doing. The ranger had rushed to the knight and was attempting to treat his wound.

Robert looked down through what was essentially a natural window of rocks and trees that formed a notch that was well hidden but allowed for seeing the victims and the other groups positions. He could see part of each of the other two groups of brigands. He picked up the crossbow the paralyzed brigand had used and quickly loosed two bolts, one at each of the other groups.

There was a lot of incoherent shouting, and it appeared he had hit someone in each group. He then stepped away from the window as a couple of bolts were returned through it from each of the groups. He didn't think they had actually seen him, and it seemed from the way they were cursing that they assumed that the brigands in his position were double crossing them.

That was just about perfect. He decided he probably needed to move, and brought out his small crossbow and used the climbing rope bolt to quickly ascend back to the ledge above him. He made sure to keep all his stealth enhancements on his clothes going. He looked out to the next group of brigands. He knew it was a long shot, but he lobbed a smoke bomb into the nearer of the two groups of brigands. It landed perfectly. It wouldn't harm them for long, but would give away their position and make it hard for them to see and breathe.

The brigands he threw the smoke bomb at scrambled from their hidden position into the clearing where the ambush was supposed to happen. The ranger quickly put an arrow into the chest of the first one, and then drew a pair of long daggers and moved almost right among the brigands. That group was larger, with six or seven from what Robert could tell. The ranger was able to take down two more before the others got their bearings. They formed up quickly, and Robert was now sure they were dealing with former or current soldiers.

Soon the other group of brigands came into view far up the trail. It was by far the largest, with nearly twenty brigands. By that time, the knight was back on his feet, but he held his sword arm close to his side and moved slowly. He had seen the larger approaching group and shouted a warning. His group quickly moved to make a retreat, with him trying to shepherd the others toward the rear. The thief girl was not having any of it. She skirted around him and went to join the ranger who was still fighting the remaining four brigands from the second group, drawing knives and a dagger.

The knight quickly directed the other three to the rear. With the help of the thief, the ranger was able to incapacitate two of the four he was facing, and the other two ran to join the larger group that was approaching. The thief and the ranger apparently decided it wasn't a good idea to try to face that many opponents and retreated to join the others. They could only go so far before they reached a point where they were trapped by a rockfall the brigands had triggered.

The remaining brigands had split in two groups and one of those had taken a shortcut to block the retreat of their victims. Now that the group was trapped, they repositioned to try to defend better. Suddenly the acrobat was seemingly flying up the side of the mountain. Robert was impressed. She was carrying a rope which she tied off on a tree and threw the other end down to the group below. The others quickly ascended, and when the brigands tried to follow, the knight, using his off hand, cut the rope with his sword.

Robert could tell they wouldn't get away without help. There really wasn't anywhere for them to go, but they had a few moments of relief. They were badly outnumbered, and their best fighter was injured and mostly out of commission. Robert didn't want to reveal himself, but he needed this group to be able to continue their journey so he could find Rhondalyn. The group was trying to work their way along the cliff sides and steep embankments of the narrow canyon above the brigands.

Robert began preparations to deal with the brigands. Once the little group of travelers was out of sight, he would act. The group moved around a bend so they couldn't see the brigands, but Robert knew it was only a matter of time before the brigands caught them. It was time to take care of the issue. He started taking various items from his storage ring.

He used a poison gas bomb and hit the group of brigands that had cut off the retreat. The wind was blowing down the canyon and he managed to get eight of the ten brigands in the group. He used poison bolts from his crossbow to get the other two. That left twelve more, if he had counted correctly, and they had broken into two smaller groups. One was trying to stay below their victims on the trail, and the other had moved further up the trail. Robert wasn't sure what that group was intending, but he decided need to speed up his intervention.

He repowered his full stealth mode on his clothes and raced up the trail behind the first group. They were not being very quiet which gave him a chance to get close. As he did, he counted eight more in this group, but they were too spread out to use a gas bomb on. He pulled out his crossbow and loaded up the poison bolts.

While he did so, he heard one of the brigands say that the other group had returned to camp to get reinforcements. He was going to have to take out all the brigands assuming he survived. He cursed silently and readied his paralytic dagger in his off hand as he raised his crossbow to fire. He managed to hit two before the others became aware they were under attack. He took out three more before they figured out where he was. With how fast the poison acted, the five he had hit were incapacitated by that point.

Just then he heard a commotion above him. It seemed one of the adventuring party members had lost their footing and was sliding down the cliffs. He ran forward, and one of the brigands had been able to pinpoint his approximate location, even with his stealth running at full power. The man tried to bisect him with a sword, but Robert was able to easily dodge, then slammed into him and threw him from the trail. Before the man could climb back up, Robert used the paralytic dagger to stun the other two. When the last brigand climbed back up onto the trail, Robert stabbed him as well and kicked him back off the trail.

Chapter Twenty-Nine

Charlotte

Charlotte was in a panic. They had escaped, but the only paths they could follow all led them back to where they had been ambushed. Nerian was injured, and even though Ewan had some healing potions, it would be a while before he was healed enough to fight properly. Somehow, neither Ewan or Cecilia had been injured fighting the brigands, but the bigger group now had them trapped. There were just too many to deal with, even if Nerian was healed.

Micaela had managed to give them a reprieve, but she knew the brigands would soon catch up to them. Behind them led only to a point on the cliffs above where some of the brigands were trying to improvise a way to climb up after them. It was a total dead end. Charlotte looked around desperately, trying to find some option they had missed.

Ahead of them was an impossibly narrow broken shelf that crossed the cliffside. It had many gaps where they would have to jump from shelf section to shelf section. If they missed, they might be able to slide, but it would take them almost to the bottom where more brigands were waiting on the trail. Even if they managed to stop or land without dying, they would be in easy reach of the brigand's weapons.

Micaela's casual confidence was the only thing reassuring Charlotte at that point. All six of them were stuck on a narrow ledge along the middle of a cliff. There was no way for them to go up, and going down would deliver them into the hands of people she was sure wanted to kill them. She watched nervously as Micaela moved to the far end of the ledge. Charlotte had no idea how she could act so calm.

Micaela went right up to the end of the ledge and jumped, landing with grace. She made it seem so easy. She acted like it was no bigger thing than going for a walk in a garden. Micaela didn't even stop, but maintained her momentum as she jumped from mini shelf to foothold to shelf until she finally reached a point that was big enough for them all to rest, then signaled them to follow.

Next went Cecilia. She looked maybe a little nervous, but mostly just focused. She made the first jump and moved along without too much problem. She landed next to Micaela and moved around her to where she could rest. Charlotte thought she saw her shiver just for a moment, but couldn't be sure.

Finn went next. Charlotte worried that he might have a hard time with it. He looked much more nervous than Cecilia, perhaps almost as nervous as Charlotte felt. At one point, his foot slipped, and he started to fall, but miraculously caught on to the next foothold with his hands and was able to pull himself up. He made it the rest of the way without issue. Charlotte could see he was relieved, but visibly shaken.

Then it was her turn. For just a brief moment, the image of her foot sliding on debris and then of her sliding down the cliff face flashed before her eyes. There was a feeling of panic, but then it was quickly replaced by calmness. She had no idea what that was about. How could she feel calm about falling down the cliff? Her anxiety kicked up and fear filled her so much that her legs started shaking.

Charlotte swallowed hard and tried to force down her fear. She had never liked heights and while strong, she had never considered herself nimble. She did her best to calm herself and slowly made her way out on the narrow ledge, leaning into the cliffside. She tried to meditate in the moment and her legs stilled, allowing her to continue.

When she reached the first gap, she paused briefly, but made herself move forward. She positioned her feet in the best way she could and leapt, barely landing on the next section leaning into the cliff harder, trying not to let her panic overwhelm her again.

Once she calmed down enough, she again began to work her way along that section of ledge. Again she came to a gap. The vision of her sliding down the cliff flashed in her vision again, but more vividly. The feeling of calm and that everything would work out came again. This one was slightly further, but she felt she had more of a feel for how to do it. She felt feelings of trust. She carefully positioned her feet, and leaned into the jump. She leapt again. Her foot landed and she immediately felt relief, but then her foot started to slide on debris toward the edge.

Her other foot was hanging out over space and there was nothing to grab with her hands. It seemed like time froze but her foot kept sliding to the edge. She started to scream as her foot slid off, but a feeling of warning cut it off before it actually emerged from her throat. She scrambled for a handhold and for a moment caught a piece of rock but it broke off as she slid past the ledge.

There was a slight slope to the cliff side, causing her to slide down it instead of just falling. She tried to dig in with her calloused hands and the rock she held in her hand. Eventually the rock caught, and she was able to stop her slide from going any further.

With her eyes wide in fear, she looked around her. Just within reach of her foot was a knob of rock that might have been big enough to get onto. She reached out with her foot, trying to be careful not to dislodge her tenuous hold. Eventually she was able to get onto the knob.

From on top of the knob, she realized that if she leaned out just a tiny bit, she would be able to see the brigands below her. The thought of leaning out came with a strong feeling of danger. She realized that then the brigands would be able to see her too. The brigands hadn't been able to see where they were on the ledge to target them with their crossbows because the slight slope of the cliff face blocked their view.

She didn't know what to do. She looked up and could see Micaela's head peek over the edge of the ledge they were on. She could see both relief and worry. Charlotte could understand, as she was feeling much the same. If the brigands weren't below, she might be able to survive the drop without being totally crippled. But they were there and she could hear them. They would probably kill her, or worse. What could she, or they, or anyone do? She didn't know.

She heard the sound of movement below change and the feeling of calm came again. She decided to peek over the edge and see what was happening, and the calm feeling didn't go away. She got a good grip on some protruding rocks, and after making sure they weren't going to come loose, leaned out to see what she could. On the trail below, she saw a brigand fly off the far edge of the trail, crash into a tree, and collapse on the ground. What? She thought, confusion reigning supreme, What is going on?

She leaned back in, and got a better grip, then leaned out again. Below her lay a bunch of brigands, but they were either dead or unconscious, she looked up the trail towards where they were ambushed. A man was there. He looked familiar, but at that moment, she had trouble remembering where she had seen him. He was not dressed like a brigand. He turned and looked directly at her and smiled. It was a friendly smile. Then he put his finger to his lips and then directed her to drop to the ground and go the direction he was going in, then he turned and sped off.

She leaned back into the cliff. Micaela was looking down at her again. She tried to signal what she saw. She pointed down below her, and tried to indicate by hand signal that all the brigands were dead. Then she signaled that they should go the direction the man went, which was the direction they were already going.

From her reaction, it was obvious that Micaela didn't understand. Charlotte whistled three chirps like a bird. Charlotte could tell that Micaela heard her, but guessed she didn't understand. Then Charlotte flipped around and started lowering herself down the cliff.

As she got over the knob she had been sitting on, she could see to the one side there were some hand holds that would help her work her way down a bit more before she had to drop to the trail below. It only took her a couple of minutes before she reached a point where she felt comfortable dropping the rest of the way. She just had to make sure she had a good landing and didn't sprain an ankle or something like that.

She had to work her courage up again, then she dropped, aiming for a smoother section of trail. She landed and collapsed to the side and tried to roll. It didn't go all that well, but she managed to not get too hurt. Then she whistled three times like a bird again. She heard a responding call, and she decided it was time to move forward.

She had to go between all the brigands on the ground, and still didn't know if they were dead or unconscious. She did her best not to freak out. She had no idea what had happened, or who the man was. Walking through the bodies was pretty creepy. Then one of them started to stir. Her whole body tensed, and she began to look around in panic. He could easily overpower her if he became conscious.

Charlotte figured she had to do something. She saw a club one of them had dropped so she reached for it. The brigand continued to move and she thought it would only be seconds before he came to. She gritted her teeth and swung the club, clobbering him over the head. He stopped moving. She was completely freaked out and she ran. She didn't know if she had killed him, and she wasn't sure if she cared. Once past the downed brigands, she slowed and carefully worked her way up the trail, trying to keep an eye out for more brigands.

When she reached the place where they had been ambushed, her blood was pounding in her ears and she carefully moved forward. There were still a few brigand corpses there from the earlier skirmish. She moved on, sure she would get shot by an arrow or crossbow bolt, but nothing happened. She continued moving forward. Since the trail was still rising, it would soon reach the level of the cliffs her companions were on.

Once she got where the rise of the trail met the level of the ledge, there was yet another group of brigands on the ground. Many of them were definitely dead, but some might only be unconscious. She poked at some of them with her club, but none of them were moving. She decided to start working her way down the ledge toward her companions. She didn't want to fall again, but she had already survived. Soon she came around a bend and saw her companions slowly working their way toward her. She waved and they saw her. Micaela worked her way forward in a couple of minutes.

"What happened?" Micaela whispered when she got close enough.

"There was a man that took out all the brigands. I don't know how, just that he saw me and directed me where to climb down." Charlotte tried to explain what she saw. "Some of them aren't dead, but a lot of them are. I have a club that I found back there that I used to knock one of them out again. If anyone is having trouble, they might be able to drop down to the trail now that it is safe." She then realized she wasn't sure of it. "I mean, I think it's safe. Maybe?"

Ewan ended up helping slide Nerian back down to the trail using what short piece of rope they had retained. Everyone else made their way along the ledge until they reached where it met the trail. Once there, they looked at the downed brigands. There were a few that were not dead, but Cecilia, Nerian, and Ewan fixed that issue quickly. They went back down the trail to make sure there were no more brigands that might recover and come back and cause them more trouble.

Once they were all back together, Ewan asked for details. "Tell me about this man that took out the brigands."

"He was dressed in plain dark clothing, tall, and had a nice smile." Suddenly something flashed in her memory. "Oh.. Oh! I think it was the man from the boat! The one Finn didn't like."

"WHAT?!" exclaimed Finn. "No, No! That guy was creepy! And if he is here, it only proves that he was spying on us!"

Charlotte didn't like how Finn was reacting, and tried to provide a different point of view, "Maybe he was watching us, but, what if he was there to protect us?" She realized she was arguing, and felt angry toward Finn. She had been worried before when she thought he might fall, but now she was irritated. Perhaps he wasn't quite as all around amazing as she had thought him to be.

Nerian disagreed with her, not really buying her idea. "Well," he pointed at his shoulder, "He sure took his time taking care of things." Charlotte looked at Nerian's wounded shoulder and grimaced. She thought perhaps she had upset him.

Ewan was also not happy. "And it looks like he was trailing us this whole time, even with me doing thorough sweeps every time we stopped or camped. I have never seen anyone who could evade my sweeps." Charlotte wasn't quite sure why Ewan was so upset, but it seemed like a big deal to him.

Cecilia laughed briefly, "That makes sense, dummy. If they evaded your sweeps, then of course you wouldn't see them." She grinned at her joke, but Ewan huffed and turned away. Charlotte tried to hide her grin at Cecilia's joke. Cecilia smiled at her and winked conspiratorially.

Micaela interrupted everyone, "Um, I don't mean to spoil your fun, but, perhaps we should see if the brigands have anything that would be helpful for us. There also might still be more live brigands somewhere, and the mysterious man is still out there, and we don't know what he wants. This" she gestured around them, "does make me feel like perhaps he isn't an immediate problem, though."

Ewan had turned back to the group. He didn't look happy, "Yeah, you're probably right. Let's check for useful supplies, but let's try to keep quiet. Then we will try to figure out what to do from there." Everyone grumbled in agreement and started moving.

Chapter Thirty

Finn

Finn tossed the load of equipment into the large pile that was forming. Just another couple of loads. They had been cleaning up after the slain brigands for over two hours. Finn could tell that Ewan was not happy, but it seemed he was upset about more than just the delay the attack had caused.

At first, it seemed that he was upset that the mysterious man was somehow able to evade his sweeps, but he seemed to have gotten more unhappy as they discovered the extent of the brigand camp. The brigands had multiple ambush sites set up on both parts of the trail and both directions of the road that traversed the low pass they were in.

The brigands in all four areas were dead or incapacitated, presumably by the mysterious man. It was evident that the man could easily have taken out their whole group, since he had taken out almost a hundred well trained and experienced brigands. Charlotte was certain it was the man from the boat, but Finn didn't want to believe that. If it was that man, then perhaps Charlotte was also right that he was protecting them. The whole thing still felt off to Finn.

He returned to his tasks. He was charged with gathering all the armor and weapons from the brigands and bringing it back to their main camp. He had two more ambush points to gather from. Charlotte and Micaela were reconfiguring their supplies, switching out anything that they found improvements for. Finn, Micaela, and Charlotte now had some light armor, and better weapons. Even Nerian had found a few small items to augment his already full kit.

Finn noticed that there were frequent looks passing back and forth between Ewan and Nerian. They seemed ill at ease, and something about the situation greatly disturbed them, but he didn't think they actually knew much more than he did. After another hour, all their tasks were done, but with the attacks and the cleanup afterward, they were getting close to sundown. Ewan had announced that they were going to camp right there in the brigand headquarters.

Finn worried that camping right there might be asking for trouble, but he seemed to be the only one who was concerned. As everyone began to settle down from the busy day, Ewan informed them that he had to go alert the local Rangers lodge about the brigands and the equipment. He promised to return as soon as he could, and then headed off down the road.

Nerian and Ceclia would be training each of them during their watch shifts, and would swap out half way through the second of three watches. Finn drew the second watch, which was the one he least preferred, but he committed to doing his duty. He climbed in his bed and did his best to sleep.

At first, he thought he wasn't going to be able to sleep because of the intensity of what had happened, but soon found himself being roused by Charlotte, who had drawn the first watch. He nodded and got up, quickly dressing, and made his way out to see where Nerian was. Charlotte wasted no time in heading to her own bed. As he watched her go, he pondered his feelings. Every time he decided he wasn't interested, he found himself being drawn back to her. It made him feel unsteady, which was unusual for him.

Nerian was slowly patrolling around the tree line and made a low whistle to get Finn's attention. Finn approached him, doing his best to monitor the area around them. "Ewan isn't back yet?" Finn guessed in a whisper. Nerian shook his head. Finn observed Nerian for a minute. It seemed that his arm and shoulder that had been injured in the attack was healing very rapidly and Nerian was able to move about with ease. Finn doubted he would be able to recover so well. Nerian must be tougher than Finn had originally thought. Either that, or had some kind of healing enhancement skill or enchantment somewhere in his equipment.

After several passes around the camp, they both retreated closer to the center. They stayed out of the light to avoid ruining their night vision. Finn observed, "So, both you and Ewan seem pretty disturbed at all of this." He gestured to the brigand camp. "What's the big issue?"

Nerian looked at him, barely visible in the darkness. "These brigands were highly trained soldiers. They might actually be brigands, or perhaps one kingdom sent them on a mission to pose as brigands to pressure another." Finn nodded, though he wasn't quite following why some shady local politics would be so concerning. Nerian continued, "The most disturbing part to me is that no one should have been able to just take them out single handedly. I have no idea who this mysterious man is, but what he seems to have done should not be possible."

Finn furrowed his brow, "So, if it's impossible, what else could explain what happened?"

Nerian frowned for a few seconds before answering. "That's just it. We have been through it several times, and we can't seem to come up with another plausible scenario that fits what we have seen. There are only 1 set of footprints that don't match us or the brigands.

"Also, the injuries to the brigands were highly unusual. It looked like small crossbow bolts for some, others were just pricks to their skin. Many seemed to have inhaled something that either killed or incapacitated them. Whoever this mysterious man is, it seems he is very highly skilled in warfare and a powerful mage. Typically, we would know about someone like that through reputation, and even then, to reach the level of proficiency they must have, it would take hundreds of years."

Finn wasn't sure if he was really following as it sounded confusing, but he still said, "Ok, I see why that's concerning." They both went back to patrolling, and a little before the middle of the watch, they heard someone or something approaching the camp. Nerian drew his sword and stepped into the deeper shadows, while Finn took up a more visible position holding his newly acquired crossbow loaded at the ready.

The sounds continued to approach and then Ewan stepped into the light. "Good evening, Finn," He said, being deliberately obvious to let him know who was approaching. "Who is on watch with you?"

"I am." Nerian stepped out of the shadows close behind where Ewan was standing. Ewan didn't even jump, but nodded and smiled, as though he knew that was going to happen ahead of time. He could tell that Nerian was slightly annoyed that he hadn't surprised Ewan.

"Well, good," he said. "There will be some of the local rangers showing up before dawn. Go ahead and wake Cecilia and you can retire, Nerian. You still have healing to do and rest will help. I will keep Finn company in the meantime."

"Ok," Nerian responded, then headed off towards where Cecilia was sleeping.

Finn moved to where Ewan had settled down, just outside of the firelight. "Nerian told me why you and he are both nervous about all this. What does it mean for us?"

Ewan looked up at him, his head movement barely perceptible in the darkness, "I suppose that is one of the most concerning parts. We don't really know what it could mean for us. This sort of thing should not be possible, and yet it was. That means someone extremely powerful is involved in our business. We know they are not one of the Halidar, since all the Halidar are all accounted for, but the power and skill level is high enough that I would think it was one of them if I didn't know better."

"I guess we'll have to ask Rhondalyn about it?" Finn didn't know what else they could do.

Ewan was quiet for a bit and answered, "We'll certainly tell her about it, but there will be some local rangers here before morning to investigate. I don't know if they will find any answers, but we will be able to continue our journey and let more qualified people deal with it."

At that point, Cecilia joined them. Ewan gave them instructions. "I am going to rest here. I won't be fully asleep, but I need rest for tomorrow.

If you can do a sweep around the perimeter every fifteen minutes, that should be good."

Cecilia nodded and turned to Finn as Ewan leaned back against a rock and closed his eyes. "Finn, we will take turns. After each sweep, I want you to then explain everything you notice, including what you should have noticed and didn't. This is still training."

Finn started his rounds, and then returned to Cecilia, who had moved a short distance away from Ewan so they didn't disturb him. Finn had thought he was getting pretty good at doing the watch, but Cecilia quickly corrected that misconception. He had no idea how much he could be aware of in walking around a camp at night, but apparently, he needed to seriously up his observation skills. The next couple of hours went by the same way. He knew he was doing better each round, but each time she came up with dozens of things he hadn't noticed, or that should have been there and weren't.

Eventually, it was time to wake Micaela for her turn at the watch. He soon returned to his bed and fell asleep again. He awoke a little before dawn to unfamiliar voices in the camp. He got up and dressed. The sky was light enough to see around the camp, and color was just beginning to seep back into the world. There were four unfamiliar men talking with Ewan. They were dressed almost the same as him with similar equipment. Each of their outfits was unique, but they certainly followed the same theme.

Ewan was showing them what had been found and explaining what had happened. They mostly listened, but asked occasional questions. Finn decided not to intrude, so instead he walked over to where Micaela and Cecilia had begun preparing breakfast. "How long have they been here?"

Cecilia looked up at him. He wasn't sure if he surprised her or not, but her reaction was more sudden than usual. She looked over at the men and then back at him, "They got here maybe twenty minutes ago. Ewan was asleep or something, but he woke up right as they stepped into camp. Sometimes his awareness is kind of creepy."

"I think that is part of what had him and Nerian so freaked out. They have trouble imagining someone who can stay outside his awareness." Finn smiled as Cecilia scowled.

"I can understand that. I thought my skills were really high, but Ewan's skills are far beyond mine. If someone is that far beyond him... well, that gets into really frightening territory." Cecilia was normally fairly serious, but she spoke with even greater gravity. It made Finn even more unsettled than he already was.

No one spoke again while they finished preparing breakfast. They made sure they had enough extra for their guests. Soon it was ready. Finn went to check and make sure Charlotte and Nerian were both awake and ready for breakfast. The rangers soon joined them in eating. After breakfast, the team quickly finished packing up everything they were taking with them, and gathered while Ewan addressed them.

"These local rangers will take care of everything here. We need to move on. I am going to ask Cecilia to act as rear guard to reduce the load on Nerian while he heals. We are going to continue on the same trail until we get to the next road. From there, we will follow the road through two towns before we start on a trail into the high mountains. Any questions?"

Nerian didn't like the change, "I don't think it is necessary to change things up. I am already mostly healed."

Ewan pursed his lips in thought for a moment and then answered. "Well, when we get to Rhondalyn, you can register the complaint and petition to be in charge. For now, I have to make the hard calls, and this is the call I am making. I need you healthy in case we run into anything like this mess. Can you accept that?"

Nerian frowned, "Yeah." Finn could tell he still wasn't happy with it, but he would go along with it. The change put Finn right behind Ewan. He would need to do his best to not get distracted or fall behind.

They headed out, and Finn felt a persistent worry that they would run into something else, but nothing else delayed them. They made camp when it was almost dark, and were up early the next morning. After three days, they reached the road Ewan had mentioned. They made better time then and after two days reached the first town. They had a lot of coin that they had claimed from the brigand camp, so they each got their own room in one of the Inns.

Nerian and Ewan talked that evening and agreed to try to make up some time by taking a coach to the next town. The next morning, they quickly ate breakfast at the Inn and then loaded up in the coach that Nerian had hired. The coach cut a whole two days off their trip, and they didn't even stop in the next town, but went half a day past it to where their next trail branched off the road.

From that point, they started switching up their formation a bit more. Finn even got to be the rear guard for one leg. He hadn't realized how exhausting it was to have to keep his awareness constantly on everything around and behind him. On another day, he heard Ewan call out ahead of them, and they soon encountered another ranger. It seemed that it was someone from Ewan's ranger lodge, so they took a few minutes discussing things privately before they were off again.

Gradually, they began to climb up into the high mountains. The nights had become very cold, and even the days did not feel warm. Ewan said that it was spring and had warmed a great deal and the truly cold period had passed. Finn was sure he never wanted to experience the truly cold period. Finally, they entered a huge valley nestled among the peaks of the High Reach Mountains.

Chapter Thirty-One

Micaela

The valley was beautiful. Ewan looked greatly relieved and had them start camp while he headed out for his sweep. His sweep was longer than usual and they were done setting up camp before he returned. When he got back, he informed them they would be resting for twelve hours that night and they would rotate everyone through solo watches. Before the watches started, they gathered for dinner.

While eating, Ewan stood and addressed everyone, "I want to commend you all on your journey. It has been very rough at times and I have heard very little complaining. For those of you who have never done this kind of thing before, you have done well in learning a lot of new skills, and I can tell that all of us have gotten stronger. Tomorrow will be the last day of our journey. There is no trail where we are going, and we want to make sure we don't leave one."

"Tomorrow may be both one of the easiest and hardest days so far. You should all get some extra rest, which is why we have twelve hours of watch. Everyone hopefully should get the chance of about ten hours of sleep. I will take the last watch and prepare a special breakfast for everyone."

Charlotte spoke up, "What will happen tomorrow, and where are we going?"

"I'm not going to tell you where we are going yet. As far as what will happen when we get there, I'm not really sure, but I am confident that there are good things in our near future." Ewan smiled big in a way that let them all know the conversation was over.

Micaela drew the first watch, which allowed her to see more of the valley as a brilliant sunset filled the sky. She was having a hard time paying attention due to her distraction from the beauty around her. It even seemed a little less cold in the valley. It soon grew very dark, and her watch continued completely uneventfully, other than one of the moons coming up and providing a little more light.. Finally, it was time to wake Finn for his shift. She found that he wasn't even asleep. She greeted him and then she went to bed.

She woke up before the sun came up, but it was beginning to get light. She could hear Ewan making food near the campfire. She waited in her bed instead of rising to join Ewan, and again enjoyed watching a vibrant sunrise. She soon became aware that several others of the company were awake as well. None of them had joined Ewan either, and it appeared they too were all lost in their own experiences taking in the beauty around them.

She could smell some kind of food being prepared. It smelled delicious, and at the same time unfamiliar. She could tell there was some kind of meat involved, along with fresh bread and various vegetables mixed in among the smells. Soon, the sunrise shifted to a more normal sky and her stomach insisted she seek out the source of the good smells. Right as she got ready to leave his bed he heard Ewan say, "Finn, can you wake Charlotte. Everyone else, breakfast is ready." Micaela had no idea how Ewan knew Finn was getting up right then, but she was getting kind of used to the strangeness of him knowing far too much or what happened around them.

They enjoyed the breakfast, which was some kind of a meat and vegetable bread pocket. It had a lot of seasonings that Micaela wasn't aware they even had. She brought it up. "You made the bread? And where did the vegetables and seasonings come from? I know we didn't have all this in the packs."

Ewan grinned, "Look around you. A place of such beauty is filled with a bounty of the world's blessings. This is my home territory, at least somewhat. I know where to find all this. I started gathering it last night. The only tracks coming into the valley are mine from a while back, which is why everyone got to do solo watches. I used the time on my sweep to start gathering this up in preparation for this morning. Even the meat is fresh."

Charlotte was awed, "Wow. This is wonderful. Thank you for sharing this with us."

Nerian asked, "What kind of meat is this?"

Ewan grinned, "What do you think it is?"

Nerian poked his knife into his food for a few moments, "Looks to be at least two kinds, maybe three. Some kind of bird, and a rabbit or something like it. Not sure what the third might be."

Ewan nodded but waited to answer until he was done chewing, "Three kinds. One is a bird, a winter goose. There is also a large hare. Any guesses from anyone else as to what the third meat is?" Micaela looked at the others. Finn was looking at his food closely and took tiny bites of each of the different kinds of meat. He had a very thoughtful look on his face.

His eyes suddenly went wide and he looked like he was going to shout it out, but thought better of it and sat smugly looking at the others. Micaela tried to clue in on what Finn had discovered and made a guess, "Is it some kind of fish?" Ewan shook his head. No one else ventured a guess.

Once everyone had finished eating, Finn made his guess. "Is it some kind of Lizard or Snake?" Micaela's stomach went queasy. Several others seemed to feel similarly about the idea as there were a couple of disgusted responses.

"You've got to be kidding me!" Cecilia looked sick to her stomach.

"Oh, Gross! Who would eat that?" Charlotte exclaimed at the same time.

Micaela swallowed hard, but didn't say anything. Ewan smiled mischievously, "Yes. That was from a large lizard that lives in some hot springs on the other side of the valley. It is considered a delicacy since it doesn't live in many places. The flavor and texture are delicate yet robust and fall somewhere between fish and chicken."

Finn looked a little smug as he said, "Yeah, it is similar to some other lizard meat I have had. It's actually quite good." It didn't calm everyone down much, maybe just a bit, but the light mealtime talk effectively ended when Cecilia stood and started cleaning up. It appeared she didn't want to talk about it anymore.

Since breakfast was over, they all started cleaning up and then packed up the camp and headed out. Ewan had Cecilia take rear guard and obscure any tracks or signs of their passing. He led them across the valley and seemed to pick at random one of the many small side canyons to go up. He worked carefully, pointing out where to step and making sure they left as little sign of their passage as possible. After a couple of hours of slow steep climbing, they came to a flatter area. In the middle was a huge boulder that was as big as an Inn.

Micaela could tell Ewan was excited, and followed as Ewan led them around the boulder. To her surprise, there was some kind of building built into the back of the boulder. Ewan led them all inside, and held the door as they entered. It was somewhat cramped to have six people with packs in the small building. Cecilia wasn't impressed, "This is it? I.. uh.. somehow expected more."

Ewan just smiled and shut the door. Suddenly, they weren't in the little shack anymore. Micaela stared and spun around to check her surroundings. They were in a large sitting room with several couches and a counter with some light refreshments on it. She wasn't even sure which of them gasped, but several people had. Cecilia's tone had completely changed. She was astounded. "How? How is this possible? That.. I don't.. " She cut herself off and Micaela chuckled internally at her reaction.

There were some grand double doors to the sitting room on the far side, which clicked and then opened silently. An elderly woman entered, smiling from ear to ear. "Welcome my weary travelers. You have done well." She looked over at Ewan, who smiled broadly. "Thank you." She waited for him to nod his acknowledgement and then turned back to the whole group. "As some of you have guessed or wondered, I am Rhondalyn. Welcome to Ashari, my home."

Some of the group murmured in confusion or awe and she waited silently until they finished. "I am not going to explain anything today, but tomorrow will be a very full day. My assistants will show you to your rooms. Dinner will be in three hours. I recommend you each stretch, clear your mind, and get ample rest. Tomorrow will be rather eventful."

Three people entered from the grand doors behind them. Rhondalyn introduced them. "These are some of my assistants. Arlista, Henry, and Betty. Ewan, if you will come with me, I will have your report now." Ewan followed Rhondalyn, while Arlista had Cecilia follow her, Henry guided Nerian, and Betty accompanied Charlotte.

Arlista turned and spoke to Finn and Micaela as she led Cecilia out of the room. "Wait here for a few minutes, and we will be back for you two."

Arlista then returned, followed closely by Henry. Henry approached Finn and said, "If you will please follow me?" Then he led Finn out. Micaela turned toward Arlista, who gestured with her hand to direct her through the doors. Arlista led him silently out the grand doors into a great atrium, and then down a large hallway to the left. They passed several doors and then Arlista turned and opened one of the doors.

As Micaela entered the enormous bedroom suite, Arlista spoke, "Unpack, clean up in the bathroom, and rest. We will return to bring you and the others to dinner in a few hours." She then turned and left, shutting the door behind her.

Micaela looked around at the room. It could be more accurately described as a palatial suite. About thirty feet away from where she stood was an alcove with an extremely large four poster bed. To her right was a sitting area with a nice couch and a couple of huge padded chairs surrounding a low table. To her left was a kitchen including an eating table with four high back kitchen chairs. There were doors to both sides of the alcove with the bed. She decided to explore a bit.

The door to the left of the alcove led to some kind of a workroom with a desk and a table. The other door led to a bathroom that defied all her expectations. It had a partitioned off room labeled 'shower' that rained water from the ceiling when she pushed a button. There was also a large tub she felt she could swim in, as well as a large vanity and sink, with a separate smaller room with a toilet.

She blinked her eyes, and looked back over everything. This was just for her? The only time she had ever seen anything approaching this kind of luxury was once when her Trapeze team had been invited to visit a king in his castle. She stood for a couple minutes, still trying to wrap her head around everything. She wasn't entirely sure she wasn't dreaming or having some kind of hallucination. Eventually, she decided to just roll with it.

There was a bin in the bathroom labeled 'dirty laundry', and she deposited her soiled clothes there. Then she filled the tub, and just soaked for a while. Eventually, she got out and decided to try the shower. The circus had a shower tent that was theoretically similar, but the difference was unbelievable.

This was more akin to being in a heavy downpour or a small waterfall, only it was comfortably hot and made her feel like a little girl playing in water again. Once she was done and wrapped in a towel the size of a large blanket, she realized that as clean as she now felt, it would just seem wrong to put on any of her clothes from her pack. All her clothes had accumulated quite a bit of dirt and grime from the long trip.

She wandered back into the bed alcove, and realized there were drawers there. She opened them hoping to find a robe or something, but to her surprise there were multiple sets of clothing already in her size and in a similar style to what she liked to wear. They were all brand new and best of all, totally clean. There was even a nice pair of shoes like she would wear around town when she had been at the circus.

Micaela took the next while sorting stuff from her bags and putting her dirty clothes in the laundry hamper in the bathroom. She wondered what she could do about her armor that she had picked up from the brigand's camp, but didn't think that it would qualify as laundry, and made a point to remember to ask about it. She also organized everything else from her pack on the kitchen table so she would know what she still had and where it was.

After she finished that up, she went to the sitting area and sat in one of the great big chairs. After fiddling with it a bit, she found that the whole back leaned back and a footrest rose up under her feet. It was amazingly comfortable, and she realized she was very tired.

The next thing she knew, she was gently shaken awake by Arlista. "It's time for dinner. Please come with me," the woman said. Micaela felt slightly embarrassed, but quickly got up and went to join her, but stopped and looked down at her bare feet on the plush carpet. Arlista followed her look, "There should be some shoes that you can wear in the closet next to the dresser."

Micaela remembered having seen the shoes and quickly headed to the alcove and retrieved them. Then she joined Arlista at the door. Arlista opened the door and Micaela was surprised to find Cecilia and Charlotte waiting there. They were dressed in their usual styles, but everything seemed clean and maybe even brand new.

She greeted them with a hand wave as Arlista instructed, "If you will follow me please." They all followed as she led them down the hall. They crossed the atrium and proceeded down another hallway on the opposite side. This one only had a couple of sets of doors spaced quite far apart. She led them to one of the doors and opened it. "Please find an open seat on either side of the table closer to the far end." They entered to find Ewan, Narian, and Finn already seated at the table. Henry stood off to the side of the room as though waiting for something.

There were ten seats on each side of the table, but the six closest to the end all had a place setting present. Three of those seats were already occupied by their companions. They each took a seat.

They only sat for about half a minute before another door opened and Rhondalyn entered. Micaela was certain she looked a bit younger than she had before. Henry and Arlista both left through a side door before Rhondalyn even sat down. Once she sat, she greeted them. "Welcome, everyone. I hope you were each able to settle into your rooms. We will discuss facilities more later. For now, we will be having dinner."

The side door opened again and both Henry and Arlista entered with large trays. They placed baskets with artisan bread in the middle of the table, and plates with salad in front of each of them. Micaela recognized most of the ingredients, but there were some she was unfamiliar with. She ate them anyway, and unsurprisingly, everything was delicious. She tore off a chunk of bread to go with it, which was also amazing.

Once everyone was done with their salad, those plates were taken away and replaced with a larger plate featuring some kind of white meat stuffed with vegetables and some kind of sauce. Micaela didn't know what it was called, but it was fantastic. Lastly they were served a dessert which was some kind of fruit crisp.

After eating, all of the companions seemed fairly satiated, and Rhondalyn used the opportunity to address them. "You all know that I knew about you before you ever came here. I have known about each of you for long before you were even born. Foresight is one of my gifts. I don't know everything about you, but enough to be able to make tools that could conclusively identify you."

She took out the stones they had all touched and placed them on the table. Instead of the five that Ewan had carried, there were now six. Six stones and six people, Micaela assumed the new one was tied to Ewan. "Even so, I did not know any of your names. While learning someone's name through foresight can happen, it is rare and not always helpful. Also, I don't know all the details of your journey. I didn't know anything about the brigand attack that you experienced on your way here, for instance."

"You have each been chosen or identified as being crucial in ending the second darkness. This one is actually more dangerous than the first darkness. If it is not stopped, it will result in the complete destruction of all people." She stopped, and looked at each one of them, going around the table.

"I want you to understand. This second darkness has been created by a new Overlord, who is none other than my fellow Halidar, Dardanos. It sounds daunting, but it is possible. I have been preparing for this for many hundreds of years. While you infiltrate his tower, I will be executing the other half of this mission. Together, me on this side of the world, and you on that side, we will end the darkness and any future darknesses in one bold stroke."

"You will not be able to do this as you are. You will need extensive training and equipment. In the next couple of months, we will be teaching and training you and equipping you with all that you will need to achieve this monumental task. It will not be easy. You must not fail."

"There will be some others who will join you for your travels and for this mission. For most of them, their job is to keep you alive until you can make it there. That doesn't mean you can ignore your own safety or can avoid fighting when it is necessary, but apart from a couple of you, there is no way to bring you up to their combat skill level in the short time you have. Fortunately, that is not necessary. For some of you, I have a pretty good idea how your existing abilities will factor into this mission. For others, I don't really know."

"Tomorrow, Arlista and Henry will help you get outfitted and equipped for your training. You will also be tested to determine your aptitudes and the best way to help you become what you need to be. Sleep well. While you wait your turns in getting outfitted and tested, please wait in your rooms and try to be patient."

CHAPTER THIRTY-TWO

ROBERT

AFTER FOLLOWING THE GROUP for several weeks, Robert was ready for this journey to be over. He hadn't been uncomfortable, but the constant need for high awareness was draining. The only real dangerous moment was when eliminating the brigands. At first, he was only going to take out the brigands who were set to ambush the group he was tailing, but then he realized that he would need to take out all of them or risk a reprisal against the group.

It had used up most of his supplies to eliminate the brigands, even though he collected what bolts hadn't been destroyed when he used them. All his poison and knockout bombs were gone, and he only had one smoke bomb left. The energy level on two of his sets of clothes was nearly depleted. If they ran into another group of brigands, he would simply have to warn the group he was following.

Fortunately, that hadn't happened. He did have to hide from another ranger that had briefly talked with them. It seemed like the group would just keep hiking forever. Finally, they had reached the top of the mountains. Robert decided to not enter the large valley but camped far enough outside the valley to not be discovered. He wasn't discovered and used his scryer to watch them. The group was up and moving the next morning.

As he scried their journey that morning, he saw them enter what had to be an uncomfortably cramped hunters shack. They didn't come back out, and so now he was approaching the shack in person. He hadn't been able to identify any wards or monitoring equipment, but he couldn't escape the feeling that he was being observed.

He stood as far back from the shack as he could while still being able to see the door. He used the multi-homed magic spectrum analyzer with the life force detector to try and determine what was going on inside. There was no evidence of anyone being inside it at all. There was also no detectable magic present. It didn't make sense, and that bothered him. Eventually, he figured he would have to go closer to find out.

When he got there, he verified the group's footprints entering the shack, and none leaving. He tried to detect any sound or life force through the walls, but couldn't get any signal at all. From a distance, he could detect nothing, but he couldn't get any of his devices to work close up to the door. It appeared flimsy, but was solid and closed as flush as any door he had ever seen. Finally, he decided his only recourse was to enter. He hoped he wouldn't regret it.

After quickly working up his determination, he grasped the handle and opened the door. It opened soundlessly. On the dirt floor he could tell where each of them had been standing, but it was completely empty. He could sense some kind of residual magic energy from whatever had happened, but they were gone. His analyzer could detect the residual energy as well, but it seemed to not be centered on anything.

Robert spent the next couple of hours searching and testing different ideas to determine what had happened and where they had gone. They had to have teleported, but without any dedicated equipment on this end. He didn't think they could have gone very far. If they were going to be transported a long distance, there would have been no point in having them make the long difficult journey to get here. After hours of work, he still had no idea where they went or how.

After exhausting his options in the shack, he decided to check in the territory around it. If his hypothesis was correct, Rhondalyn's base would be somewhere close. He began to search the area around the shack. He spent the entire rest of the day climbing up and down steep embankments and cliffs while trying to identify any presence of anyone or any source of magic. Eventually, he found some cracks in the rocks with strange airflows that didn't match the patterns around them, that might be part of a ventilation system.

He used his scrying gnat to search the airflows and cracks and eventually found that there was a huge facility underground in the mountain. The cracks weren't actually part of the ventilation system, but the presence of the facility affected the airflows and temperatures in unnatural ways. He couldn't get through most of the wards, and hadn't been able to find any kind of physical entrance. He finally found a fault in one of the wards and made it through with the gnat and took a look around the small part of the base.

The part he could get into appeared to be staff quarters where there weren't a lot of people going in and out. Based on how big the overall facility seemed to be, there should be more people than that. However, the people who used this section seemed to be high level and influential people. At one point, he even saw someone who he suspected might actually be Rhondalyn.

He monitored them for a full day, and got a general feel for what they were doing and was able to confirm they worked for Rhondalyn. There was one woman that he noticed who seemed to be frustrated a lot of the time. It appeared she wasn't listened to as much as she thought she should be and there were frequent orders from two other individuals. From the conversations he heard, he believed her name was Betty.

Robert decided it was time for him to find a way in. If he could get to know Betty, he might be able to get her to disclose what she knew about Rhondalyn's activities. Even more so, he might even be able to recruit her to be an active and ongoing agent for the Overlord. The only thing that bothered him was that he was unable to identify where the group he followed here had gone to. It probably didn't matter, since he had found Rhondalyn's location and potentially someone who could reveal what she was up to.

Based on what he had detected about the facility, he now knew what direction most of it lay in, and would search that direction to try and find an entrance. He decided to use his scrying flyer at first, since it might be faster. It only took him about forty minutes to find what looked like a promising opportunity. There was some kind of long warded tube buried just a few feet underground that stayed mostly level and extended from the far end of the larger warded facility and went several miles before ending in another mountain side. That mountain contained a network of warded tubes or tunnels that seemed connected to a large mine.

That had to be how they got supplies. It was unlikely that they could be truly self-sufficient in the facility, though it certainly was large enough. The entrance to the mine was many miles away from where he was, and it would take him a quite a while to get there. Then he had to find where the wards started and find a way through them. It appeared that the wards covered mine tunnels, and they formed some kind of maze. Once he found his way through the maze, then he could make his way into the facility.

Unfortunately, the journey to the mine entrance required him to either cross some glacier covered mountain peaks or journey back down the mountain and circle around a good number of mountains to get there. It was times like this that he really wished he could fly. He decided that time was of the essence and chose to go over the glaciers. Not many people would consider that the preferable route, but he was thoroughly protected from the elements and had tools that would speed his journey that would make it better for him.

He had to change into his more formal outfit, since it was the only one that had enough energy. He figured the journey would take three days, and a long three days it was. Despite not getting cold, walking on ice and snow was never a fun time. Finally, he descended on the mine entrance. It wasn't super busy, but it appeared to be some high value asset for one of the local kingdoms. Robert didn't have time to go through the local political structure. He was already far behind where he needed to be. He had lost four days already.

The sun was already getting close to setting, and he wanted to make sure he was inside before they closed it all up for the night. He had to sneak in when the miners were leaving. He activated all of his stealth and camouflage enhancements. In keeping to the shadows, he was able to avoid notice by anyone.

Finally, he got far enough into the mine that he was able to find a spot where it appeared that no one had been in a long time. He set up his scrying tools again. He needed to make sure he knew his route, and scrying would be much quicker than physically hoofing it. He figured out a way to get the mapping tracker to work with the flying scryer and was able to map out the tunnels fairly quickly, but only until he ran into warded sections.

Soon, he was able to chart out the route to the nearest wards. Out of caution, he finished mapping out the rest of the tunnels and soon found there were seven places where wards started up. He carefully analyzed each of the wards and the ground going into them. There seemed to be several that had evidence of heavy traffic. One had very frequent heavy traffic, but he suspected that it was an active mining area. Not that they couldn't be mining in the same place as the supply entrance to the facility was, but he suspected it wasn't the case. He would try the other high traffic areas first.

That left only two of them. Both of the wards were the same type. Very powerful and impossible to crack from a distance without sending out alerts. He wanted to get in unobserved, so he began the hike to the nearest ward. When he got there, he realized that it wasn't close enough to the warded tunnel to the facility to be what he was looking for. Then he backtracked and made his way to the other one. It seemed much more plausible that it went where he hoped.

As he got right up to the invisible ward, he carefully began to examine what he was dealing with. Once again, he used the multi-homed magic spectrum analyzer, which let him determine how many overlapping wards were there. It also let him know exactly what type he was dealing with. He was impressed. Rhondalyn certainly hadn't gotten rusty.

He brought out the ward piercer that Terlan had given him. He hadn't thought he would need it, since he had a lot of experience with getting through and around wards, but these wards were beyond him. He wondered how Rhondalyn had missed the flaw he exploited earlier when he had monitored some of the facility staff. *Well, no one is perfect, not even Dardanos. I know of at least three flawed wards in the new tower. I just haven't gotten around to reporting them yet.*

He continued working on the wards. Eventually, he was able to create a small hole in the wards and scry through it and was able to ensure that it went where he hoped it would. Then came the delicate process of enlarging the hole enough for him to pass through without breaking the wards and alerting people to his presence. Fortunately, he was able to get it the first time, even though it took a couple of hours.

He followed the path he had mapped through the many tunnels and eventually came to a new set of wards that surrounded the tunnels. These ones were different, and he could tell that this tunnel was completely artificial. He must have reached the long tunnel near the surface he had originally followed to find the mine. He started his walk. It would take a couple more hours to walk the distance to the facility. He checked again to make sure scrying would not reveal himself.

Then he scried down the long tunnel to see what kind of entrance there was into the facility. He could see a large heavy metal door in what appeared to be a solid stone wall. *Hmm, going to have to get much closer to that to find a way through that.* Then he started walking.

Being in a winding tunnel, and even with his enhanced night vision, the walk seemed to take forever. He knew it only took the amount of time he had estimated, but the tunnel made it drag out. Finally, he came up to the door. He checked it over, and it didn't seem to have any wards on it at all. That seemed strange to him, since that would be an easy place to put wards that would be highly effective. Not putting wards there was just asking to be exploited.

He double checked everything. He couldn't scry behind the door or the wall, but he could walk in. So that was what he did. Behind the door was a short entry tunnel. There was another door at the end of it. He could see the mechanical locks in place. The two doors could not be opened at the same time. He worried that it was some kind of trap.

Regardless, he shut the outside door. He could hear the heavy duty external locks clank into place, but to his relief, he could hear the ones on the other door open. The difficult thing was that the darkness was absolute. It seemed that all frequencies of light, radiation, and even magic were reduced to nothing, so he couldn't see or detect anything using sight or even his equipment. He could hear, smell, and touch, and he was able to assure himself that there wasn't anything to worry about.

He reached the other door by feel, and was able to open it. Behind it was just as dark. He hoped that once he was through that he could find or create some kind of light source, or at least navigate by magic. He stepped through. The floor was still just solid rock. He shut the door behind him and heard some heavy locks clank into place. Then the lights came on, and he wasn't alone.

"Uh-oh" he mumbled. He knew he was in trouble.

"Hello Robert." The woman standing there said. "You are Robert? Correct? One of Dardanos's chief assistants for the last two hundred plus years?"

Robert nervously nodded his head. She knew his name and who he was. It had to be Rhondalyn. She continued. "Yes, well, you have sought me out and intruded on my domain. You could have just asked me to come and visit. It would have saved you four days of surveillance and infiltration work." He felt like a small child being reprimanded by a teacher for making elementary mistakes.

She started to turn, "Well, come along, no need to keep waiting out here. Can I have you stand over right there for a minute?" She pointed to a marked spot on the floor over to the side of the room.

He looked where she indicated, and could see it was some kind of scanner. "Um, what will that do?" He hadn't moved.

"Oh, come now Robert, you are in charge of Dardanos's security in that awful new tower of his. I am sure you have similar security protocols. It's a scanner. It will let us know everything you are carrying, to make sure you don't have anything nefarious in mind with your little visit."

He hadn't expected to feel like a little child, but couldn't escape the feeling that she viewed him as such. Reluctantly, he stepped over to the scanner. "Do I need to raise my arms or anything?" he asked in his most bored voice, trying not to show how intimidated he was.

She smiled patronizingly, "No, just stand there, this will be painless and only take a moment." Then a bright flash happened.

Robert looked around. He wasn't in the same room anymore. He was in some kind of bedroom. All his equipment was gone too. How could he have been so foolish? Then he noticed his ring was also missing. "Arrgh!"

he growled. That was entirely new tech. How did they notice that? He looked around the room. It seemed very comfortable, much more so than his normal quarters in the new tower or even the old tower. At least he wouldn't be miserable.

Then the woman's voice spoke from everywhere around him. "I apologize for the inconvenience, but you will need to stay in the room we have assigned you. As you can see, we have removed your equipment. You might get it back when you leave. We'll see. For the meantime, get some sleep, you have had an exhausting last several weeks. Betty will be in soon with some breakfast. It might seem a bit early, but it is almost sun-up."

Betty? He thought. That has to be a coincidence. There is no way for her to read my thoughts, so she couldn't know that I intended to try to recruit her. Could she? Determined to carry forward with his mission, Robert was still bothered by how uncanny the situation was.

He soon found out that he was unable to leave the suite. Food was provided and plenty of comfort, but he did not get to leave. He was doing his best to build a positive rapport with Betty, but she only came twice a day. He was also certain that he was constantly being watched. This was proving more challenging than he had expected.

Epilogue

The Overlord sat at his desk, looking out the window from his office at the Storm as it spread and did his bidding across a large portion of the world. He smiled for just a moment. The experiment has been adequately successful and things were mostly going in the right direction. The storm he was watching now covered hundreds of thousands of square miles and was nearing forty percent of global coverage.

He was on track to have completely covered the whole world within the next six months, exactly as scheduled. It was the key to resolving most of the worst atrocities known to man. War, oppression, inequality, unfairness, theft, crime, and a host of other problems would mostly end. There would of course still be some problems, but he would work through those as he got to them.

One big concern was famine, but that seemed like it was being effectively handled where he had things organized. The workers were certainly functional enough. That part had turned out even better than he had hoped, but he needed more of his forces to keep up with the growth. That was one of the major headaches that was plaguing him. His forces were not as effective as he anticipated.

He had dedicated an unbelievable amount of resources to preparing his forces, but having to keep them covert for so long had caused a lot of issues. Now that it was overt, things should have been going much better. But they weren't. Somehow he needed to find better ways to keep track and organize his forces and make sure things didn't fall apart too much in the transition.

He looked at his clock, and realized Kaltha would be there in less than twenty minutes with her weekly report. She was very capable and was handling a significant portion of Robert's work while he was gone on his special mission. He was grateful for Kaltha, but she wasn't Robert. She kept the tower operations running. It was often thankless, but she was doing a pretty good job of it.

Still, it wasn't enough. He needed someone who could work administrative miracles. He needed Robert. But Robert was out on a mission of utmost importance, and he had disappeared. Normally, Robert was extremely punctual with reporting in daily, but it had been a couple weeks and there had been no contact. Dardanos had even tried to contact Robert directly, but there was no connection. He wasn't sure how that was possible.

Robert seemed to have dropped off the face of the world, and Dardanos needed him. He tried to think what could have happened, but he didn't have enough information. He hated doubting himself, but perhaps he had been unreasonable to send Robert on this mission. He needed someone with the utmost competence. Someone who could defuse tense situations and solve nearly impossible problems. That person was Robert. It has been Robert for a very long time.

Now Robert was missing. The energy and power emanations from Rhondalyn were also getting stronger. He needed answers. He needed them, but had no way of getting them. He tried to calm himself as he felt the lines of uncertainty and worry slowly etch themselves into his face. There was nothing he hated more than uncertainty.

– TO BE CONTINUED –

CHARACTERS

ARCHMAGES AND HALIDAR

Vlastorn - First Overlord, Arch-necromancer - Destroyed at end of first darkness

Evander - Light archmage

Dardanos - Earth and energy archmage

Rhondalyn - Healing and scrying archmage, secretly a seer too

Sidoran - Rogue Shadow Archmage, husband of Rhondalyn, Reported deceased after first confrontation with Vlastorn

Aspheron - Elemental Archmage - Died collapsing the sides of the pit

Thelanor - Arch Paladin - Killed by Vlastorn at end of the first confrontation

Ferozel - Arch SpellSword - Killed by Vlastorn at end of the first confrontation

Nitara - Void archmage - Killed by automated protections triggered by attempting to destroy the core crystal

Catamus - Air and Water archmage – Killed by Vlastorn during the first confrontation

CORE TEAM

Nerian – Royal Knight at the Tower of Light

Micaela – Circus trapeze artist

Finn – Jack of all trades

Cecilia – Master thief

Charlotte – Milk maid

Ewan – ranger of Isalor

RHONDALYN'S PEOPLE

Henry

Arlista

Betty

Banosh

DARDANOS'S PEOPLE

Robert

Kaltha

Geron

Terlan

OTHERS

Freya - Matron of the circus

Korel - Wagon driver for the circus

Pentar - Father of circus family

Segrid - Mother of circus family

Thanosh - Pentar and Segrid's son

Frieda - Pentar and Segrid's daughter

Vipora - Pentar and Segrid's daughter

Gaiten - Circus worker

Koz - Injured royal knight at the palace gates in Zentel

Theibold - Royal steward in Zentel

Karl - Injured royal knight in the throne room in Zentel

Jeffrey - Royal knight lieutenant in Zentel

Nerian's Mother

Master Ganslow - Blacksmith in Mijople

Carlisle - Blacksmith's apprentice in Mijople

Isan - Carpenter in Mijople

Bojerus - Tavern keeper in Mijople

Gesh - Hunter from Mijople

Staynor - Traveling merchant from Mijople

Orvindo - Tavern keeper in Beaumont

Finnias - Bard encountered in Beaumont

Isolde - Barmaid in Beaumont

Janice - Duchess of Beaumont and Cecilia's mother

Brone - Duke of Beaumont and Cecilia's father

Rasdal - Cruel bodyguard assigned to Cecilia

Kolana - Assistant in a dress shop that helps Cecilia

Janora - Dress shop owner in Beaumont

Hank - Thief in Merdal

Verlina - Stewardess of Ethalor Manor

Leofric - Larder keeper of Ethalor Manor

Smat - Pickpocket in Parnul

Scritch - Pickpocket in Parnul

Rolund - Thieves guild leader in Parnul

Janice - Thieves guild secretary

Bruno - Thieves guild guard

Jans - Refugee heading into Mijople

Asheena - Refugee heading into Mijople, married to Jans

Elanor - Refugee and former teacher

Edmund - Guard in Mijople

Paulino - Man from Mijople

Walter - Wagon master heading to Port Yadzul

Rostella - Woman in Mijople

Matilda - Woman in Mijople, Elanor's cousin

Captain Hallin - Guard captain in Mijople

Joben - Guard in Mijople

Captain Yermont - Ship captain of the Grudge Merchant

Seeley - Foreman on the Grudge Merchant

Captain Drogo - Ship captain of the Silent Star

Bosun Jostor - Bosun on the Silent Star

First Mate Rheshak - First mate on the Silent Star

Mr. Trefaris - Sailor on the Silent Star

About the author

Will Groberg has been telling fiction stories to his family for more than three decades, but only recently started putting them down in a written format. He is a consultant, programmer, educator, entrepreneur, inventor, gamer, avid reader, economist, and wannabe philosopher. He has lived in more than 34 places and visited most of the states in the US. He has worked in a wide variety of industries coving everything from engineering to medicine to tourism to public safety. He is the father of six daughters who love stories and whose support has been fundamental in getting his stories into writing. He currently lives in rural Arizona with his wife and his youngest daughters, where they enjoy the beautiful mountains and from were they can look out their front window and see Mexico. Even though none of them have ever been there.